Christos Tsiolkas is the author of five novels: *Loaded*, which was made into the feature film *Head On*; *The Jesus Man*; *Dead Europe*, which won the 2006 *Age* Fiction Prize; *The Slap*, which was published in 2009 and has since been published all over the world; and *Barracuda*. *The Slap* won the 2009 Commonwealth Writers' Prize, the 2009 Australian Literary Society's Gold Medal and was longlisted for the 2010 Man Booker Prize. Tsiolkas is also a playwright, essayist and screenwriter. He lives in Melbourne.

merciless gods
CHRISTOS TSIOLKAS

ATLANTIC BOOKS
London

First published in Australia in 2014 by Allen & Unwin.

First published in Great Britain in 2015 by Atlantic Books, an imprint of Atlantic Books Ltd.

'Petals' first published in *Overland 216 Spring 2014*

'Hung Phat!' first published in *Below the Waterline*, ed. Garry Disher, Harper Collins, 1999

'Saturn Return' first published in *Blur*, ed. James Bradley, Random House, 1996

'Jessica Lange in *Frances*' first published in *Pub Fiction*, ed. Leonie Stevens, Allen & Unwin, 1997

'The Disco at the End of Communism' first published in *Brothers and Sisters*, ed. Charlotte Wood, Allen & Unwin, 2009

'Sticks, Stones' first published in the Get Reading! collection *10 Short Stories You Must Read in 2010*, The Australia Council, 2010

'Civil War' first published in Picador *New Writing 3*, eds, Drusilla Modjeska and Beth Yahp, Pan Macmillan, 1995

'Porn 1' first published as 'The Pornographic Scientist' in *Readings and Writings: 40 Years in Books*, eds Jason Cotter and Michael Williams, 2010

10 9 8 7 6 5 4 3 2 1

A CIP catalogue record for this book is available from the British Library.

Trade paperback ISBN: 978 1 78239 727 4
E-book ISBN: 978 1 78239 728 1

Printed and bound by CPI Group (UK) Ltd, Croydon, CR0 4YY

Atlantic Books
An imprint of Atlantic Books Ltd
Ormond House
26–27 Boswell Street
London
WC1N 3JZ

www.atlantic-books.co.uk

For Wayne van der Stelt,
who has been there from the beginning

Contents

Merciless Gods

I WANT TO TELL YOU A story about an evening many years ago. I hardly see anyone who was at that dinner party anymore; apart from the occasional email we have all disappeared from one another's lives. I dare say it could be argued that our drifting away from one another is not extraordinary, that it would have occurred in the normal course of events—the raising of children, changing address, moving away, stagnating friendship—but I am certain that the events of that evening had no small role to play in the fracturing of our group.

There were nine of us seated around the table. We had been to university at the same time, some of us had worked together, we were a group of young professionals just beginning to pair off, find lovers, even think about marriage. Serena and Ingrid were the hosts that evening and the dinner was in honour of Marie, who was soon to leave for San Francisco to become an editor for a leading publisher of travel guides. I was there with Mark—we had just celebrated the first anniversary of our relationship—and there was Antony and Hande, and Madeline and Vince. We were also celebrating the news that Hande had just been accepted as a solicitor in one of the city's major labour-law firms; we were all keen to toast her and Marie's good fortune.

We had all dressed up for the occasion; it was the first time I had seen Mark in a suit and a tie. The women had all bought new outfits for the evening and were complimenting each other and striking model poses. The men looked debonair and rather splendid in their dinner suits and crisp white shirts. We looked as though we belonged in the elegant apartment that Serena and Ingrid had just moved into on Collins Street; their view across the illuminated cityscape was dazzling. The Cold War had only recently been relegated to history, technology was promising boundless opportunity and the recession had not long ended. Our generation was buoyant. We owned the future.

Mark nominated himself DJ that night (a beatless house track would follow Pearl Jam or the Screaming Trees—it was the season of grunge and Café del Mar compilations), Antony had scored us some ecstasy and Serena had spent the day cooking us a feast. That night was a film. We were a sophisticated art-house movie; we were chic and we were young. We were beautiful.

Though the setting was perfect it could not be said that we were all completely at ease as we popped the cork from the first bottle of champagne and filled our glasses. I think now that we never really settled that night, never quite managed to give ourselves over to the abandonment that beckoned, even with all that fine food and the elation of the stimulants and intoxicants. It seemed that the evening had begun with a faint tremor of anxiety, and somehow that sense of unease never quite retreated; we never managed to banish it. It entered our drinks and our food, we breathed it in. It was a mild early-autumn night, the breeze was cooling without chilling us, but even with the balcony doors wide open, the air in the apartment seemed inordinately heavy.

You see, although we were all there to celebrate with Marie, we also knew that she had beaten Vince for the job. Since university they had both pursued careers in publishing. Vince initially backpacked through Indonesia and started filing travel reports on Flores, Borneo, Java and Sumatra for the nascent travel-guide industry. His writing was pungent, informative and free from cant or cliché, and before long he was editing and writing the guides to Oceania and the Pacific. Marie began working as a copy editor in a small publishing collective that was riding the last dying swell of second-wave feminism. When the press folded, Vince let her know there was an opening at the company he worked for. She got the job. Good-natured rivalry had defined their professional relationship for the first few months, but none of us were surprised when it became more competitive. Vince was brilliant, sharp, quick-witted, a child of migrant factory workers who wore his entry into the bourgeoisie as both a chip on his shoulder and a badge of honour. He had a wicked temper that made him unpopular with those not seduced by his charm and intellect. He did not hide his contempt for intellectual laziness. When the position in San Francisco came up, he had applied for it and so had Marie. It was Marie, whose father was a diplomat and who was fluent in three languages, who'd got the job.

'I don't mind,' Vince had barked at me when I'd brought up the subject in the locker room after our fortnightly game of squash. 'She fucking deserves it.' But he had played like a lunatic, the ball rebounding furiously, whipping towards me at such speed that I thought it would slice me. He did mind. He was proud and arrogant and hated being beaten. He minded deeply.

So, there we all were, Vince barely able to conceal his envy, Marie resenting her feelings of guilt, Madeline attempting to be the appeaser and the rest of us pretending everything was fine. It was fortunate that Hande was so excited that night. We could all rejoice in her happiness. The food that Serena had prepared was exquisite: fresh seafood from the market, lamb marinated in wine and with a crust of feta and herbs, an alcohol-soaked tiramisu for dessert. After the first few bottles were drunk the initial stiltedness of the evening seemed to vanish. At one point, between the entrée and the main course, Vince, Hande and I were smoking on the balcony, looking across into the empty lit-up offices across the street. Between draws, he said,

'Well, it isn't quite New York.' Hande and I looked at him for a moment, then she replied, 'At least it isn't Beirut.'

'Or Adelaide,' I added.

It felt good to finally laugh. The smells, the tastes, the music, the clothes, the conversation—I can remember everything about that night except who suggested the game. I suppose if I were to meet up with any of those old friends they would probably all guess that it had been Vince. I am also tempted to say it was him. But I think that is too easy. Mark would say that I am giving him the benefit of the doubt, that of course Vince had planned it all from the beginning; that I was letting my feelings for Vince get in the way.

It is true: back then I was in love with Vince. Mark was never convinced that it was possible to be in love with two people at the same time. It is, I still claim that truth, though now I know that such a divided loyalty can never be equal. Vince and I had fallen into an easy camaraderie from the moment we'd met in our first tutorial at uni. By the end of that first week I was in love. It was adolescent love, impossible, destined to be unfulfilled and unconsummated, but university had emancipated me from the evasions and dishonesties of high school and I made an obsession out of that first liberating rapture. Vince tolerated my puppyish devotion, though we never spoke about it. One night on holiday in Bangkok we had got paralytic drunk and I had given him a blowjob after we'd miraculously managed to find our way back to the hostel. He claimed no memory of it the next morning but was surly with me the rest of the day. That very evening he went off with an American girl and I didn't see him for three days. When he finally came back to our room I pretended to be unconcerned. Mark was right: I could forgive Vince anything.

Yet, yet, yet . . . I don't believe it was Vince who suggested that damn game. If I had to nominate someone I think it must have been Ingrid. As host of the evening she would have been especially conscious of the underlying tension, and might have suggested a frivolous game to steer the gathering away from argument. We had taken the drugs and the first euphoric wave had passed through us; we had danced wildly to the music, and were sweating and laughing on cushions on the floor, our ties and heels and jackets discarded. I recall that Vince had kicked off his shoes and was sprawled on the sofa, his shirt unbuttoned, Madeline running her fingers through the wet curls on his chest. I recall it because I wished it were my hand there. Mark was no longer playing punk and hip-hop but acoustic songs and mellow electronica. Hande had her head on my shoulder, Serena was in Ingrid's embrace, Marie was listening dreamily to the music and Antony was rolling a joint. Someone suggested Charades and we all dismissed the idea. Exquisite Corpse? Truth or Dare? Botticelli? Then someone suggested the game.

I had not ever heard of it and I have not heard of it since. Everyone has to write one word on a scrap of paper that is placed in a bowl. The word should, we were instructed, denote an emotional state or a category of morality or experience, like one of the seven deadly sins or a phase of maturity.

Then it's like Scruples? someone asked.

No, once all the words go into the bowl we choose one and then we have to go around and each tell a story based on that word.

I don't get it.

Okay, let me explain. Say I pick out the word 'masturbation'... We would have all laughed. *... Shut up, don't be such children! Say the word is 'masturbation'. We all take turns to tell a story about masturbating ...*

So it is *like Scruples?*

No. No. This is what's so great about it. It doesn't have to be your own story. It can be a story you heard, something that happened to someone else ...

God, it sounds so complicated.

No, it's a load of fun, I promise you.

How do you win?

At the end of the round we all vote on the best story.

A few of us groaned. The ecstasy was lovely; my skin seemed to shimmer; the last thing I wanted was for us to fall into trying to outdo each other. I just wanted to lie among my friends and sink into the night.

I think we should give it a go.

That was Vince, that was definitely Vince. One by one we all reluctantly agreed.

I remember when it came to Mark he shrugged his shoulders and looked at me. 'You interested?'

I looked at Vince. 'Yes. It could be fun.'

•

We agonised over finding that one damn word that would work for the game, a word that would both entertain and impress. The buzz of the drug was now flooding out of my belly and rippling through my whole body. I looked over at Marie, who was biting the end of her pen, and she gave me a sheepish smile in return. So much of what we did then seemed to be an effort to convince our friends that we were witty and erudite. Conceited though it might sound, we did believe ourselves to be special, that we stood apart from the common herd of twenty-somethings in our city. That all seems so absurd to me now, but in our defence it must be remembered that we had not yet found ourselves at the other end of stagnant occupations, or relationships that had failed through inertia and predictability, we had not yet discovered that we were as mundane and trivial as everyone else. It could not be an ordinary word that was placed in the bowl: it had to be superlative, breathtaking, a word that challenged and astonished.

Vince was the first to crumple his scrap of paper and throw it in the bowl. Mark was next. Hande and I were the last. My word was simple but telling and I blush to think of it now. What did I expect to happen when it was read out? The word was 'unrequited'.

'Marie should pick the first word,' announced Ingrid, always mindful of her role as host. 'Marie or Hande. It's their night.'

Marie lazily shook her head, tucking her feet under her and reclining further back in the armchair. She waved at Hande, who was still sitting on the floor beside me. 'You do it, babe, the table's too far.'

'You lazy bitch.' With a laugh and a flourish as though she was performing a conjurer's trick, Hande picked out a tightly crumpled piece of paper. It's Vince's, that was my immediate thought. I looked across at him. His face was impassive, but I sensed an almost imperceptible tension grip his body. I don't think anyone else would have been aware of it, not even Madeline sitting next to him would have been conscious of the agitation he was hiding so well. They had been lovers for only seven or so months; she might know his body intimately but she had not followed him, coveted him, adored him for nine years. In that time I had closely observed his every mood, coming to understand his likes and dislikes, his fears and ambitions. I *knew* Vince. I was the only one who really knew Vince.

Hande was unrolling the paper. She looked at it and dropped the paper to the floor. 'The word is "Revenge".'

Were there cruel angels in the apartment that evening, malevolent ghosts dictating how the night was to unfold? But as I have explained, it was a cool evening with only a slight breeze coming through the open doors to the balcony. It was accident, chance; and possibly any word would have led to the same conclusion.

'So who goes first?'

Serena shrugged. We were all suddenly struck by shyness.

It was Antony who finally raised his hand. 'I'll go.' He took a last pull of the joint and rested his hand on Hande's thigh. 'I'm going to tell the story of what I did to Peter Rothscomb.'

Hande scowled. 'Do you have to?'

'It's the only revenge story I have.'

'It doesn't have to be your own personal story,' Ingrid interjected.

Hande made a dismissive gesture. 'He can tell it.' She slapped his hand off her thigh and got up. 'But it's a horrible story.'

'Is it okay if I tell it?'

Hande had gone to the fridge for another bottle of wine. 'Tell it,' she called out. 'Bloody men,' we heard her add as she kicked the fridge door closed.

'It isn't a particularly edifying story,' began Antony sheepishly as he watched Hande refill his glass. 'But it is about revenge.' He cleared his throat. 'You all remember Peter Rothscomb?'

We all nodded. Rothscomb was a member of the Young Liberals on campus, a pale effeminate man who was always putting forward conservative arguments in the political science tutorial I attended with Antony and Ingrid. He was perfectly harmless but I think we all detested his smugness, his unapologetic assumption of inheritance and the right to rule. Our hatred of him was only exacerbated by the fact that his arguments were usually informed and cogent. Antony's animosity towards Peter was even more pronounced as they had both gone to the same private boys' school together and had been in competition with each other for years. Since the fucking sandpit, Vince would often observe.

'In our honours year there was a prize for the best thesis in political science.'

I nodded again. Antony and Ingrid had both submitted their thesis for the prize. I had not. I'd been lucky to scrape through.

'My thesis was on the conditions that led to Perestroika in the Soviet Union. I slaved that year, I read anything and everything I could.' Antony was getting increasingly animated, as if in the telling he was becoming the student he'd been four years before.

'Remember how I hardly went out that year? I became obsessed with it—it seemed momentous to me, the crucial subject of our age. It felt impossible to keep up with the events that were unfolding so rapidly in front of our eyes. It was 1989 and the Communist regimes had started to collapse.' Antony slammed his right fist into his other palm. 'Bang, bang, bang! Everything that was solid seemed to melt into air, as if democracy was collapsing Marxism into itself. I think it was the first time I discovered what it really was to study, not to parrot information by rote, but to really develop and express an argument.' Antony paused and sipped his wine. Mark had crawled along the floor to the stereo to turn down the music.

'Anyway, I was frustrated by the banal analysis that was coming out of Western journalism and equally annoyed by the confusion of the left. Euphoria on one side, apocalypse on the other. I was convinced that the reduction of Russian history to a narrative of tyranny and oppression was only one side of the story, that there was an equally important history of dissent and opposition that informed the actions of people like Gorbachev.

I worked and reworked and reworked that thesis. It was the best work I had ever done. It will be the best work I ever do.'

We were now all seated around the coffee table, some of us on cushions on the floor, Vince and Madeline sharing the sofa, Marie on the armchair across from them. Antony's story was making me melancholy as I recalled that period when experience occurred in a rush, when I seemed to be learning something new every moment. There was an elation and excitement to life that Antony had reminded me of: his words were the first premonition I had that it would not always be so, that time had already passed.

'I got second prize.' Antony sculled his drink and lit a cigarette. Ingrid let him smoke inside. She too seemed lost inside her memories of that time.

'I bloody came second and that knob Peter Rothscomb won with a thesis on Menzies.' Antony's face was so incredulous that I couldn't stop myself bursting into laughter.

'It's not funny, mate. I was livid.'

'So what did you do?' asked Serena.

'Yeah,' Vince said. 'How did you get your revenge?'

It was at this point that Hande grabbed a cigarette and headed out to the balcony.

'It's okay, you can smoke in here,' Ingrid called out to her.

'It's alright,' Hande replied, 'I can hear everything from here.'

Antony was blushing now. I felt for him. Hande's reaction had unnerved him and it was clear he was reluctant to continue.

'Go on, Ant,' Hande's voice rang clearly from the balcony. 'Tell them.'

He took a deep breath. 'I fucked Sally St John.'

'Who?' Serena didn't know that crowd.

Vince's laugh was loud and coarse and abrupt. 'You fucked her? When?'

'At her hens' night.'

We all exploded into laughter. Even Hande, her back against the balcony rail, watching us all, even she was trying hard not to smile.

'Who the fuck is Sally St John?' shouted Serena.

'Hon, she was this guy Peter's fiancée. They'd been together for years,' Ingrid explained.

'Since the sandpit,' Vince and I said simultaneously, which made us collapse into laughter again.

Serena was shaking her head in bewilderment. 'What were you doing at the hens' night?' Her face lit up in delight. 'You were the stripper!'

'No.' Antony was laughing and blushing, stealing glances at Hande, who had stubbed out her cigarette in a pot plant, and now came back inside and sat herself next to Antony. She laid a hand on his shoulder, flicked him gently on the cheek with a long scarlet-painted fingernail.

'Remember how he used to work at Mietta's?' Hande asked. 'The most handsome waiter in the world? Well, Sally's hens' night had their dinner there before they headed out. Sally got wasted and Antony here fucked her behind the garbage cans out on the street while one of the sous-chefs kept watch. Isn't that right, darling?'

Serena giggled. 'She sounds like an easy lay.'

'It wasn't the first time though?'

It was one of those moments when the sound of the traffic on the streets below seemed to cut out at exactly the point when a track on the CD fell to a close.

'What do you mean?' Hande demanded of Vince, her voice furious.

'It was a question,' he answered, holding up his hands defensively. 'I assumed that if she fell into his arms so easily there was previous history there.'

'There wasn't, alright?' Antony growled.

'I didn't mean anything by it. I just knew that she and your sister were friends. They went to the same school, didn't they?'

'They weren't friends, they were classmates.'

'My apologies then. I was only asking.'

The tension that had seized us all was broken by Hande's hearty laugh. She shook her head and leaned across the coffee table to clink Vince's wineglass with her own. 'Well spotted,' was all she said.

Antony had the good grace to blush, then threw up his hands. 'Okay, okay,' he confessed. 'We might have fooled around as teenagers, but we never had sex. But I knew she liked me and I might have—yes, I might have played on those feelings that night.' He grinned proudly and began rolling another joint. 'What can I say? I'm irresistible.'

We all groaned at this and Hande playfully smacked the top of his head with a cushion.

'Who's next?'

Serena's hand shot up at Ingrid's question. 'Me, me. I want to go next.'

Serena was one of those people who couldn't relate a story or tell a joke without falling into fits of giggling. If the anecdote wasn't funny she would sometimes fall silent in mid-sentence, collect her thoughts and then continue. The result was that everyone felt the need to encourage her when she took the floor; her lack of confidence coupled with her sincerity and kindness meant that we all felt great goodwill towards Serena. It was a relief for all of us that she was willing to be the next player. For one, we knew that her story wouldn't make anyone uncomfortable as Antony's story had: she would never deliberately embarrass Ingrid. Also—and I am sure I was not alone in this—I was desperately trying to think of a story to tell which would be sufficiently daring to compete with Antony's revelations. As a child I once snapped off the head of my sister's most beloved doll in retaliation for her dobbing on me when I'd accidentally broken a crystal vase playing footy in the sunroom, something which was explicitly forbidden. But that was so prosaic and uninteresting. Should I make something up instead?

'Who is it?'

Madeline's question snapped me to attention. Serena was telling us about someone she knew and refused to name, who was a writer and married to another writer. Now Antony was urging her to divulge the woman's name.

'I'm not going to tell you that.'

'So we do *all* know her,' he concluded.

Serena, giggling, glanced over at Ingrid, who quickly shook her head.

'No,' said Serena with finality. 'I'm not telling. You don't know her personally, though you all know her by reputation. Anyway, that's not important. As I said, she's older than us, was just about to turn forty when her husband confessed to an affair with a mutual friend. Shell-shocked, as you would be, she decided to accept an invitation to a high school reunion. Usually she would hate going to such a thing but she was feeling shitty, broken-hearted, and the last place she wanted to be was home . . .'

'Had they split up?'

Serena shook her head at my question. 'No, but her husband had just confessed, and she felt gutted and in no state to make a decision. Anyway, she attends the reunion, gets drunk and ends up sleeping with a man she had a crush on when she was at school.' Serena took a sip of her wine. 'From what she told us he was a typical suburban jock, handsome in a blokey way, and now working as a tradie of some sort. His wife wasn't at the reunion, she was back at home in the city minding the kids, so our friend ends up back at his hotel room and they fuck their brains out for two days before she goes home.'

'Where was the reunion?'

The tip of Serena's tongue slipped through her teeth and licked at her upper lip. It was a habit of hers, something she did whenever she was anxious or unsure. To this day this is the image of her I carry with me, the pink tongue worrying at her top lip.

'I don't know, I can't remember.' She giggled again. 'Somewhere in the country? Anyway, that's not important.'

'Is that it?' Vince rolled his eyes. 'That's not much of a revenge story.'

'No, no, no! I haven't finished.' Serena had become so excited she was jiggling up and down in her seat. 'So she gets home, tells her husband everything, they fight, they scream at one another, they cry, they make up and all is finally forgiven . . .'

'Yeah right . . .'

'Six months later there's a short story competition in the *Age*,' Serena's words spill over Madeline's objection, 'and her husband submits a story that gets published.' Serena paused, her eyes shining. 'This is where it gets interesting. She opens the newspaper on Saturday morning, her husband hasn't said a word to her that he's submitted the story, he wants it to be a surprise . . .'

'Remember,' Ingrid interrupted, 'this friend of ours is a writer as well.'

'Shut up, shut up,' Serena wailed. 'This is my story.' She paused again, to make sure we were all listening. 'So she starts reading her husband's story . . .'

'Wait, wait.'

Serena frowned at Hande. 'What?'

'Where's the husband?'

'Jesus, I don't know. In the kitchen? Taking a slash?'

'But he is there?'

'Yeah, of course . . . will you all just shut up and let me finish? He's there. So she begins reading and it's a story about a man who on his fortieth birthday is told by his wife that she has been having an affair with a mutual friend. He's upset—very upset. His high school reunion is coming up and he decides to go. He goes, he gets drunk and hits on a girl he used to have a crush on. She's married, with kids, leading a very suburban life. They fuck like rabbits and then he comes home and tells his wife. They fight, they argue, they cry, they make up. Our friend finishes reading *that* story.'

We had all fallen quiet. Serena sat back with a jubilant grin on her face.

'My God,' exclaimed Madeline. 'What did your friend do?'

At this point Serena started laughing so hard, so convulsively, that we couldn't help but all laugh ourselves. She couldn't speak. She pointed at Ingrid. 'Finish it, finish it,' she managed to stammer out. Ingrid wrapped her girlfriend in her arms and took over the story.

'She doesn't say a word to her bloke. Or maybe she says something like, good story, congratulations. She's cool, pretends to be unconcerned. But she gets up and goes to his study, climbs up on his desk and proceeds to take a dump right over his keyboard and his computer. She shits and pisses all over his desk.'

There was stunned silence for a moment—even Serena had gone quiet, looking at all of us expectantly—then the moment was broken by Vince loudly clapping.

'Now that,' he said, 'is great revenge.'

Hande was clapping too. 'Good on her. Bravo, bravo. That's exactly what the creep deserved.'

'Why?' It was Marie.

We all turned to her in surprise.

'Don't look at me like that. Why did he deserve it?'

'Because the prick stole her story,' Vince said through clenched teeth.

Marie shrugged. 'That's what writers do, they steal stories. She's a writer, she knows that.'

'No, no.' Hande had crossed her arms. 'He betrayed her.'

'Oh, come on,' Marie groaned. 'What probably pissed her off is that she didn't write the story first. Women do that all the time. We think that because we're in a relationship we shouldn't compete.' I remember how furious she seemed as she spoke, how her voice rose, that she wiped away spittle from the edge of her mouth. 'She's an artist involved with another artist. She can't run away from competition. She just can't.' Possibly aware that we remained unconvinced, she lowered her voice. 'I understand her reaction. Her husband should have told her about the story, shown it to her before it was printed. But I'm not going to blame her husband for writing it. That was his right.'

I was looking at Vince while she spoke; I couldn't read his face. He had no idea I was so focused on him. He was staring intently at Marie.

Serena reached over and took the joint from Antony. 'But you have to admit, it is a great revenge story.'

Vince was now nodding his head slowly. Suddenly he looked over at me. His eyes were gleaming. 'It is a terrific story, revenge on revenge on revenge.' He nodded once more. 'And I do believe that Marie is right.' He raised his glass to her. 'Everything is fair in love and art.'

His comment unsettled us all. I lowered my eyes to the floor.

Ingrid tittered nervously. 'Who's next?'

She looked across at Madeline, who shook her head violently. 'Not me, not me, I can't think of anything.'

At that precise moment I looked up and saw that Vince was about to speak. But before the words could come I heard Mark's voice. 'I'll go next.'

Mark was on his knees, scanning the CD collection on the shelves. He pulled out a disc, slotted it into the player, then came and sat beside me. His knee lightly touched mine and as it did so I knew immediately the story he was going to tell. I knew it so well I could have told it myself.

He had first told it to me when we had just started sleeping together. It was in what is lazily described as the 'honeymoon period'. But it is not a honeymoon, it is not a holiday. It is the ardour of love, it is sweat and labour and exertion, it is boundless energy, when lovers are consumed by the project of understanding one another, discovering one another, of forging union, when every inch of the lover's body is new territory to be discovered and claimed, when their scent is as necessary to one's life as air, the time when the rest of the world vanishes and all those things that once seemed important no longer matter: not friends, not family, not work, not study, not sleep, not food; when what matters most is their eyes, their smell, their skin. He had told it to me after a night of making love. We were smoking cigarettes in bed, waiting for sleep or waiting for the dawn. In that act of narration his story had become my story as well, one of those acts that bonded us to one another; but I am being honest when I write that his divulging it to our friends did not make me feel betrayed or jealous. They too were part of our lives, and it seemed to me that in telling it to them all, with me beside him, Mark was further cementing our union. I think this was what his knee glancing mine was all about. I had never loved Mark more than I did at that moment; I was never so proud of him.

Before we became lovers Mark had been living in a flat in North Fitzroy for three years. It was basic, one bedroom, with a tiny kitchen. But though it was poky and unattractive, he was loath to move out. It was, for all its shortcomings, home. The apartments were across the road from a park and in the middle of that park was a toilet block that was a notorious homosexual beat. Not long after Mark had first moved into the flat, a middle-aged man was viciously bashed in one of the cubicles. When he was discovered he was in a coma, a sleep from which he never recovered. The police found his killer, a young father in his

twenties who was arrested and charged with murder. When the
case came to trial the defence lawyers argued that their client's
assault had been precipitated by the dead man's soliciting of him
at the urinal. Mark became obsessed by the trial, took the tram
into the city every day to sit in on the deliberations. It could
have been me, he would always say, I used to go across to that
beat on a weekly basis, it could have been me bashed and left
dying on that concrete slab, it could have been me that bastard
punched and kicked and pissed on. In the end, the killer pleaded
guilty to manslaughter with diminished responsibility. It may
seem strange now that such a cruel crime could lead to such a
verdict, but it occurred at a time when sexual minorities had
not long been demanding a space within mainstream culture;
and the law, being the law, being slow and cautious, took pity
on a father. The killer walked away with a suspended sentence.

'You have to understand,' Mark was saying, 'that for the
first time in my life I understood what it meant to be outside
society.' He looked directly at Hande and then at Vince. 'I was a
middle-class white kid who had an intellectual understanding of
oppression but I had never felt the outrage of injustice. The man
who died was just like me—a little older, sure, but a professional
white middle-class guy who happened to be a faggot and because
he was a faggot his death was permissible.' Mark drew a breath
and held back his tears.

'If that bastard had apologised once, if just once he had said
sorry for what he did, I think my anger would have dissipated.
But he was in that courtroom day after day and behind him

was the lover and the brother and the sister and the mother and the friends of the man he had killed and he didn't look at them once. And they had to hear every sordid sexual story about their lover and their brother and their son and their friend. He was portrayed as a pervert, it was implied that he was a paedophile because he visited beats. *Well, I visit beats.*'

He spoke the words with molten fury; they rang through the apartment. *I visit beats.*

'I remember the killer's face when the verdict was read out, how he was beaming, how he looked vindicated. He hadn't done anything wrong, and as far as our society was concerned, he was right. He had done nothing wrong.'

Mark, who rarely smoked, reached over for a cigarette from Hande's pack. She lit it for him. Her eyes were wet; she stroked his hand before flicking the lighter. A wave of euphoria rushed through my body.

'He had two children,' Mark continued, the first intake of nicotine steadying his voice. 'A girl of about seven and a boy about five. They were there only the first day of the trial, to make a fucking impression I guess, and they never showed up again. But I realised I knew them.' Mark handed the cigarette to me. 'I was working in that coffee shop in Victoria Street at the time and I realised I had seen them at the primary school down the road, that I had even seen their father pick them up.'

This was where it got hard. This was when his voice began to tremble.

'I'd finish my shift at Time Out and I'd walk down the street to the school. I'd look through the bars of the playground and watch the kids play. I didn't think about the girl; it was the boy I was looking for.'

I didn't dare look away from Mark. He was searching the floor as he spoke, his voice muffled, not braving the faces of our friends.

'I knew that if I did something to the boy, that would hurt their father the most. I just sensed it, he was the kind of guy who would feel it the most if something happened to his son. Sometimes they would walk home from school alone, they didn't live far. I followed them once: I now knew where they lived. There was nothing that didn't go through my mind, how I could hurt that little boy, make him suffer, destroy him, punish him for what had happened to the dead man. There was no terrible thought that didn't cross my mind. I wanted to do it. I wanted to do the unimaginable to him.'

'My God, my God, what did you do?'

Mark looked up, he smiled at Ingrid. A wide, humble, relieved smile. 'Nothing.' He squeezed my knee. 'I did nothing. I walked away. I quit that job, I went back to study, I fell in love. I didn't do anything.' He let out a rush of breath, wiped the sweat from his brow and tipped his head onto my shoulder. 'I came to understand how you could do the most terrible things because of hate.'

I smelt him, the sweat and the smoke and the fear in

him. I could smell the perfume of relief. How I miss that smell, how I still long for it.

Hande crawled on her knees and collapsed into us, her arms around his and my shoulders. 'You are such a good man,' she whispered to my lover, holding his face and kissing him, her tears falling on both of us. 'A good man doesn't let hate dictate what he does. You are the best man I know.'

Vince's voice called out, cold and clear and hard, 'But if you had done something to that boy, bashed him, fucked him, killed him, I wouldn't have blamed you.'

The words were too harsh. Even Mark recoiled.

Hande swung around, furious. 'That's because you are *not* a good man.'

It was exactly what we needed. She sounded so incensed, a mother defending her brood, that Mark burst into laughter. He hugged her, tickled her, until we were all on the floor together, giggling like children. Mark extricated himself from the melee, going to sit on the sofa. He put an arm around Vince. 'He's alright, is our Vince.'

I never loved him more, I was never so proud of him.

The laughter had not quite died out but Vince's voice, assured and clear, sliced through it and we all fell quiet. 'I'm not a good man,' he agreed with Hande, unsmiling, looking at me, looking only at me. 'It's my turn.'

I believed I was the only one among our friends who understood Vince, even though the unspoken undercurrents of our friendship, his indulgence of my obsession, might have indicated to anyone with any insight that our relationship did not rest on an equal footing. I was a fool, but that I did know him well. As he started telling his story I was aware that though he would have appeared calm to everyone else, assuming the unconcern of the born raconteur, there was a certain relish in his performance that evening. It wasn't just the drugs: Vince Varkos had the constitution of an ox, I never once saw him lose control on drugs. This evening, though, there was perspiration on his upper lip, a tremor to his voice. Vince was flushed with exhilaration; he couldn't wait to tell us all his story.

'Revenge is a dish best served cold,' he began. 'Isn't that what they say?' I found myself nodding, as always his best, most attentive audience. 'This is a story,' he continued, 'of how I exacted my revenge years after the fact. I should warn you that I am not proud of what I am about to tell you.'

That was a lie. His gleeful tone betrayed him.

'As Hande will attest, having also grown up in Westmeadows, our schools were full of migrant kids. There were poor Anglos, of course, but mostly we were Slav and Islander, Italians, a scattering of Greeks like myself, and lots and lots of Turks. The Turks dominated the schoolyard—wouldn't you say that was true, Hande?'

'Yes,' she answered, 'we were definitely the majority.'

'I had no idea you went to the same school.'

Vince dismissed Serena with a wave of his hand. 'We didn't, but we were just down the road from one another. Broadmeadows, Westmeadows, Campbellfield, Fawkner, they were all close together. Wogs ruled. Unlike in your schools,' he added.

I caught the shared grin between him and Hande and a spike of jealousy went through me.

'Now you have to understand, in this environment the fact that my mother was a widow, and an attractive young widow, was already a sign of difference. That I was also an exceptional student, a reader with little time for the sporting obsessions of my fellow students—that simply accentuated those initial feelings of being an outsider. For my classmates I was a soft Greek pansy and my mother was a slut.'

'Surely the other Greeks didn't think that?'

Vince raised an eyebrow. 'Hande, don't be so fucking naïve, you're from that world as well. My mother wore make-up, she took great care of her appearance and she refused to wear mourning black for more than forty days. The Greeks did not hide their envy and dislike for her. No, the Greeks were the ones who were most vile to her.'

'Your poor mother.'

Vince smiled once more at Ingrid's comment. 'My poor mama, indeed. By the end of fifth grade I found myself being bullied by three boys, all in my class, all Turks, all stronger and bigger than me—Omet, Hussan and Serkan. The one I hated the most was Serkan. He was the ringleader and he was the cruelest. Their teasing of me was relentless. On my way to school, at school, on the walk back home. They would steal my lunch, stop the other boys from playing with me. I didn't mind their hitting me, their spitting at me, what I detested most was their constant slurs against my mother.' His voice was raised and contemptuous. *'Your mother's a slut! A whore! You're the son of a whore!'*

Vince drew a breath, that chilling smile still on his lips. 'I used to wet the bed at nights, I even had thoughts of suicide. I know this all sounds melodramatic, but there you are. That is the cruelty of childhood. I offer you my experience as a counter to that noxious ignorant lie that childhood is innocent.'

'Did your mother do anything?'

Vince seemed taken aback at Serena's question. He gave a curt shrug. 'I said nothing to my mother. To tell her would have increased my torments tenfold.' Vince's smile was now a smirk. 'Of course, it might have been different for you at a private school, Serena. I'm sure all your schools were much more civilised.'

I blushed. I tried to catch Vince's eye but he was deliberately avoiding my gaze.

'One teacher did attempt to intervene. I still remember his name: Mr Clifford. He took me aside, told me that I needed to become more resilient.'

'That's a fucking stupid thing to say to a child who's being bullied,' said Ingrid.

Vince seemed genuinely surprised. 'On the contrary, it was good advice. To survive I *had* to become more resilient.' He butted out his cigarette. Madeline's hand reached for his but he moved away from her. I'm ashamed to admit that I felt a stab of pleasure at this.

'It lasted a year. Those three boys were ignorant and dumb and are, I presume, still in Westmeadows, breeding further dumb and ignorant children. I went to the local high school until I sat an exam in year nine and won a scholarship to University High. And here I am, very far from the Omets, Hussans and Serkans of this world. But I won't ever forget the agony and humiliation of that year.'

I was concentrating so intently on what Vince was saying that Marie's snort of exasperation took me by surprise. 'Really, Vince,' she said, 'we've all been bullied at school. You surely can't still be wanting revenge on three primary school boys, can you? My God, after *all* these years?'

There were very few occasions when Vince was lost for words, or betrayed any weakness, but this was one. But, almost immediately, he regained his composure. His lips formed a tight snarl as he turned to her.

'You're so the model of the university-educated left-wing feminist, Marie.' He tilted his head then, in mock deference. 'Compassion and forgiveness for the nameless and the stateless, righteous piety and judgemental moralism for everyone else.' He turned to face Ingrid. 'I'm sure Marie here would have agreed with Mr Clifford that all I needed was resilience.'

Marie seemed to want to interject at this moment but Vince spoke right over her. 'No, I bear Omet, Hussan and Serkan no ill will. That would be churlish. Those *cunts* mean nothing in this world.'

'So what's all this got to do with revenge?'

'Ah!' Vince looked delighted. 'Now we can get to the nitty and the gritty. Now I have described to you the world I lived in, the world dominated by Omet and Hussan and Serkan. I got the scholarship and left that pathetic world behind.'

His voice had returned to its usual sardonic tone but I was not at all fooled by the casualness of his speech. There was real pride in him now; he sat with his legs apart, his white shirt open at the collar, his dark tie loosened. He possessed the sofa as he possessed the room, and I wanted to kiss his neck and his handsome, serious face.

'I think it was the happiest day of my mother's life, even more so than when I graduated from university. By then she already knew that I had escaped the working class. Her mantra throughout my school years, from the earliest age, was that I should study, read, better myself.' He turned to Marie. 'I'm sure you'd deconstruct her aspirations as insufferably phallocentric and bourgeois, but she didn't want her child to be condemned to the same monotony that characterised her working life. The day I got accepted into Uni High was the happiest day of her life.'

'I don't condemn your mother's aspirations.'

Vince hardly seemed to notice Marie's objection; he continued, his voice still infused with pride. 'She wanted to take me to dinner. There were two cousins I was close to and she also asked that I invite friends from school. My closest friend was called

George, another Greek and another bookworm.' Vince glanced casually at me, then looked away. 'I think, looking back on it, he was gay.' He shrugged. 'That doesn't matter. The person I most wanted to be there was Nazin. She was a Turkish girl in my class, the only other student who came close to equalling me scholastically.'

There would have been a few catcalls at this unself-conscious vanity—from Ingrid or Antony—but Vince would not have cared. He had no idea why conceit would be considered a negative quality.

'Nazin once received a better mark in a maths test than I did and I was gutted for days, just gutted. From then on I resolved to do better than her. I do believe that this competition spurred me on to be an even better student, and I thought that even though we rarely talked to one another she too understood and enjoyed the thrill of our intellectual combat. Because of it I became obsessed by Nazin—I believed I loved her. I dreamt about her, created conversations between us as I walked to and from school. In my fantasies we both had brilliant futures in the arts or the sciences or in politics, we would get married and we would have many, many kids, we would travel the world, we would be famous.' Vince's eyes were closed and I doubt that any of us had ever seen him so transfixed. He had never once in all the years I had known him talked about love, of that experience and of that emotion. But it was clear as he spoke that night that he did indeed know something about love.

It hurt me, I am ashamed to say. Even without looking at her, I knew it hurt Madeline as well.

Vince opened his eyes. They were cold, hard, unyielding. 'Your typical self-obsessed teenage fantasies, of course. But this was how I felt and I was convinced Nazin had to be there at dinner, to celebrate with me. I mustered all my courage and one day after class I invited her. It was awful. I stammered and I blushed and I could hardly get the words out. In the end she took mercy on me and explained that she could not come to a dinner with me, that her father would never allow it. *But it's okay, it's okay*, I told her. *My mother will be there, I'll get her to phone your dad and he'll know there's nothing to worry about.*' His voice calmed again. 'But this seemed to agitate her and I said nothing more.' He turned towards Hande. 'I put it down to another example of Turkish girls being enslaved by their fathers. It didn't once occur to me that Nazin would not want to celebrate with me. But a few days afterwards I was in the locker corridor talking with George about the dinner. An Omet or a Hussan or a Serkat overheard us and started teasing me. I didn't care, I was soon to be out of there—what harm could their words do me? Noticing that his abuse was having no effect, he called out down the corridor.'

Vince leapt to his feet and began baying. He held us captive, an actor on a stage. I could see the claustrophobic narrow corridor, feel the rush of bodies around the lockers. '*Hey, Nazin, didn't this poofter Vince invite you to dinner?* I wanted to die, not because of what he had said about me, but I would never have

wanted to humiliate Nazin. I think at that moment I was prepared
to punch him: I would have been beaten but I would have been
defending her. So idiotically romantic were my fantasies. Except
he went on, shouting, laughing: *As if Nazin would ever accept
a dinner paid by a whore's wages, as if.* As if! Those last two
words he literally sprayed across my face.'

Vince sat back down. I could not look at him. None of us
dared look at him.

'I was looking straight at her.' His voice had lowered, he
once again sounded unconcerned. 'She said nothing but for a
moment I saw a small sly grin that told me everything I needed
to know. She agreed with him, she agreed with all the Omets
and Hussans and Serkans of this world. That grin disappeared
as soon as she saw me looking at her but I was never to forget
it. That afternoon I went home, waited for Mum to get there
and told her I wanted dinner to just be us. She protested, but
I convinced her that was what I really wanted. For the night of
the dinner she bought a new dress, I still remember it, a white
frock with red floral swirls, she did her hair and she bought
me a new jacket and new shoes. I laughed and talked and was
excited all through dinner, not letting on that inside all I could
think of was Nazin and that cruel disdainful grin. I've never
been able to forget that grin.'

'How did you get your revenge?' Mark's question was so
quiet that we almost did not hear it. He seemed fearful asking
it, as if Vince's story had taken us far from the confines of a
parlour game.

But Vince clapped his hands together and grinned at him. 'Yes, yes, of course, revenge. Let us get to what really matters.' He leaned back in his seat, his finger tracing the stubble under his bottom lip. I thought he was figuring out how best to resume his story, but now I wonder if he was gauging how far he had reeled us in, whether we were there for the taking. In the pause, Serena rose, grabbed more bottles and refilled all our glasses.

Vince watched her fill his glass, then raised it, sipped, and began to speak. 'As you all know, I had a great time after I finished my studies, travelling in Indonesia and Thailand. I'd hooked up with a German girl there, Angela, and she invited me back to West Berlin. I loved Asia but I was hanging out for the bright lights and flushing toilets of Europe. Berlin was astounding. The wall hadn't fallen yet but you could tell there were seismic shifts just about to happen. It was crazy, I didn't sleep, I took a shitload of drugs, I partied every night. It was the most decadent place I have ever visited. Angela knew this DJ, a Kurd called Rajan, and he threw the best raves, they went on for days. He and I hit it off immediately. He was a migrant kid as well, we understood each other. Soon after I got there, Angela left me for a woman—'

'Score one for our team!' yelled out Ingrid.

'Yeah, yeah, yeah, so I decide to head to Greece. Rajan tells me he is holidaying in Turkey for the summer and we decide to meet up in Istanbul.' All of a sudden, with great force, Vince slapped his knee with the palm of his hand; it cracked like a gunshot through the apartment.

'Fuck,' he muttered. 'Fuck, we are so far away here, so far away from life.' The look he threw Marie was fierce. 'You don't know how lucky you are.'

'I think I do,' she replied calmly.

'Didn't you just love Istanbul?'

Vince grinned at Hande. 'Yes I did—it was the second most decadent place I have ever been. Rajan took me to these raves there, to gigs where two hundred screaming Turkish punks in Che Guevara T-shirts and anarchist tattoos were jumping around like it was 1977 while all the time behind the bar a picture of bloody Atatürk hangs on the wall.' He grimaced at Hande. 'What is it with you Turks and that arsehole?'

She shrugged. 'It's the law. Every venue has to display his picture.'

'I couldn't bear his weasel eyes always looking down at me, wherever I was, whatever I was doing.' He shrugged, in imitation of Hande's nonchalance, and returned to his story.

'I danced, I ate, I fucked and I danced some more in Istanbul. The one unintoxicated moment I had I wandered into the Grand Bazaar to buy my mother a necklace. My grandmother always used to say that the best gold in the world comes through Costantinopoli, and it must be true because there is stall after stall after stall of gold being weighed and displayed. I finally found a beautiful crucifix for her, simple but solid gold, and I bought it for her as well as a solid gold chain.' As he was speaking he seemed unaware that his fingers had reached for his exposed neck, that he was softly stroking the underside of his chin.

'After a week in Istanbul, Rajan invites me east to where his family are from. We travelled on buses for days until the West just disappeared. It was mountains, desert, mountains, desert and soon there are signs pointing to Iraq, Iran, Syria, and all these places in the Soviet Union I've never heard of. We're on this 1950s bus with Turkish peasants staring at us as if we've just descended from the stars. Not just me, they think Rajan is an alien as well. We might both look like wogs but he's got brand-new Adidas runners on his feet, a Happy Mondays T-shirt, a mohawk, plugs in his ears. He's a Berliner through and through. I want to laugh, I want to hoot, I'm in the backblocks of Turkey and having a wonderful time. But I notice that the closer we are getting to Rajan's home the angrier he gets, the more he's telling me in his German English that he can't stand the Turks, that they stink, that they're inhospitable, that they're savages. I realise that this dude hates the Turks with a red-hot hereditary passion. They've imprisoned my uncle, he tells me, they've stolen our lands, they are murderers, animals.' Vince had thrown his arms in the air, was gesticulating wildly; I could see the bus, the scorched open road, the Kurdish friend next to him, I could see it all. *Yunan, Yunan*, he kept saying to me, gripping my arm, *you and I are Greek and Kurd united against the Turk*. It's like the further east we head the less of a German he became. The more he remembers his hatred, the less a European he is. I myself don't give a fuck. Omet and Hussan and Serkan are a lifetime away, I left them dying a long slow suburban death in Westmeadows. I want to sing, I want to breakdance, I want to fuck every single one of these peasants, every toothless man, every covered woman, every bright-eyed child on that bus.'

His eyes that night were burning. I finally understood his zeal for travel, for not standing still, for bursting through walls. I could see the desert landscape of eastern Turkey, touch it, smell it.

'The bus stops in the middle of fucking nowhere and we have a few hours to wait till we get on the next one that will finally take us to Rajan's home in what he no longer calls Turkey, in what he insists is Kurdistan. I am in this town with literally one street, there's an old woman herding goats down it, there are snow-capped mountains in the distance. "That's Persia," Rajan tells me. "Or so they say. But that's also Kurdistan."

'Next to the bus stop is this small bazaar and we wander through it. The men are open-mouthed, wondering what we are, men or women, human or alien, the women cover their heads and faces as soon as we approach them, while the kids are all following us, touching us, asking for money, for cigarettes. I'm hungry and thirsty after the long, dirty bus trip and I start bartering with someone for some food when I hear Rajan shout out and I turn around. His hand is gripping tight onto this young boy, he can't be more than seven or eight, who is struggling and kicking at him. Then I notice that the boy has my money belt in his hand, that he must have stolen it off me while I was pointing to what I wanted to buy.'

Vince stopped and looked around at us, as though reminding himself that he was no longer there in Kurdistan but back here in boring and safe Melbourne. 'I rush towards him and grab my belt from him. I didn't care about the money or the traveller's cheques or the passport, all of those could be replaced, but I didn't want to lose the crucifix I'd bought for my mother. I open the money belt and everything is still there. I am about to turn to Rajan and tell him to let the kid go, that there's nothing to worry about. But at that moment, with the gold cross and chain heavy in my hands, the kid looks up at me and grins. A sly mocking grin. And it is as if Nazin is in front of me, not this little kid. The little bitch is laughing at me. I flick the chain and the crucifix whips across his face, and the grin disappears alright—he's not yelling or cursing after that. There's blood on his chin.'

Marie flinched. Vince continued, now speaking directly to her. 'The kid's gone quiet but everyone else is shouting, all his beggar friends, they're all around us, yelling, trying to grab him, but Rajan still has a grip on him and I can't stop myself, I start hitting this child, slapping him, on the face, on the head, on the neck and shoulders. By now all the women are crying and screeching, the kids are screaming louder, the men are walking towards us looking like they want to slit our throats. I know we could be in terrible danger, that what I am doing is unforgivable, but I don't care. I just want to punish the little bastard, I want to make sure that he never grins that grin again.'

Then Vince suddenly leapt up and shouted so loudly that Marie jumped back in fright: '*Polizia! Polizia!*' He was laughing, towering above us, alive and on fire. He sat back down, his voice softening as he spun us back into his net.

'Everything goes quiet, there isn't a sound. The gods are smiling on us—Rajan has just yelled out the one word that can silence them. Everyone suddenly looks terrified and it seems that half the market has just vanished. Then from the middle of this crowd an old man emerges, like some kind of apparition, with a long grey beard, a turban, robe and sandals, like he doesn't belong to our century at all. He comes up to us, grabs the kid, and then *he* starts laying into him. He is screaming abuse at him, he's hurting the kid much more than I was, but the child is too scared to complain. He just howls and takes his punishment. The old man looks at me and starts speaking and Rajan translates. "This child is cursed! This child has the demon in him. Call the police, arrest him if you must." He gives him one final slap and then throws him at our feet. The old man is looking at me and his eyes are full of tears. He is asking me to do something, he's begging me, but I can't understand a word he's saying.

'"What's he saying? What's he saying?" I ask Rajan.

'"He wants you to punish this child. He says he doesn't know what to do with him, that he is his poor departed brother's child, may God have mercy on his soul, that he cannot do anything to discipline the child, that he will only bring shame on them all. In the name of God, will you do something?"'

I had somehow become conscious of Madeline. She had wrapped her arms around her knees, dug herself deeper and deeper into the sofa, moving further and further away from her lover. She was entranced and fearful. I knew this because I was in exactly the same state. We were all mesmerised.

Vince didn't look at any of us as his voice lowered. 'It must have been the heat. The heat and not having eaten and the burning sun and the noise and the sheer animal stench of the place, but above all it was the old man appearing out of nowhere as if he were some Old Testament prophet. It was all of that and the kid being the exact double of Nazin. Her eyes, her face, her softness. I wasn't in time, I was out of time, and I was looking into this old man's eyes, this old man who looked like Moses, who looked as if he had spoken with God and he's asking me what to do and all I can see are his Old Testament eyes and all I can sense is the crucifix in my palm and I just say, "An eye for an eye." That's all, I don't know where it comes from but it does. An eye for an eye. The old man looks across to Rajan, who translates for him. Then it is as if all the fear and anxiety in his face disappears. There is still weariness and sadness but there is no longer fear. He grabs the kid with one hand and my arm with the other and we start following him.'

At that point Hande rose, took a cigarette and went out to the balcony. Mark told me later that she had gone utterly pale, her face drained of all colour and life. It was strange, he told me: Vince was talking about the old man's face being weary and despairing and that was exactly how Hande looked at that moment.

'I am following the old man, Rajan is behind me and behind him is all of the marketplace, all of the village. The little boy is now walking in front of his uncle and what astonishes me is that he doesn't make a move to run away. We haven't gone that far when the old man opens a door in a wall that leads into a courtyard. A group of women and girls are standing around a stove but they cover their heads and go indoors as soon as they see us. The old man pushes his nephew through the door, lets Rajan and me through but closes the door to anyone else. Some of the village kids have climbed the wall and are sitting up there cross-legged, looking down at us.

'The old man picks up a hatchet from against the wall and hands it to me. The blade has been recently sharpened but there is rust at the base, the handle is made of knotted wood. He then grabs the kid and pushes him down so his arm is lying across a stone block that one of the women had been sitting on. He points to his nephew's wrist. The boy is crying now, so hard that the cries are soundless. It is as if he can't breathe, and there is piss running down his legs and wetting the earth under his bare feet.

'Rajan is saying to me, "No, enough, what are you doing?" but the old man keeps pointing to his nephew's wrist and ordering me and it is as if I can understand him, that he is saying this is justice and I am thinking the prophets have walked this land, we are where gods were born and destroyed and resurrected, and I am thinking about how Nazin hurt me, how she scarred me, and I am thinking of how that evil grin of hers hurt me and can still burn, can still burn through me, and I think, this punishment is just. I raise the hatchet.'

'You're a fuckwit, mate, you are such a bullshit artist!' sneered Antony as he stumbled away to join Hande on the balcony.

For the first time since beginning his story, Vince looked directly at me. *I'm not making it up*, he mouthed, shaking his head.

He raised his arm, bent at the elbow, swung it down through the air. 'The axe is old.' His arm swung down and up once, twice, three times. 'It takes me three blows to sever the boy's hand.'

It was Madeline I was thinking of: for the first time since she'd been with Vince, it was Madeline I was thinking of. I haven't been able to shake the memory of her as she was at that instant, her body trembling, her lips trying to form words. If it was a lie he had been spinning, it was a lie that had entrapped his lover as much as it had any of us. If it were truth, she had no more claim to it than any of us there. Madeline had realised at that exact moment what we had all known and had been too cowardly to admit: that Vince did not love her at all. Vince didn't love any of us. He did not love me.

I said it softly. 'You're an evil man. Whether it is true or not, you are an evil man.'

His eyes met mine. His face was flushed, his expression grateful. He nodded his assent. I recall his relief and the wretched sadness in his eyes.

•

What was there to say after that? Did we believe him? Of course that was the question we all wanted to ask ourselves but then was not the moment for asking it. Our first concern was Madeline. She had started crying as soon as he'd finished speaking, but he didn't comfort her or even touch her. Ashamed of her reaction, she fled into the bedroom and the women all followed her.

We men sat in uncomfortable silence. Then Mark pointed towards the hallway. 'You have to go in and talk to her.'

Vince was nodding, as if in agreement. But then he jumped up off the sofa, searched for his shoes, put them on and grabbed his jacket. I had to look away. 'I don't have to do anything. She's hysterical, I can't abide being with her when she's like that.'

Antony rushed in from the balcony. 'You useless, selfish prick. You can't walk out on her—go into the bedroom and talk to her.'

Vince's eyes were glistening. 'What are you going to do, Ant? You going to defend her honour?'

It was clear that Vince would have loved nothing more than for Antony to punch him, that it would have been the fitting antediluvian response to the night. Vince was already victorious, I doubt he would have felt the need to return the punch. But we were not such men. I was ashamed, as were Antony and Mark. Vince shrugged. He turned to leave.

I followed him, I believe Mark did call out, 'Jesus Christ, just let him go,' but I followed Vince.

'Stay, Vince, she'll be alright. It's the drugs and the shock of the story, you hooked us all in, mate, just stay, please stay.'

He patted my arm but did not reply; I watched him throw his jacket over his shoulder and walk down the stairs.

He patted my arm. I remember this now and I am mortified. He patted my arm, like a dog.

•

While we men cleaned up, the women managed to calm Madeline, convincing her to stay the night in the spare bed. We all slowly took our leave. Marie, Hande and Antony shared a taxi while Mark and I decided to walk home through the city.

The last thing Serena said to me as she kissed us goodbye was, 'It's not true, you know. None of it. Vince wouldn't do that—none of us are like that.'

'Of course it's not true,' scoffed Ingrid. 'He did it because he couldn't bear the attention to be on Hande and Marie. Bloody vain up-themselves conceited men.' She took the bowl from the coffee table and hurled the remaining scraps of paper off the balcony. They fluttered in the breeze then spiralled down to the street below.

'You don't think it's true, Mark, do you?' Serena had grabbed hold of his arm.

Mark hugged her close to him. 'He just wanted revenge, baby, and he got it. Vince always gets what he wants.' I tried to catch his eye but he had moved past me in the hallway.

'But it's funny, isn't it,' Serena continued, not wanting to close the door, not wanting the evening to be over like that. 'How is it that the first word we picked out was exactly the one he wanted?'

'Any word would have done,' Mark answered as he kissed her goodbye.

•

That evening marked the end of our social group, the setting of
the sun on our intimate, privileged world. Not that it all ended
abruptly, that we stopped seeing each other then and there. We
stayed in touch for a while, in time even managed to make jokes
about that night. Antony began referring to Vince as Hatchet
Man. *Here comes Hatchet Man. How's it hanging, Hatchet Man?*
Keep your children away from Hatchet Man. But no one ever
really laughed at it. We fell apart slowly. Vince and Madeline
inevitably split up not long after that night, and she moved to
Sydney. I've heard nothing of her for years. Hande and Antony
married and had two children. I heard recently that they have
divorced. Serena and Ingrid are still together and now have a
daughter. Marie lives and works in New York City. Mark and I
lasted for seven years, until I ruined it by having an affair with a
work colleague. He couldn't bear to see me for a few years. But
recently I called and suggested we meet for drinks after work.
We laughed and chatted without acrimony; and alas, for me at
least, not without regret.

Vince is in Athens. He is married, he is a father. In Europe
on a work trip two years ago, I sent an email to the last address I
had for him, saying I'd be in Athens for a few days and suggesting
we catch up. I did not receive a reply.

Marriage, children, divorce, affairs, travel, work. It was
inevitable that we would all drift apart. I once thought our group
unshakeable but that was a delusion of youth. We were far more
ordinary than we believed ourselves to be.

•

That night as Mark and I walked home, out of the city, through the gardens, I don't recall that we talked much. The exercise stilled the chemicals in our blood, brought us welcome fatigue. While he showered, I had a cigarette on his small balcony. In the waning of the night I watched a car pull up across the road; a young man got out and walked over to the toilet block in the park.

While I brushed my teeth, Mark stood at the bathroom door. I could see his reflection in the mirror. He was naked, his hair wet, his skin flushed from the hot shower.

'What word did you write down?' he asked me.

My mouth was full of toothpaste, I had to spit into the basin before I could answer. 'It was silly,' I said, 'I couldn't think of anything so I just wrote down "childhood".'

He smiled at this, a small tender smile, but when I turned to him I don't think I'd ever seen him look so sad.

Tourists

AT THE END OF THAT LONG day, as they fell into bed, exhausted, they both agreed that it had all been worth it, if only for Edward Hopper's *Early Sunday Morning, 1930.*

'You know,' Bill said, cupping Trina's body into his, his left arm gently curving around her belly, 'I'm always a little scared when I finally get to view a painting I've always wanted to see that it will never be as good as my anticipation of it. But the best paintings never disappoint you, do they?'

'Mmm,' Trina answered, welcome sleep only moments away. 'That's so true.'

His friend Brendan had emailed him from Sydney, had written, *Dude, you have to go to the Whitney. It's one of the things you HAVE to do in New York*. Their friend Clare, who had recently returned home after a year in the United States, had told them the Whitney was fabulous. And their Rough Guide to the city had made special mention of the museum. They had to go to the Whitney.

Their first mistake had been to think that they could walk there from their hotel, which was just south of East Houston. Though it was only late May, they had woken to a muggy morning, the light conquering the city's seemingly impenetrable layer of haze to bathe the streets in hues of orange, gold and yellow.

They had forgone breakfast at the hotel in order to find a café in Little Italy, but when they got there they all seemed to be shut. A skinny blank-faced girl was wiping down a table on Mott Street but when they went to take a seat she had shaken her head and said, *Sorry, we're not open till eleven*. It was a curt, dismissive statement and it had given him the shits. They had kept walking and ended up in Starbucks. Their croissants were dry and their coffee bland, and he couldn't stop complaining.

'You're such a snob,' she laughed.

'We got rid of Starbucks in Melbourne,' he reminded her.

'Bully for Melbourne.' She laughed again. 'We're in New York City—how can you even try to compare it to Melbourne?' She struggled to find an analogy that would do justice to her feelings. 'It's like . . . like . . . It's like comparing a village to a metropolis.'

That had put him in a sulk. Then by the time they had reached 23rd and Third Avenue, the back of his shirt was damp with sweat. She seemed not to notice the heat, had not slowed her pace to accommodate it.

'I think we should take the subway from here,' he announced.

'Oh, are you sure?' She sounded disappointed. 'I'm so enjoying the walk.'

He hadn't pushed it. But he quickened his steps, letting her fall behind, so that she had to call out to him to slow down. 'Walk with me, don't run ahead.'

He heard it as a whine. 'Well, stop fucking dawdling.'

She said nothing but at 42nd Street she inexplicably turned right.

'What are you doing? That's the wrong way.' He wanted to consult the map in his back pocket; he was sure they had to head towards Fifth Avenue, but he didn't want to take out the map and look like a tourist.

'We're getting the subway.'

They didn't speak a word to each other on the train. She motioned for the map and he silently took it out, inching away from her as he did so, turning his back to her as she unfolded it.

A young Hispanic couple, the youth with his arm around the girl's waist, both of them listening to music through their earphones as they rested their heads against each other, watched her reading the map. The boy lifted the earphone away from the girl's ear and whispered something to her. Bill blushed and turned his body further away.

At the 77th Street stop she got up and he scrambled to follow her. His right hand was held awkwardly against the front pocket of his jeans; every few minutes he would brush it against the pocket, making sure the wallet was still there.

Back at street level, she handed him the map. 'You know,' she said, 'we *are* tourists.'

Pissy bitch. He deliberately dawdled, letting her walk ahead, but as they crossed into Fifth Avenue his bad mood vanished. He quickened his step and reached for the bottle of water in the pocket of her backpack. 'Hey,' he said, smiling, 'look up.'

They stopped, looking down the avenue, at block after block of stately nineteenth-century facades that disappeared into Harlem. It was a workday, and grim-faced New Yorkers in business suits jostled past them. A middle-aged woman, svelte in a tight black dress, held out her hand for a cab but it whipped past her. 'Fuck this,' she drawled, putting her sunglasses back on in one quick graceful movement.

Trina slid her arm through his. 'Isn't it the most fabulous city?'

A previous night, in a bar in SoHo, he had been waiting to catch the eye of the bartender when he overheard a man beside him say, 'God, I hate Midtown, it's full of tourists.' He and Trina had just spent the day at the top of the Empire State Building, listening to the audio tour, gazing down at the astonishing city encircling them, so moved he had found his eyes welling with tears. But at the bar, he cringed. The bartender had cocked an impatient eyebrow at him, waiting for him to order, and Bill had been embarrassed by his own accent. He had to repeat the order, the harsh Australian consonants and chopped vowels sounding grotesque to his own ears.

But now, with the valley of the avenue chopped into alternating geometric shapes of light and shade from the sun straight above them, he realised that he *loved* Midtown, the fantasy of it, the romance of it, the cinematic sweep of it. They were still arm in arm when they reached the Whitney.

There was a queue. Bill went to the front to read the sign on the glass doors and a stout older woman in a dark blue uniform approached him.

'You can't go in there, sir.' She was shaking her head. 'We don't open till one today, sir.'

Bill joined Trina at the end of the line.

'What's wrong?'

'She was such an officious bitch,' he answered. 'And I just hate how she kept calling me *sir* in that rude, supercilious way. It's so fucking false.'

At a minute to the hour the glass doors were still locked and the stern woman guarding the entrance still had her arms crossed. A woman in the middle of the queue had just sighed loudly, *Oh for God's sake*, when the guard, as if taking pity on them, pushed open the doors and gestured for the queue to start moving. Even so, they were ignored by three young staff at the front desk, a man and two women; they were laughing and logging on to their computers, refusing to look up. Then, almost in unison, their smiles disappeared and they turned to face the waiting line. To Bill, the young man appeared particularly irritated, as though the visitors were an unnecessary imposition. He hoped they didn't get him.

But as they moved forward he was the next attendant free. He was handsome, immaculately dressed in a crisply ironed fawn shirt.

Bill had his wallet open and asked, 'How much for the two of us?'

And then the little prick rolled his eyes and tapped the notice in front of him.

Bill felt sweaty, was sure that there were damp patches under the arms of his T-shirt. He was all too aware that, unlike the other visitors, New Yorkers in smart summer wear, his and Trina's T-shirts and shorts, her backpack, marked them out as outsiders. Fumbling with the money, Bill handed forty dollars across the counter.

Trina stepped up beside him. 'There's a Hopper on display, isn't there?'

And then the little fucker did it again, rolled his eyes. 'Yes,' he answered her, not hiding the contempt in his voice, 'but we are a museum of *contemporary* art.' He drew out the penultimate word as though Trina might never have heard it before.

Bill felt Trina flinch beside him and when the man handed over the two paper tickets, Bill grabbed them out of his hand. The young man's distant demeanour wavered for a split second, then he recovered and the sneer returned to his face. 'The Hopper is on the top floor.' Then a pause. 'Sir.'

They walked towards the lift, then as they waited there behind an elderly couple, Bill exploded. 'What a stuck-up black cunt,' he hissed at Trina.

The old woman turned around, stunned, looked at him and then quickly turned away, taking a step as though recoiling from him. Trina had also shifted away from him and was looking at the floor. In the lift to the top floor, she stood in the corner opposite him, her eyes fixed on the numbers lighting up above the door.

She waited till everyone else had exited and then she turned to him, her eyes furious. 'You Neanderthal, how dare you?' He couldn't answer her, he couldn't find the words. She almost ran from him and disappeared around a corner. He knew better than to follow her.

For the first few minutes he wasn't even aware of the canvases on the white walls, the sculptures or the mobiles. As much as he was hiding from his wife, he was also avoiding the elderly couple from the lift. He couldn't stand seeing their distaste, their revulsion. And he did feel revolting; the shame that was blinding him to the world in front of his eyes seemed impossible to quell. His body felt lumpy and awkward, misshapen and clumsy, as if the insult he had uttered had physically altered him. He felt unclean.

For fuck's sake, he rebuked himself, thinking of the man's arrogant dismissal of him and Trina, *why didn't I just call him a spoilt cunt, or a rude cunt, or even a faggot cunt?* All of them were inexcusable, but none was as disgraceful—no, as *blasphemous*—as what he had said.

He turned into a small alcove off the main gallery and that was when he saw the Hopper, a row of tenement shopfronts, the red and yellow pigments bold and earthy at the same time, the blue of the morning sky repeated in a stretch of awning, in the hues of the curtains of the apartments above the shops. The beauty of the painting stilled the chaos inside his head; he forgot about the heat of the day, the insulting behaviour of the young man, the wretched abasement of his own response to it. The melancholy of the painting, the quiet, empty street, the evocation of solitude, made him long to be back home. He had to stop himself reaching out to touch the painting, seeking its solace.

Trina had come up next to him. He smiled at her wide-eyed admiration of the work. He leaned across to her and said softly, 'It's beautiful, isn't it?'

'I'm not ready to talk to you yet.'

His shame had vanished completely. 'Fuck off then.' He didn't care if he was overheard.

So this is contemporary art. The top level consisted of works in the collection that had been exhibited in biennales over the last forty years. Though Bill was no expert in art, he knew enough to recognise the beauty in the Rothko and the Johns, the Bourgeois and the Kruger. But in the gallery he had just entered, a large flat-topped cubicle took up most of the floor space. Branches and twigs had been arranged around it but seemingly with no attention to line or design. It looked as primitive as the little sculptures his niece brought back from kindergarten; except, at four years of age, his niece already had a more developed aesthetic eye than did the sculptor of the work in front of him. The walls were made of the thinnest chipboard, unpainted and untreated. Bill walked around the cubicle. An unsmiling security guard was standing watch and as he walked past him, Bill playfully rolled his eyes. The man did not blink, continued to look determinedly ahead. He turned around to take a quick peek at the man but the guard's face remained stony, there was no shift in his straight-backed stance.

There was more wood and metal and wiring haphazardly thrown together as sculpture on the lower level; there was also an early sixties Mustang convertible, the inside gutted, and a video projection of a desert highway flashing across the windscreen, random Polaroids of the desert landscape around Joshua Tree stuck along its chassis. In another room, a DVD on a loop played what seemed to be a harshly over-lit video of a woman's hand grating a plastic toy; it was not a doll, which would have at least made some kind of sociological sense; nor was it a war toy, which would also have had a discernible purpose. Two women, plump and silver-haired, dressed as though they had set off for church or temple that morning, were looking quizzically at the screen. *There's nothing there*, he wanted to say to them, *don't bother*, but if the day was teaching him anything it was that he should just keep his big stupid fat mouth shut.

He wandered into a passage that led to a large darkened gallery in which one long wall was divided into two screens.

On the first panel a dignified old man, in a thick checked shirt buttoned at the collar, was answering questions from an off-screen interviewer. Something about the old man's suspicious but dignified manner in front of the camera spoke of a much earlier age, as did the vivid colours of the image, shot on film, pulsating with depth. On the second panel an abstract collage of found footage—from nature documentaries, educational instructions, old family Super 8—reminded Bill of his early childhood, as did the whirring of the projector. The second panel played silently while on the first the old man struggled to answer questions about himself. Within minutes Bill recognised that the old man had dementia, that his memory had been ripped from him the way his own grandfather's memory had been stolen. The strain in the old man's voice, the unsettling fear in his eyes as he tried to recall if he did indeed have children, was almost unbearable to watch.

Bill let his eyes rest on the footage of a man and woman setting up a tent by a river: the saturated colours of the Super 8 stock, blown up to fit the wall, were as rich and brilliant as the brushstrokes in the Hopper painting. There were footsteps and he turned to see the elderly couple from the lift enter the room, hesitating for a moment as they adjusted to the near darkness.

Bill slipped out, terrified that they would recognise him, walked quickly to the stairs and straight down them to the ground level. It was only then that he regretted not finding out the artist's name; the installation about the loss of memory had moved him. The three young attendants were still seated at the counter but he couldn't face asking them, didn't want to have to deal with their rudeness, the insinuation in the young man's tone that he was somehow not worthy to bear witness to such art.

He pushed through the glass doors and took in breath after breath of the hot dirty air. With the exception of the Hopper and the unknown artist's video installation, the Whitney had only offered him emptiness. He hoped Trina would feel something of how he felt, agree with his reaction. If she didn't, if she liked that place, responded to that art, it seemed to him impossible for them to trust one another's feelings again. He felt it would separate her from him forever.

He was awaiting her exit from the gallery with such eagerness that her sudden appearance and grim silence momentarily confused him. Then he remembered and he couldn't suppress a groan: she hadn't forgiven him.

She took out the bottle of water, drank from it, and returned it to her pack without offering him any. 'I'm hungry,' she announced. 'There's a place Chloe told me about, she said it was a fantastic old-school kosher deli.'

'That sounds good. Where is it?'

'On the Upper West Side.'

It was already close to two o'clock and it would mean having to walk all the way across the park. Or catch a cab. He didn't want to go but he didn't want to upset her further, so he just stood there looking indecisive.

She looked at him as if he were some idiot. 'You don't want to go there?'

'No, no,' he lied, 'I do.'

She slipped the backpack onto her shoulders and started walking. He called her name and she swung around, her annoyance evident.

'I think we should get a cab.'

'I want to walk.'

'We're hungry, it's hot, it's across Central Park. Come on—let's get a cab.'

'No.' She was shaking her head, her arms folded. 'I want to walk. So I'm going to suggest that we split up and we'll have lunch separately.'

'No, I think we should have lunch together.'

'I'm not sure I want to have lunch with you.'

For God's sake, they had just been words, about a preppy stuck-up shit who had insulted her. And the little prick hadn't even heard them. But Bill knew that there was no possibility of winning that argument, knew that he didn't deserve to.

'I'm really sorry. It was an awful, idiotic thing to say.'

'It was more than that,' she spat out. 'It was a racist thing to say.' Her voice wasn't raised at all, but he was conscious of the delivery van that had eased into a park behind her, and that the driver was black. 'I feel like I don't know you.'

The driver had opened the back door to the van and was lifting boxes onto the kerb.

'I feel terrible about it, Trina, I really do.' Bill found he was whispering. 'I feel really ashamed.' He offered her a shy apologetic smile. 'Let's get some lunch, eh?'

She shook her head. 'I want a couple of hours alone. You actually repulse me at the moment.'

If he spoke he would cry. He stood there, nodding, as she told him to meet her in three hours at a bar on Mulberry Street that they had discovered their first night in the city. If he spoke he would cry.

He wandered the city, looking into the windows of cafés and restaurants, unable to decide on any of them for lunch. He walked in the shade of the cross streets of the Upper East Side, past Lexington, past Third Avenue. He found a small deli and ordered a pastrami and salad roll that turned out to be enormous, and sat on a small stool outside to eat it, but could only manage to eat a third of it. Down the street he could see a man wheeling his belongings in a trolley, stopping every so often to check through bins and gutters. Bill wrapped the roll in a napkin and perched it carefully on the edge of the stool for the homeless man to find.

Bill walked all the way to the edge of the island, hoping to find a park, a space, some kind of solitude from the roar and bustle of the metropolis, but at the edge of the city a motorway, ugly and relentless, barred any access to the river. His shirt was now sticking to his back.

He wandered back to Second Avenue and scanned the sign above a bus shelter. An elderly man dressed in a light brown suit, a fedora in his hand, looked across at him and smiled.

'Excuse me,' Bill said to him, 'can I get a bus here to go downtown?'

'Where do you want to get to, son?'

'Allen Street.'

'It's the right bus.'

They waited, standing next to each other.

'Are you English?'

'No, I'm Australian.'

The old man smiled. 'I've always wanted to go there. I've heard Sydney is beautiful.'

'I'm from Melbourne.' The old man kept smiling and nodding. 'It's in the south,' Bill explained.

But the old man had looked away and was holding out his hand to hail the bus. Bill climbed the steps behind the man and held out a five-dollar bill to the driver.

'Allen Street, please.'

The driver was shaking his head. 'Exact change, sir.'

Feeling foolish, feeling like everyone's eyes were on him, Bill fumbled through his pocket. He had to re-count his money, confused by the foreign coins. He had only a dollar fifty in change. And a two-dollar Australian coin.

The old man had made his way back to the front of the bus and tapped Bill on the shoulder. 'How much do you need, son?'

'Fifty cents.' Bill gratefully accepted the two quarters, took his ticket and moved down the aisle. The old man had sat next to a young woman who was listening to her iPod. As he passed, Bill said thank you to him, and the old man replied, 'Don't mention it.'

Bill took a seat down the back and then stood up again, balancing carefully as he weaved down the aisle to stand next to the old man. 'Excuse me, sir.' Bill took the gold Australian coin from his pocket and handed it to him. 'This is a two-dollar Australian coin,' he explained, 'for you to use when you make it to Sydney.'

The old man beamed as he accepted the coin. 'Thank you, son, you're a mensch.' He laughed at Bill's puzzled expression. 'It means you're a good boy, son.'

Bill didn't dare say a word for fear that if he did he would burst out crying.

He got to the bar fifteen minutes early and Trina was twenty minutes late. The first time they had come across it, it had been evening and the place was full. There was a crush to get to the bar and the music was loud; they had thrilled at ordering martinis and sitting at the bar, watching the mating rituals of the fashionably dressed young New Yorkers. They had sat in a blessed jet-lagged torpor, every so often looking at each other and laughing, *We're in New York, we're in New York!* But that afternoon the bar was empty except for the sullen-mouthed young bartender, her hair dyed platinum in a pageboy bob. Bill ordered a beer and took a seat at a front table.

When Trina did arrive she offered no apology for her lateness. He jumped up to greet her. 'Do you want a beer?'

Instead of answering she threw her bag on a chair, barked at him to look after it and walked over to the bar herself. She returned with a white wine, placed the backpack between her feet and took the seat.

He leaned over to her, whispered, 'I missed you.'

And he had, he really had; he had pined for the presence of her by his side. The city he had wandered through that afternoon had seemed grimier and far less miraculous than when she was with him, when she was seeing what he was seeing, taking in what he was taking in. He was jealous of all that she had done that day without him.

'I didn't miss you at all.'

The bar, the city, everything fell away and there was only a rising panic, a fear of what she would say next. During and after their worst rows, their most cauterising arguments, he had fantasised about life without her and had decided it would be possible. He knew he could survive leaving her. It was a truth that he zealously kept from her, a trump card that he would only play if she dared him with the threat of walking out. In the past, that certainty had warmed him: that he could answer back that he didn't need her. But now, for the first time not assured of her devotion to him, he realised it was not the truth. He could not live without her.

He dared not speak.

A black youth, a khaki satchel flung over his shoulder, was running against a red light, crossing the road towards them. The youth jumped onto the kerb and walked over to the table.

'How you all doing?' He was remarkably handsome, still only an adolescent, with an open sincere smile. His clothes stank of his sleeping in them. 'I am very sorry to disturb you but I was hoping you might have some loose change to give me.'

Trina had already brought her backpack to her knee, was opening it. Bill pulled out his wallet. He took out a ten-dollar note and handed it to the youth.

The smile widened. 'Sir, I am so very grateful.'

There was a whistle from behind the bar. The three of them turned; the bartender was gesturing to the young man that he should leave. He dipped his head, almost a bow, and sauntered up the street.

Trina was shaking her head. 'Was that some kind of fucking absolution? You think that makes up for what you said?'

Before he could speak, before he could even begin to think about what a possible answer could be, two older gentlemen came into the bar and sat at the next table. They were both slim and dressed in fine linen suits. The taller man was wearing a beret, which he placed on the table as soon as he sat down. He took off his jacket and carefully folded it across his knees. They were both softly spoken but Bill was sure that they were speaking Italian. One of the men took out a small map of the city and examined it while the other went to the bar, returning with two glasses of beer. He nodded to Bill and Trina. The two men clinked glasses and took a sip. Bill watched as the tall man leaned over and very tenderly wiped a line of foam from the other man's top lip. Oh, he realised, they are lovers.

Trina got up and went over to their table. He heard her introduce herself and the three of them began a conversation in Italian. He did not feel slighted at all: he adored it when his wife spoke the language. She seemed more animated, more alive, when she spoke in her parents' tongue. At one point one of the men pointed to Bill and she said something that made the three of them laugh. Bill lifted his shoulders and frowned in pretend annoyance.

Trina sat back down beside him. 'They came to New York twenty years ago,' she explained, 'and they haven't been back since then. Vincente,' she indicated the taller man, 'is from Abruzzo, not far from where my father was born. Carlo is from the Veneto. They met in university, in Padua, thirty-five years ago. Isn't that wonderful?'

Bill wished she had said that without sounding so melancholy. 'It is wonderful.'

Trina smiled at him, the first smile she had offered him all afternoon. 'Carlo said that you are very handsome and I said that you need to keep your weight down.'

Bill laughed, heartily, hungrily; he tilted his head back and roared. He was sated by her smile.

After their second drink he asked her what she had thought of the Whitney.

'The smug emptiness of the work stunned me.' Trina gazed out onto the street. 'I thought it was art that suited a city that had brought an entire economy to near collapse by speculating on the value of nothing.'

Trina shook her head as they both watched an old Chinese woman walk by carrying an enormous plastic bag full of empty aluminium cans. 'I thought the art there was arrogant and vain and that none of it will survive. I don't think any of it deserves to survive.'

He listened, wanting to tell her about the video installation, how that had not been cheap or inert, that it had moved him. But he dared say nothing.

After dinner they took the lift to the rooftop bar of the hotel for one final drink, a whisky for him and a vodka and soda for her. But a DJ was playing relentlessly anodyne house music, it was crowded, with every sofa and chair taken, and the bouncer at the door had moved to forbid them entry till Bill flashed him their room key.

They stood with their drinks in a corner, crushed against each other, looking east along Houston to the shadows of Alphabet City.

'This was probably a really tough neighbourhood.' Trina was shouting to be heard, her words sliding into each other. 'Imagine what it would have been like when Vincente and Carlo came here twenty years ago.'

He could only nod. The pulsating drone of the music, the constant motion of a train of people pressing by them, the semi-darkness which strained his eyes: he wanted it all gone, he wanted only to be alone with his wife.

Her lip curled, her face fell and he thought for a moment she was about to cry. 'You bastard,' she said up close to him, 'when we do have kids, you dare say one racist thing to them, just one, and I swear I'll leave you and take them away from you.' She was thumping his chest, hard.

Next to them, a young woman giggled and whispered something to her boyfriend.

Bill took hold of Trina's hands. 'I promise,' he repeated, frantically, earnestly, like a schoolboy pledging a vow on his mother's life. 'I promise, I promise.'

He had never been so desperate to assure her—and himself—of anything.

When they got back to their room, they found that the maid had scattered a handful of mints on the pillow where they had left the tip.

The Hair of the Dog

MY MOTHER IS BEST KNOWN FOR giving blowjobs to Pete Best and Paul McCartney in the toilets of the Star-Club in Hamburg one night in the early sixties. She said that Best's penis was thicker, the bigger one, but that McCartney's was the more beautiful. 'Paul's cock was *elegant*,' she liked to say. I know too that she had spat both men's semen into a tissue, and that neither man had looked at the other while she took turns servicing them. Afterwards, she had shared a cigarette with Paul.

There is no exact date for when the above incident took place but we do know that The Beatles were performing in Germany from 1960 to the end of 1962. The musicians would have not yet been twenty; my mother, born towards the end of the war, would have been even younger.

My grandmother was a widow when she gave birth to my mother, having lost her husband in the battle for the Dukla Pass. Even on her deathbed my grandmother refused to name my mother's father, preferring as she did the entire time I'd grown up in her house to remain silent about the war years and those following.

I know that much of my mother's bitterness about her own mother arose from the obduracy of this denial. My mother saw it, as did many of her generation, as an unwillingness to face the past, as a denial that went beyond the personal and embodied the collective stink of German history. But I don't see it that way. It was painful for my Oma to stir up those memories. Though she never told me of it directly, I sensed her loneliness. I was not burdened by it; I think it made me want to please her more. I do know that she loved her husband; the way she sighed when she spoke his name, Manfred, when she remembered him, told me that. And she must have remembered him every day of her life, or at least every day of those eighteen years I lived with her. Until I was an adult and left home, I would hear her sigh his name at least once a day.

•

My own father was called Eddie Price. He was a booking agent for nightclubs and music halls in England. My mother had already had two terminations by the time she was pregnant with me and there is no doubt I would have been her third but for a dream she had on the eve of visiting the abortionist. In the dream, she was back in the science laboratory of the *Realschule*. All she remembers is seeing two jars, each containing a foetus suspended in formaldehyde, and that next to them there was a third jar smashed on the shelf. She awoke convinced that if she had another abortion, she would never be able to bear a child again.

I met Eddie once: we shared an uncomfortable lunch in a pub in Manchester. A handsome man in his youth, he was by then obese, his face destroyed by too many years of drinking, smoking and God knows what other excesses. He had married an English woman, Louise, but his wife knew nothing of me. Eddie died in the early eighties and I am still in contact with my half-brother, Alan, who is a generous, stolid northern Englishman. My two half-sisters, Bernie and Alice, still want nothing to do with me.

As I did not live with my mother as a child, what I know of her life over this period comes from reading her first book, the memoir *Der Tropfen der das Fass zum Überlaufen brachte*. In English this literally means 'the drop that made the barrel run over', and has the sense contained in the phrase 'the straw that broke the camel's back'. But I think my mother's English translator made the right choice rendering the title as *The Hair of the Dog*, for that is indeed the sense and the spirit of the book. It is just under ninety pages in the original German, a fiercely honest account of an addict who is unashamed of her drinking, who makes no apologies for her ferocious love of alcohol. It was difficult for me to read it at first—shocking, really—for very early in the book she describes how, faced with the choice of sobriety and motherhood or abandoning herself to the bottle, she chose the latter.

She calls herself Maria in the book, and she doesn't use my real name or that of my father, but she does call my Oma by her name, and she begins the book with what has become its most notorious passage: on her knees in the filthy toilet at the back of the Star-Club in Hamburg, sucking off two of The Beatles. I guess that also must have been a shock to read when I was fifteen, but it is the cavalier abrogation of any responsibility towards her child that of course hurt me the most.

'It's just a book,' she would say to me, and would then turn to her mother. 'It's just a fucking book, don't take it too seriously.'

'Your mother takes responsibility for nothing.' My grand-mother would spit out those words like a curse.

They would have no effect on my mother; she would just turn around and laugh. 'That's a good one, you old witch. I love the audacity you have to talk to me about responsibility.'

I have reread *Der Tropfen der das Fass zum Überlaufen brachte* recently and now I can see that it is indeed a marvellous book, written with that stupendous combination of arrogance and self-revelation that makes the first work of any writer with genuine talent such an electric experience to read. It is also undisciplined: the best writing in it is about drink, about chasing drink, about the euphoria that comes with drinking. But there are also rants in it, ill-informed condemnations of West German politicians and artists, long patches of repetitive exploits. There is righteous fury in it as well: her character Maria would gladly incinerate the whole of Western Europe for the inhumanity of the Holocaust and the cowardice of collaboration—but there is not one scrap of genuine kindness.

Victor thinks me too critical. He says that though the writing is sometimes incoherent, he admires the avenging urgency of my mother's tone. 'What else could her generation do?' he asks, always rhetorically. 'They had to create an art that punished the poisonous legacy of National Socialism.'

I don't bother arguing with him. He is an Australian, of European heritage admittedly, but his knowledge of European history is limited to the broad brushstrokes of a television documentary. I have learned not to labour the point with him; he gets childishly irritable and offended when I counter that he wants history to be written at the level of good guys versus bad guys, when I reproach him for not being subtle in his thinking. I once accused him of thinking like an American and, my God, was that a mistake. He refused to speak to me for a week.

It is not only with him: I have learned that discretion is necessary here in my adopted country when it comes to politics. But occasionally I will meet a German traveller to Melbourne and it is blissful to talk our language for an hour, to give vent to all my dissatisfaction and annoyance with Australia.

But always the traveller will ask, 'So, do you want to come back home?' and I'll answer, *Nein. Nein nein nein.*

I wish that Victor had met my Oma.

•

My mother adored Victor. 'He's such a beautiful man,' she would say to me in German, loudly, so he could hear. 'He is a god.'

She flirted with him and he basked in her admiration. And of course he loved her notoriety; I'm sure that he was writing letters back home nonchalantly mentioning that his German lover's mother had sucked off Paul McCartney and was a celebrated cult writer. But he also saw how mean alcohol could make her. One terrible night, in a bar on the Dudenstrasse, my mother flayed me viciously, insulting my looks, my intelligence, my beliefs, my hopes, my dreams.

'You are a nothing,' she accused. She prided herself on being non-violent—oh yes, she was all peace and fucking love—but I'd rather she had smacked me or punched me or scratched my face. It would have been easier to bear.

Victor shouted at her, I had never seen him so furious, and he led me away as I wept, my eyes swollen, everyone staring at us.

It was a bitterly cold night. That ruthless Berlin wind was carving right through us and I just kept saying to him, 'Take me to Australia, please take me away from here, please take me to your home.'

And Victor, who had been dreaming about the romance of Europe since adolescence, who had read across philosophy and philology in order to be an intellectual in Europe, agreed. He held me in his arms that night on a bench in the Britzer Garten, and told me about swimming in the savage ocean, about the smells of the desert, about crocodiles and wombats and kangaroos.

It was February and I worked double shifts at the bar to save money. In April, two years before the fall of the Berlin Wall, I bought my one-way ticket to Australia.

•

My mother's second book is called *Brüderchen und Schwesterchen—Brother and Sister*. It is a dark, unsettling fable, pornographic and compelling. It begins with two adolescent siblings discovering that their mother has disappeared. The father is long dead and there seems to be no one else in the village they trust or who shares any kinship with them. No location is named, nor a year, but through some carefully placed clues—the styling of the boy's collar; a film magazine with Fredric March on the cover—we know it takes place in the early 1930s. Left alone, Rolf and Lisbeth, the brother and sister, begin to play at marriage, first cautiously, then passionately, and finally, desperately. The danger and release of their fucking is intoxicating but very soon they begin to tear at each other, wanting to destroy one another. By the end they have starved to death, Rolf expiring first as Lisbeth lies next to him. She hears his final breath and she also believes she can hear the first soft murmurings of their child's heartbeat deep inside her.

It is, of course, perverse; the unrepentant eroticism of her portrayal of incest was deemed outrageous, but by the end of the twentieth century, scandal no longer necessarily meant being an outcast. The book was a tremendous critical success. And that is how it should be. *Brother and Sister* gets under your skin and remains there; after reading it you want to raise your head and gulp for air, so entirely has her writing seduced you and dragged you into the siblings' squalid, hermetic world.

Many critics wrote of the novel as some kind of allegory of German history, sifting through the text to uncover metaphors for Weimar or for the divided Germanys of the Cold War. Undoubtedly such readings are accurate, but I am not a critic. My mother always had too much to say about history. But I think that novel is her finest work not because of the ferocity of her writing but because it is not a story about herself. I can read it without seeing her, something I cannot do with the memoir. I wonder too about the dead father in the novel. By the fogginess of the children's recollections of him it is clear that he died in the Great War. Their memories of him are tender. We understand that the mother's desertion of her children may have arisen from her inability to come to terms with the loss of her husband.

The story is oblique but, as it was written after my grand-mother's death, I'd like to believe that *Brother and Sister* was also a rapprochement with my Oma's ghost, that for the first time my mother could look at her personal past with some tenderness and could admit to her own mother's suffering.

We never really had the chance to have that conversation. I didn't return to Germany for the publication of the second book, though I sent her a long lauding letter when I read it, and when I started to speak about it that last time in Hamburg, she dismissed my question with an exaggerated groan. *'Mein Gott!* It's just a fucking book, don't take it too seriously.'

Victor, of course, who desires happy endings in reality if not in fiction, remains convinced that the novel proves that my mother had forgiven her own mother. All I know is that the morning we had agreed to visit my Oma's grave, my mother rang, off her face, incoherent, to say she couldn't make it.

Unlike Victor, I am sceptical of happy endings.

•

My mother died just after her last book was published. It is a self-lacerating story, another memoir, about the destruction of age. It is merciless and very funny. She describes what it is like to try and masturbate when your cunt has become so dry that even poking one little finger up there causes unbearable pain, how the smells her body emits disgust her, what it is like to wake up after a night of boozing with excrement caking your buttocks and your thighs. She describes hiring a young Turkish man to touch her, to just run his fingers across her tits, her stomach, her cunt; how she witnessed the grim concentration in his eyes as he fought back his aversion to her body. The author is aware of the great cosmic joke time has played on her, leaving her lust and her fantasies sharp, youthful and intact, while deracinating and drying up the ageing body. And that is its title, *Zeitlich. Time.*

My mother was out of time.

•

Victor and I had a terrible argument that last trip to Germany. Dismayed by how feeble and ill my mother was, he wanted to bring her home with us. When I demurred, he accused me of abandoning her. I thought him ridiculous. He had just read her fucking book. Was he prepared to clean up her shit every morning? Did he really believe she would be happy in our California bungalow in Melbourne? Did he really think my mother would be content tending to the vegetable patch and pretending to be interested in the endless stories from Mrs Koulouris next door about her grandchildren?

He didn't want to listen. 'It's our responsibility,' he insisted. 'We have to take care of her. Don't you love your mother?'

'I do,' I yelled back, 'but I don't particularly like her.'

His face was purple with fury. 'You're inhuman,' he spluttered, 'just inhuman.'

We thought my mother was asleep in her bedroom but at that moment she came into the living room wearing an open robe and nothing else, and filled a dirty glass with the cheap red wine she loved drinking. Victor turned away, embarrassed by her nakedness.

My mother gulped hungrily from her glass, finished it and refilled it. She wiped her cracked, wine-stained lips with a sleeve. 'Victor, darling,' she said, 'I think you are adorable, but for Christ's sake, stop being so insufferably *petit-bourgeois*.'

Danke, Mama, danke schön.

She died in her sleep. Her wish was to be cremated. I returned to Germany for her funeral and it was during that time that

I discovered for myself the wonderful numbing panacea of alcohol. Throughout the organisation of her funeral, the endless conversations with journalists and critics, I drank. I drank from morning to night, I was drunk at the service, I was drunk at the wake, I was drunk on the flight home.

I was sitting next to a slim young thing, a blue-eyed pale-skinned woman returning home after five years in Europe. She asked me if I was visiting Australia for the first time.

'No, I live there,' I explained. 'I've just been back to bury my mother.'

'Oh,' the young woman said with wide eyes, then added timidly, 'I'm so sorry.'

'No, no,' I slurred, and then giggled. 'She had an interesting life, my mother, there is no reason to feel sorry for her.' Then I said it, wanting to be wicked, wanting to see how she would react. 'She once sucked off Paul McCartney in the toilets of the Star-Club in Hamburg, many, many years ago.'

The young woman stared at me. 'Oh,' she said again, and then sighed, no doubt thinking of her own mother, of returning home. 'She sounds amazing.'

'Yes,' I answered, indicating to the steward that I wanted another drink, 'yes, indeed she was.'

Petals

I am imprisoned. I am in here for three years. I am having to endure two years and three months longer. I don't know if I can endure. I don't speak. This is a curse and there is no reply to make back to a curse.

They are blaspheming all the time in here. They are beasts, and not only the imprisoned ones. The ones with the keys, they too are wild. The master too and those who are working here, they all have the stare of a beast. This gaze they all share, it doesn't come from in here, it is carving on their faces from long ago. Their fathers too have the same stare and their grandfathers and the grandfathers before them.

It tells where they come from and what they are.

I sing yesterday. I don't know why, I no sing from the first day here. No, from even before. From the moment when I open my eyes in the peace and in the calm and I am hearing a song from inside my body. Not from outside me but inside, a melody that is being sung by my blood and my bones. I hear my voice and I open my eyes and all is mud and dirt.

She is white, as if a leech has drunk all of her juice. I am killing her. The singing stops. She falls, a bird I shoot with my sling. Then I see that her fingers on her left hand are twitching, that her eyes are opening and closing and opening and closing. I have not killed her. I lay her before Death but He does not take her.

For bringing her to Death's door I am here for three years and I must endure two years and three months more.

I have no hunger for song and I have no right for song. Even my pain and my solitude do not deserve a song.

Even so, I sing yesterday. My voice is a clarino.

Where are the greens of the meadow, the water from the well?

Stiv hears. Stiv is the name of that poofter, sometimes they call him Stivi, the little Stiv. It is not possible such a pollution is once a child. I struggle to say their names, they makes my mouth twist, like a stone is caught there. Stiv Gharin, such a name tears at my throat. Stiv Gharin shouting at me, *What's that shit you are singing, dago? Who said you're allowed to sing?*

—I don't need permission from you to sing, you fucking animal.

—What was that, you reffo?

I say again in Greek.

And that is when his eyes go the glare of his race and of the demons, and I swear to all the gods and all the saints and to the Mother of us all that I am speaking the truth. They are all devils, him and his father and his grandfather and their grandfathers before them. Till you reach the end of their line and you find the Satan. That is their start and that is their story. It is written in their eyes.

He makes a scream, from deepest hell. Each word is a gob of spit at my face, at my brow, at my cheeks. *Speak English, you dirty fucking wog!*

Where are the greens of the meadow, the water from the well?

His forehead smashes into mine and there is pain, then black, then a yellow light. Then I am throwing up an ocean of blood. Stiv Gharin, that obscenity, that demon, he is gone.

I see it then that I will kill him. A vision of a prophet, ancient and built by the gods.

I have two years and three months. Why do I care, what is there to seek from a future? I have no future, I only have fate. All future is gone now.

I see this written as if a commandment from our God.

—Are you hurtin'?

It is Tzim. He is a good lad. It is him and me and the poofter Stiv, we are the three in this cage. Tzim is good, he is tasty, he is sweet and he is handsome. He is half of that race of beasts and criminals and he is half of that black race here that is made a misery. He is good and he is handsome but the drink in here has made him slow and the pooftering here has made him a whore. That is as it is. I too jump the kid but only when we are alone. Of course I jump him. He is tasty and he is sweet. When I kiss him, his lips are soft, they are as a child. He tastes like a child. I kiss him. The others only jump him, they are a gang and they jump him together. One is in his arse and two are in his mouth and the others spill themselves all over him. But I am a man, I am still human and I kiss him.

—I no hurt.

He doesn't believe in me. He brushes his finger on my nose and pain makes tears in my eyes. And I curse, I curse the Christ and the Mother and I curse my balls.

Tzim jumps back, a shadow in his eyes, the mark of the beast of that damned white race. And even him, even him that they spit on and they fuck and they bash and whose arse they have made the same as the cunt of an old woman who has birthed a dozen children, even he does not bear it when I speak my tongue.

That is what every stranger is like. I understand it first on the ship that takes me to these dark horizons, I understand it that the stranger cannot bear our tongue. Of course, I understand it. I too do not want to hear a stranger's tongue. That is God's law everywhere.

I speak in English. *Thanks, mate.*

He is again sweet. He smiles. He takes a scrap from his pocket, a cloth that is a handkerchief also and full of his sweat and his spit. The cloth is red now with my blood. He gives it to me the cloth.

—Come on, I'll take you to the sick room.

Butchers they have here, not doctors. The doctors and nurses here they too have that wild stare. I don't want to go but there where Tzim touches it my nose it begins to swing like a bell.

Fuck bloody God, I want to hear the peal of bells on the mountains and through the valleys! I want to hear a chant from a priest, even though them I can't bear. I leave Greece and in here I leave one more time my homeland. There is no Greece anywhere left for me, not even in that toilet of shit they call Melbourne. Even there I am exile.

Two years and three months. What does that matter?

—No sick room, no bloody doctors, I say to Tzim. I tell him I want to go to the desert.

—Go bush, I go bush, I become black bastard like you.

He doesn't like it. I take his hand.

The dog with the keys, that outrage, he laughs when he sees me.

—I want sick room.

—And I want cunt. What are you going to do about it?

Two years and three months. I slaughter him now and then they hang me with that beautiful lad, Ronilt Raen, handsome that one, a man that one, I am proud to swing next to a man like that. And I will meet Death with at least one cunt cop head hanging from my belt.

Tzim lets go of my hand.

•

The doctor is new, only here four months and not yet savage. He is a kid, he is a little darling. He has red hair and he has blue eyes. It will happen, it will happen. He is of their race, soon he'll be a beast.

—What happened, Arthur?

He says our names, the animal with the keys doesn't like it. I don't speak.

—What happened to him, Donaldson?

—He fell.

And with that the monster with the keys, he pushes Tzim out of the room. The doctor and I only alone.

Tzuli too has red hair. Tzuli too has blue eyes. Before I making her eyes black, before I am killing her.

Slowly, slowly the doctor fixes me up. He is taking my nose and pushing. There is a pain, it is burning in fire but I am not even one breath leaving to escape. I do not move at all.

—You really need a hospital.

That makes me laughing. I am eleven years old when I first coming to Athens and having my nose breaking in a boxing match. There is no hospital for me then and there is no hospital now. Hospitals not belonging to us.

To forget pain I looking up at the icon of the Queen on the wall behind the doctor. She is not beautiful but she is young and she looks like one of them but not with that ugly savage stare. It is this forsaken land that making them beasts. It will make us all beasts. Her skin is white, I'd like to touch her skin, to put my hands on her tits, to make her cunt lick my fingers.

The doctor is noticing my staring at the Queen. Not for him, he doesn't like her. He talks of my homeland, he starts to say big words I can't understand, I hear democracy, I think I hear fascism. I think. I don't know, they are big words and I have no appetite to answer him even if I did understand him. Why is he asking me questions? What does he want from me?

Tzuli too asked me questions. All the time, asking me questions. About the wars, about Greece, about politics. Tzuli is a student and wanting to know everything. In the end, she betray me.

Best not to say a word to no one, that's the first and best lesson I taking from Greece. Best to not say one damned word.

Tzuli wanting to know everything. And in the end, in court, she tells them everything. How many times I am hitting her, how many times I am kicking her, she tells them everything. She is tasty and she is sweet, she is beautiful and she is good. But in the end she is a betrayer.

I pretending I am mute and I am dumb. I pretending I don't know one fucking thing about politics.

I can see, that young, sweet doctor, he is not happy in me. What the devil does he want from me?

He is not happy in all of us Greeks in here. There are four of us, we all pretending we are hicks from the mountains. The devils with the keys and the demons with who we share our cages, they don't want us together. *Speak English, you reffo cunt!* They don't want us together and we don't want to be together. We reminding each of us of what each of us is losing.

None of us answering the doctor's questions.

Two years and three months. I will go to the desert. Black I will become.

He bandaging me up.

I makes my way to the yard. In the far corner, where there is some soil and garden, there is the old man with his roses, colours I have before never seen. I like the old man, he is timid and he is gentle, he is sweet and he is soft. I have never heard him blaspheme. I go to help planting some more flowers. A thorn pricks my skin and I damn the rose and the garden and the prison and the world. He laughs but then quickly stopping, he looking away. I see that there is fear in his glance.

He doesn't stare as the beasts do, he stares as the frightened do.

He jumps children, that is his sickness and his fate, that is why they have imprisoned him. All of them hate him, those animals despise him. The murderers and the rapists, the thieves and the forgers, the drunks and the drugged, the dogs with the keys, all of them hit him and bash him and spit him and curse him and rape him, and again and again they bring him just to reaching Death. They make him look at Death, then bring him back. Again and again. That is his life. The beasts say of him, He is the worst, the most ugly and vile thing in here, that there is nothing worse.

I don't believe it. He is gentle and he is upright. I think those little girls are fortunate to being broken in by a good man, it is no problem if I is a boy fucking a gentleman like him. He is tender and rare is tender. That is why the wild men with those venom stares can't stand him. It is the tender they hate. They don't have it, their fathers never have it, not their grandfathers or their grandfathers before them.

Pink and yellow like the sun; white as Tzuli's skin. There are blue roses here and purple and gold and red. I like working in the soil and the mud and the ground and the dirt with the old man. Silent, our hands and knees graze the flowers and the musk of the petals flies all around us. Everywhere else here stinks foul; here, in this small patch, there is perfume.

—I heard you had an accident, Luigi.

It is Stiv, Stiv and his arsebuddies. A gang of wild beastly glares. I don't pay him attention. He is pissed off.

With one hand he grabs the flowers, the thorns cut his skin, but he not caring. He tears them from the earth.

One small bit of land, one bit of good in this hell. Even that is too much for him. He is not from family or society, he does not know of welcoming or duty. He is an animal in the wild, he is savage.

Stiv rips apart the flowers. His arsefriends take hold of the old man from behind and Stiv opens the poor old fool's mouth, the old fool who doesn't cry out, doesn't say no, doesn't say a word, the old fool who suffers this every day, and Stiv fills the old man's mouth with flowers, with the petals, with the thorns, with the stems and with the dirt. They are laughing. Blood on the lips of the old man, blood like tears running from his mouth.

Stiv to me turns next. He is pulling out the remaining flowers. He is not laughing.

Where are the greens of the meadow, the water from the well?

I wish to sing, to sing so loud that the mountains fall. But there are no mountains here. I cannot find my voice. And it is the old man stopping me. His eyes pleading for me to not do a thing, not say a thing, not make movement. His eyes are terror and helpless and understand all together. The old man is stopping me.

Stiv throws the flowers in my face. With laughing, as always with the most vile of words—*dago* and *reffo* and *wog* and *poofter* and *cunt* and *fuck* and *shit* and *piss*—Stiv and his arsebuddies are not here.

Tzim's cloth is still in my pocket. I clean up the old man, I pull out thorns from his lips and his tongue, pull one from the back of his throat. What a worthless race black Fate has sent me to dwell with. Whatever the old man is doing before, his body now is frail and it is dying. How can they do this to old men? There is nothing of knowledge or respect here, I say into my own mouth, just poofterism, alcohol and violence.

—Spit, I tell him. And he spits in Tzim's handkerchief.

•

The nights inside here sicken me. The minutes pass like hours and the hours are infernal and eternal. We playing cards, we listening to wireless, but most of all they are evil cursing. The black bastards too, they curse. The Yugoslavs too, that spat-upon and lost race, they are shouting and blaspheming. We Greeks and the Calabrians, we letting out vileness only under our breath. Otherwise, *Shut your mouth, you bloody dumb dago*. It is the race of the savage glare that create the din of hell. Every second word a foulness, every other a blasphemy.

The old man alone he sits, always alone. If I having real balls I should be sitting with him but it is not worth it. They will give it to me day and night and night and day. He is scratching at his lip, taking off the skin where the thorns is been biting him. The little skins float into his lap like dying petals.

Stiv Gharin gets up from the table of card players and asks the filth with the keys he wants to go to the toilet.

I get up too, I ask the filth with the keys that I must go to the toilet.

In the latrine I can hear Stiv Gharin pissing a fountain. Then he lets drop a foul fart as he shits.

Two years and three months.

I kick door and he has no time. Brow meets brow, and I am hitting him so hard with my forehead that the sound is a clean Orthodox bell ringing on the mountains. He places a hand to the wall of the latrine, he has courage this beast, he will fight Death, but he cannot go to his feet before I pulling at his hair and bringing his head down hard on the concrete slab of the toilet. I do it again. And again, the bells ring.

I pull his head up by his hair to give it to him a third time.

He is a caught fish, a dying fish, his mouth opening closing opening closing.

I let go of his hair.

He is seeing black and in the black a yellow light. He can't get up, he is there around my legs, twisting like the damned adder he is. I let him squirm. I wrap Tzim's cloth around my hand and I dip into the latrine, I grab his three fat shits.

—I hears you have accident, Stiv.

He knows what is awaiting for him. He is trying again to go to his feet but I smack him hard and he falls back on the latrine. I pull his mouth, he is a frightened dangerous serpent but I am now having the hunger of a god and I don't care that he is bite me and scratch me and punch me. I am opening his mouth, I am seeing right down to his black heart and I am grabbing the shit and pushing it all the way down, I am filling his mouth and I am filling his throat. I fill the animal's lungs with the shit.

Two years and three months.

I leave him, let him drop. I go to wash my hands. I clean them and I clean them, I don't want his stink on my skin. I clean them and I clean them and I can hear the Stiv is making retches and then I hear him vomiting. He is on his hands and knees. He retches again and then the vomit is coming, all that shit but also there is pink and there is the yellow of the sun and there is blue and there is orange and there is purple. So many colours for this shadow place.

Mother of us all, where have you taken me, that vomit is beautiful here? Stiv is taking a breath, still on all fours and looking up at me. Black his eyes, dark the wild stare in his eyes: I am not managing to conquer that.

I close the tap. I open my lungs and I start to sing.

Where are the greens of the meadow, the water from the well?

—Who said you can sing, wog?

Two years and three months. I'll go to the desert, that most bleak of seas, I'll become a black bastard. I'll make that my home.

—This is Australia, wog! We speak Australian here, wog!

Every hour of every day. Every hour of every day, dear God, these condemned, these barbarians, these animals, they cannot take breath without curses falling from their mouth.

Two years and three months.

I am walking back to the latrine. He is a snake, that is what he is, he is venom. I am kicking him, he falls. Then I am raising my right foot, our boots in here they are thick-soled and they are heavy. With all my might, with all the strength that God has given me, I am smashing my foot down. I am Bobi Mor, I am Eusevio and that miracle child, I am Pelai. I am sing, *Where are the greens of the meadow, the water from the well?* With every kicking of my foot on his head, I can't do anything but singing.

All around me, just for a moment, one blessed moment, there is the sweetest scent of roses.

Written in Greek and translated into English by the author

Hung Phat!

SHE NAMECHECKS HYPATIA AS A HERO. She wraps herself in white cloth: scarves and sheer shawls. 'You know how they killed Hypatia,' she asks me, 'do you?' I don't.

She tells me. They stripped her and hacked away at her skin with shards of broken pottery. 'They ripped her skin off.' She shudders. 'Can you believe that?'

Hypatia was head of the library at Alexandria, keeper of knowledge for the whole of the ancient world. They burned down the library, destroyed the scrolls. They skinned her alive.

'Who's they?'

She shrugs. A scarf is wound theatrically around her head. 'They is *they*: the Pope and the Emperor, their priests and their soldiers. The same *they* as always. That's the part of history that never changes.'

She's a pessimist. It comes naturally, she says, she doesn't have to bullshit to be it. But she can't shake her addiction to astrology and will always read a horoscope if she comes across one. We're walking down the street, oblivious to the movement around us, we are together in her world. I'm guiding a path and she's reading aloud from a *Woman's Day*. 'Crap, crap, crap.' Her voice is a stiletto. 'Horoscopes are just another lie,' she loudly tells the street. She throws the magazine onto a bench and we keep walking. A few steps on and she's changed her mind, turns back to grab the magazine, to have another look. 'It's because I'm a Virgo,' she explains. 'We're hard to please.'

Virgos are hard to please. Virgos make enemies easily. They love to talk but they're not subtle, and at their worst they are just plain fucking rude. The ones I know are all independent. They're virgins, untouched. I don't know shit about astrology but my best friends are always Virgos. It is the only sign I can pick. I can always pick a Virgo.

'I can piss standing up,' she tells me.

'Bullshit.'

'Wanna bet?'

'Okay. How much?'

'Five dollars.'

She's got her feet wide apart, knees slightly bent, leaning over. She's doing it. I rub the bottom of my chin with my thumb. I've lost the bet and the piss is sinking into the dirt.

She hitches up her undies.

I hand over the money.

•

We've known each other from day one. Which is not quite true, but true enough. We met in school when we were fifteen. She had been a student in some hippie institution, and wore colours and beads. She and I liked each other immediately. We fell upon each other. We were misfits but we desperately wanted to be liked.

I was very young when I worked out that I preferred spending time with girls. Kid-in-the-sandpit young. At fifteen, it was a little bit different. I was kissing girls as well as hanging out with them and that was changing everything. She didn't care; sex didn't muddle us up. We knew it straight away, just by looking at each other. She made me laugh, and she seemed like a sister to me. I don't have a sister but I imagine her and me is what it would feel like.

She gave me good advice about sex, about love, about the differences between men and women. Much better than anything I received from other girls, from guys, from Mum, Dad, from my teachers; even better than the television. I had another friend, Jessie, and we used to talk, but one night we rolled around together drunk at a party and pashed on. They were only alcohol kisses. The next day at school, we avoided each other. My crush was on Bella, big, beautiful, black-haired, long-legged Bella. But Bella never looked at me.

I was also close to Derek. We were cool. He was okay, but he wanted to fuck me. That sounds up myself but it was true. He told me and I said it was alright, that I didn't mind, that I was kind of flattered. But that changed things too. Again, I just wasn't interested. I did have sex once with a guy, Dominic Borstino. I guess it was sex. We wanked together watching porn. His dad was out and we found the pornos under Mr Borstino's bed. We watched them and touched each other's dicks a few times. We didn't look at each other. As soon as I blew, he jumped up and left the room. He spent ages in the bathroom. I heard a flush through the porno-disco music and he came out with a towel, all zipped up. I was pissed off. I had wanted to see him come. I never told Derek about Dominic. But I told Zazie.

That's her name. I should tell you that. Her name is Zazie.

'Did you like it?'

'Dunno. Don't think so. It was strange with no talking, no kissing.'

'Did you want to kiss him?'

'Nah, not really, but I still wish we had. I didn't really want to kiss him but I wanted there to be kissing.'

The bell whistles the beginning of class and she jumps off the fence, tramples the cigarette. 'Would you do it again?'

I shake my head no. 'I like girls,' I tell her.

We head for the lockers.

•

The name Zazie has no history, she tells me, none at all. Her mum made it up, plucked it out of the multicultural air. Zazie's mother has a mix in her. Scottish, English, some French and maybe something Spanish, but she shed her European skin long ago. She had got pregnant at twenty-four, two years out of uni, one year into a research job on radio. She decided to keep the baby. The father was doing a PhD in agricultural science, measuring and counting the land. Neither wanted marriage. But Zazie's mum wanted the baby. Every summer after New Year, Zazie would go up north to stay with her father, his wife, and their two children. I'd miss her like crazy. My suburb's asphalt streets stank from the heat. There was nothing to do.

She would come back bush-brown. 'Fuck, it was boring up there,' she'd always say, and straight away she was back to watching videos, smoking cones. I always envied her those summer escapes. It was nowhere, a farmhouse amid a numbing puzzle of paddocks, but it wasn't home, it wasn't the suburbs. It wasn't fucking Blackburn.

Blackburn used to be orchards. Shady fruit trees, apples and oranges. But I never knew the orchards—they got taken over by supermarkets. There was one magic spot left, a hillside that ran into a creek. I walked up and down along that creek, winter and summer, fleeing the wearisome suburban grind. I saw a snake once. It was thin and shone a brilliant black. I had jumped on a log and it slid away from underneath, flashing into the undergrowth. It was a tiny thing really; my fear was only momentary.

I told Zazie about it. She laughed. 'You should see the whoppers I've seen in Queensland.' Another reason to be envious.

In the library, flicking through film books, I came across an entry for a film called *Zazie in the Metro*. A French film by Louis Malle, the guy married to Candice Bergen. I showed it to Zazie. She got all excited. 'Did you name me after that film?' she asked her mother when she got home. Her mum had never heard of it. But Zazie was not convinced. She must have come across it at some stage. Zazie must have come from somewhere.

'So you do have a history,' I told her.

'Yeah,' she laughed. 'I'm related to Murphy Brown.'

•

Our last summer at school I had sex with Kayla Robinson. I forgot the condoms and splashed all over her stomach. We lay close together afterwards, listening to each other breathing. The radio, whose sound had disappeared while we were fucking, came back slowly. I gently pushed her away from me, wanting to get up, and our skin had stuck together. Patterns were forming across her stomach, her breasts were wet. I kissed her and she tickled my dick.

'It's droopy—it looks tired,' she giggled.

I didn't say anything, I grabbed my T-shirt. The drying semen looked odd on her body, on her soft skin. I cleaned her up.

•

Kayla, Zazie and I were watching *The Color Purple* on video. I was a little stoned, a little bored and flicking through magazines.

'They've changed it,' Zazie complained. 'The women were lovers for ages in the book.'

'Hey, Zaz, you're a lesbian, aren't ya?' asked Kayla. The question was straightforward, interested. There was nothing sly or malicious about it. But the room became dangerous.

'Yes,' said Zazie.

We didn't look at each other. When the movie finished we went out to get smokes. Zazie was strolling the aisles of the 7-Eleven, shoplifting chocolates. The three of us were walking around the shop, hand in hand.

•

A girl at school got murdered. Her body was dumped on the train line. She was younger than me, two years below, but Kayla was good friends with her sister. Zazie was angry, not scared like Kayla, but furious. Cops came to talk to students, to teachers, news crews would follow us home.

'I want to get out of here,' Zazie started saying. 'I've had it with this place.'

The murdered girl was Orthodox. Kayla and I went to the funeral. The church was weird, smelly but wonderful. I got high on the incense, on the colours and gold of the icons. The saints looked poor and tired, some of the holy pictures seemed weathered and damaged. The dead girl's mother was hysterical. That was the part of the ceremony I hated the most;

she was falling and twisting into cracked shapes, supported by her sons. She was howling. Beside me, Kayla was crying softly. I tried to cry, I squeezed my eyes tight, but nothing happened. I wasn't sad.

●

Zazie moved. Her mother sold their place, got a flat in Brunswick. That changed everything. I was a regular house guest, crashing out on the sofa in the lounge room. I loved Brunswick, the small houses, the trams and the streets. It was noisy and the air there smelt like a city. I was looking for work, Zazie was studying. It was just one year really, one small year, but we had tremendous fun. There was always speed and there were always parties. Strange beds all the time. Kayla and I broke up, Derek moved to Sydney. It was just me and Zazie.

She has a photograph of me from that time, standing outside a Victoria Street grocery. I'm in a black T-shirt and my arms are crossed. The sign above me reads, HUNG PHAT! It's Vietnamese and we don't know what it means. But she thinks it's funny. 'Are you hung?' she yells at me. We're at Luna Park, off our heads, riding a roller-coaster. I scream back, 'You'll never know!'

We've never seen each other nude. I have imagined it.

The photograph of me rides her wallet. It's the only photograph there.

●

Work changed me. Zazie said that about me and I guess she was right. I was working in the city, selling phones and faxes, the odds and ends of communications. I sleepwalked through it, putting money away each week, cutting down on going out. I was determined to travel and Zazie slipped out of my life. She was studying, meeting people, fucking women. I receded from her world. From time to time we'd ring. I'd leave messages on her machine and she'd leave messages with my mum. She got tattooed and nose-ringed. Work had me in a white shirt and a tie.

She came in one day to take me to lunch. The guys I worked with stared hard at her.

She kissed me across the counter. 'Can I take you away from here?'

'Please do.' I was in the middle of a sale, spinning bullshit about mobile phones to a nervous carpenter who was sniffing the air. It was Zazie he could smell. She smelt of sweat and incense, of dope and cigarettes. Herbal cigarettes. She walked through the store, caressing the hardware.

Lunch was three quick pots and a packet of Twisties at the Charles Dickens. She told me about a video she was making, asked me how my savings were going.

She pulled at my tie, poked fun at me. 'You look so straight.'

'I have to look straight.'

I promised to send her a postcard from America. She'd always been in love with the myth of New York. I was visiting America for her, she was making me do it. 'New York, now that's a real city,' she said, 'the only real city.' She promised to write to me while I was away.

I returned tipsy to work, chewing on some PK, fingers yellow from the Twisties. I could no longer smell Zazie in the shop. Only the dry odour of plastic.

•

I ring her on a Friday night. I leave this message on the machine: 'Zaz, it's me. Got a call from Kayla yesterday. She's getting married. She'd like you to come along. It's a small do, no big church bullshit. Call me.'

On the following Thursday, Dad tells me Zazie called. She wants to know when the wedding is.

I call back, leave this message: 'Zaz, the wedding is on March twenty-third. Can you make it? Call me. I want you to be my date.'

Three weeks later I get a call. I'm home alone, watching a porno. I pause the video and grab the phone. The TV screen flickers on a bright yellow image, a close-up of a woman's face, her eyes closed, her head tilted back, simulating ecstasy.

Zazie rushes into a conversation, stumbling and sliding through words and emotions. She can't make the wedding. Too much study. She's in love. Her video is going to be shown in some festival in St Kilda. Anyway, she doesn't like weddings. Tells me to give her best to Kayla, bitches about her buying into the suburban dream. She sounds as if she's speeding. Abruptly she tells me she has to go. Someone's at her door. I say goodbye. There's a click, then the dial tone.

I continue the video but I'm wanking without a hard-on. When I come, it's nothing, a zero instead of a feeling; it's like taking a leak but there's less sensation.

•

There were between seven hundred thousand and a million scrolls in the ancient library in Alexandria. Writings from Phoenicia and Persia, from across the Mediterranean. Mathematics and astrology, plays and epics.

In Zazie's video, simply called *Hypatia*, a woman is seen walking through a library, touching the spines of books. A security guard comes into the library and arrests her. There is a fire and books are thrown on it. Then the video cuts to the woman's head being shaved; her hands are cuffed and her clothes are stripped away. Cut. A scroll is thrown on the fire. A flash to a computer screen being logged out, then a hammer smashes through the screen. The end.

There is light applause after the screening. I cheer, I whistle, I stamp my feet. Zazie is in the row in front of me and she turns around with a wicked smile. 'Quiet, you dag,' she whispers. She's blushing. I keep cheering. I am—there is only one possible word for it—I am proud.

•

Five postcards and a letter.

Greece, 5 May 1992, a statue of Athena on a suburban roof, crisscrossed by television aerials. I write: *Zazie, this place is chaos. The banks are always on strike, the streets are always crowded, day or night, and it stinks. I kind of like it. I met up with a German woman who speaks very good English and what sounds like passable Greek. She and I are going to travel to some of the islands together.*

Lesbos, 23 May 1992. Three naked women, all blonde, lying on a beach. *Zaz, saw this card and immediately thought of you. I've spotted many dykes here but there doesn't seem to be any Museum of Lesbian History. Did you make that up? It is stunning here, but I miss Australian spaces. You can't get away from anyone here, too many tourists. All the Greeks seem to have a brother or sister or cousin in Melbourne. Write to me at 17 Rue d'Alsace, Paris. Claudia, who I'm travelling with, has got a friend who'll put us up there. Write.* I underlined this final word twice.

Paris, 8 July 1992. The Eiffel Tower. *I love this city. It is beautiful in the morning light, in the bright sun, it's glorious at night. I feel cheap and nasty, everyone else is dressed so well. Australia seems very far away and Melbourne seems so limp in comparison. The flat we're staying in is small and cramped, it overlooks the railyards. But I don't give a damn. It took less than a minute, Zazie, less than a minute to love this place. P.S. Visited Morrison's grave. Placed flowers on Oscar's tomb, from both of us.*

Dublin, 16 October 1992. An A4-sized advertisement for Sinéad O'Connor's new CD, I ripped it off a shop window and I write on the back. *Gorgeous, isn't she? I'm so glad to get out of London. Everyone was whingeing and gloomy. Ireland is obviously poorer but people are friendlier. Also, too many Aussies in England. I wanted to escape all that. I'm going to Belfast, to visit some of Dad's family. I feel at home here in Ireland. Does that sound weird? I don't think it's a pretence. I am relaxed here. There's a Palestinian student I met at the hostel that you'd really like. Her name is Anna and she's doing a PhD on Gertrude Stein. Do you know her? She was a dyke writer long ago. Of course you probably know her. I've got one of her books,* QED. *I'm sending it to you surface mail along with some other things. Anna is good to talk to. She talks about Israel, Palestine, war. She explained to me the differences between Christians and Muslims. I just listen to her, keep my mouth shut. I'm realising I know nothing.*

New York City, 3 January 1993. The Chrysler Building. *Happy New Year, Zaz. It's fucking freezing and the hotel room is sucking up all my cash. I'm going to try and hitch down to the south tomorrow. Is the Chrysler still your favourite building? I keep trying to look inconspicuous on the streets but I can't help looking up and then standing like a stunned mullet in awe of the architecture. Don't write now, I'll be back home soon. Unless some rich yank wants to be my sugar mummy or daddy (at this stage, I'm open to all offers). You'll have to visit here. You'd love it, it is so exciting.* At the bottom of the card, two sentences are scrawled out with heavy ink.

This is what I crossed out, what I couldn't send to Zazie: *Mate, I hate this place, I hate NY, I am lonely and I'm cold and no one speaks to me. I hate their fast chicken, fast ribs, fast burgers, fast fries, fast lives.*

And from San Francisco, 10 January 1993. A crumpled paper napkin. Across it, scrawled in blue pen, were the words: *Zazie, Australian girls are cool.* It was signed Jennifer Jason Leigh.

I add a note. *Zaz, she was sitting, reading a paper, in a booth across from me. I felt like a deep dag but I had to get her autograph for you. You're absolutely right. She's fucking beautiful! The USA, mate. What a trip!*

•

She picked me up from the airport. She had her hair shaved. I hugged her tight. Driving into Melbourne, the city looked fragile, deserted and flat. We had a coffee in Smith Street and all I could think of was how big the streets were, and how white everyone's face was. Zazie was very white. Not just pale, but skin that came close to the perfection of white.

'Sorry I didn't write. I was so busy, I'm making another film, a real film this time.'

'The other one was a real film.'

'No, that was video.'

She kept talking, I sat there watching Australia go by. Home. I was missing Europe.

•

Her film is called *Trace*. It's eight minutes long and shot in black and white. It opens on an old woman's face; in voiceover we hear her talk about an old pub in Richmond where dykes used to hang out. It was called the Kingston. Then we see the old woman climb some stairs and enter a dance club. The music is loud, something not quite techno, not quite house. The old woman takes a seat by herself and watches young women in leather and vinyl on the dance floor. Another close-up on her face, lashed by the strobe. The music fades. She starts talking to the camera, telling us about the Kingston. There's a cut to a group of women sitting around a pub table. The camera pans across their faces. Some are middle-aged, the others are much older. They are drinking and laughing. Two of the women kiss, a long, passionate, wet kiss. Then up come the credits.

Zazie's film did have an effect on me. It was the kiss. There was something unique in that screen kiss. It wasn't that they were women; it was that they were old.

'That's the best bit,' I told her afterwards.

'Yeah,' she answered, 'I know.'

•

My wedding was small, a ceremony in a garden and lunch at a pub. I invited Zazie but she couldn't make it. She sent us a card, addressed to me and Tania. *Good luck, kids*. That's what it said.

•

Tania comes into the bathroom. I'm taking a shower. She's got the *TV Guide* in her hand. She says something but I don't catch it. She pops her head in and I kiss her on the lips. The *Guide* gets wet. 'Look,' she points to the page, 'next Friday they're playing *Zazie in the Metro* on SBS.'

I jump on the phone as soon as I get out of the shower. I ring, there's a long wait, and some guy answers.

'Is Zazie there?'

'She doesn't live here anymore. I don't have a number.'

I watch the movie with Tania, tape it. It's about a young French girl who always misbehaves. She even looks like Zazie—I mean, the real Zazie. It is shot all around Paris and I turn to Tania. 'We should go. I'd like to take you there one day.'

Tania says, simply, 'We will.' I rub my face all over her, smell her, touch her, kiss her, and I forget about watching the movie.

•

I come home from work and the house is empty. Tania's still at college, evening classes. The answering machine is flashing three messages. After a call from Mum and a message from the plumber, Zazie's voice crackles and laughs.

'Anyone there? Anyone there! Jesus, this is costing a fortune. I'm in Alexandria—it's ugly. They've ruined it. They must have burned down everything, it's all fucking concrete boxes. Except for the Mediterranean. Now, that's beautiful. I got my tarot done by this Egyptian woman. She spotted I was a Virgo straight away. Probably all crap but it was fun. She let me videotape her. Jesus, I wish you were home. We haven't talked for ages. I don't know when I'll be back. Maybe never. I'll write, I promise I'll write. Or maybe I'll phone from New York. Sorry, this is costing a fortune. Love to Tania. Goodbye.'

The machine spurts out a few weak beeps, the tape wheezes back on rewind and then clicks to a stop. I make myself a sandwich, munch on Vegemite and bread. I go outside. There's still a few hours of light. I start digging and planting.

Saturn Return

I wish William Burroughs had never done the Nike ad. As Barney says, he lasted into his eighties without compromising his credibility and then he blows it all to sell sports shoes on television. Trying to be generous, I argue that the approach of the millennium is screwing with lots of people's heads.

'Sure, sure,' mutters Barney, 'but how's he going to stand up now and recite poetry that tells multinationals to fuck off and go to hell?' He bangs his fist on the steering wheel.

'Why does everyone end up disappointing you?'

I've come to expect to be disappointed by people. The faces that stare down on me from my bedroom wall are all dead. I mean the famous faces: Monroe, Clift, Rainer Werner.

Janis, River and Jean Seberg. They are all dead and they all died young. I'm much harder on the living: not so much with family and friends; you learn to tolerate the vulnerabilities of the people around you. It is harder to do that with those beautiful faces caught timelessly on film, photograph or screen, who one moment are expressing their love of art, or talking passionately about their dreams, about changing the world; then flick, another image and they have reneged, become fake. There's a photograph of Jane Fonda, black and white, limp hair over her face, her fist raised in support of the Vietcong; and then there's that video of her, with her airbrushed body outstretched, doing aerobics to bad disco. Once you lose someone's respect it is the hardest thing to win back.

•

We are travelling to Sydney. The sun is beating down on us and the inside of the Valiant feels like an oven: our skin sticks to the vinyl seats. Barney is driving, his hands steady on the wheel as the sun tans his naked torso.

'Whoo hoo, baby,' he sings out to me, 'ain't it fucking great to be out of the city?'

It takes around eleven hours to get from Melbourne to Sydney, nine if you put the foot down on the accelerator and evade the cops. We take three days. The first night we stop at Bonegilla, just before the New South Wales border. Barney wants to see the skeleton of the migrant camp. It is an obsession for him. Many nights at dinner at my folks' he would spend the evening asking my father about his life in the camp, his voyage to Australia. I would let the two of them talk, occasionally butting in with an observation they would both ignore. Often I'd leave them talking in the lounge and I'd go in and help Mum wash up. Their intimacy never disturbed me. I never had a close relationship with my old man but through Barney's persistent questioning I discovered my father's history.

The sun is retreating when we arrive in Bonegilla. Barney wants to go straight to the camp but we can't see any signs showing where it might be. When we book into a caravan park on the edge of the lake, I ask the owner if she knows where the old camp is located.

'Love, it was over there,' and she points across the lake to a small stretch of land jutting out into the water. 'But there's nothing left, you know. It all belongs to the army now. Were your parents at the camp?'

'My father was,' I reply.

•

That night we get fish and chips and watch a science-fiction movie on the TV. I roll a joint and Barney pokes fun at the stilted dialogue. I lie next to him and blow smoke into his face. He cradles me in his arms and kisses me softly. I taste the beer, the nicotine, the marijuana. A thin layer of grease and salt lines his lips.

'Baby,' he tells me, 'I can't believe they haven't put up some kind of museum here. Think about the fucking history.' He shakes his head and goes back to watching the movie.

I finish the joint and lie back in his arms. As the drug begins to take effect I can hear sounds outside: ghosts murmuring in a discordant chorus of many languages. But it is only the wind blowing over the water and through the trees. The nocturnal music is punctured by staccato bursts of gunfire coming from the television.

Barney whoops with exhilaration every time there is a glorious, bloody death. He tickles me and kisses me again. 'Hollywood is bullshit, ain't it, mate,' he whispers to me, and he returns to watching the movie. I don't answer. It isn't a question.

•

Next morning it takes me a long time to wake from the depths of sleep and enter the real world. I drag myself into consciousness and Barney is above me, video camera in front of his face.

'Happy birthday,' he yells and I pull the sheet over my face.

'Fuck off,' I manage to say in between fits of giggling. He drags back the sheet and films up and down my body. He hands me the camera and I focus on the top of his head as he licks my thighs, rolls his tongue over my balls and cock. I film myself shooting cum over his face, onto his neck and shoulders. A little unsteady, I zoom into the white patches of sperm. He wipes his face and body with the sheet and stands above me on the bed, holding his hard cock in one hand. The roof of the caravan is low and he has to crouch. I film his face, move down his body and zoom into the wrinkled skin of his balls; they flap wildly as his masturbation becomes more vigorous. As he nears coming I zoom out and frame his upper body. He is silent until a trickle of clear liquid coats his cockhead. He comes in a small white spray and I cut to his moaning, sweating face. He kneels next to me, covers the camera lens with his hand and whispers, 'That's enough.' I turn off the camera.

We have a hurried breakfast and set off for the camp. He whistles as we walk along and I remain a few steps back, watching the rhythm of his shoulders as he strides along the edge of the lake. I fell in love with this man's walk. His walk, and the soft melody of his baritone voice. He keeps looking back at me, eager, smiling.

'Excited?' he keeps asking as we draw ever closer to the peninsula. I don't answer him, just return the smile.

The truth is that the closer we get to what may be the old camp the less sure I am about what I'm expecting to find there. When I listened to my father's stories I imagined Bonegilla in black and white, imbued with a melancholy mid-century European sadness. The sharp summer colours of the land and the sky do not fit the images in my head. As we approach the peninsula, a congress of black birds takes flight and sweeps in a curve above us. An army van sits still on a dirt track in front of us. A young blond soldier is sitting on the bonnet rolling a cigarette and watching the lake.

Barney walks up to him. 'Hey, mate,' he says, 'we're looking for the old migrant camp. Know where it is?'

The soldier rubs his brow and stares listlessly at us. He looks very young; his eyes are clear blue and his skin is soft and hairless. He finishes rolling his cigarette and jumps off the bonnet and walks towards us. He points to the video camera hanging off Barney's shoulder. 'What's that for?'

Barney smiles even more widely. 'My friend's dad was at Bonegilla. We want to make a video for him. That's alright, isn't it?'

The soldier shuffles uncomfortably for a moment, then shrugs and grins, won over. He waves towards a timber fence in the distance, behind which a row of tiled roofs is visible. 'See those houses? Behind them is where the camp used to be. But there's shit there now.' He draws deeply as he lights the cigarette. 'Have a look around, but you'd be better off going back towards town and checking out the old administration hall. The railway used to run into Bonegilla and that's where the ethnics got off.' He rubs his brow again. 'Fuck-all really to see.'

When we get to the site of the camp I have to agree with him. There is fuck-all there except for a few corrugated-iron huts. They are dirty, ramshackle, with broken windows, and they all smell of urine. But Barney is excited and immediately starts filming.

I walk into the largest hut. The timber floor is littered with old newspapers, rat shit and cigarette butts. Graffiti is scrawled on the shattered walls. I walk past what must have been an old kitchen and notice a syringe dumped in the filthy sink. The deep cavern of the hut is cool and dark. The sun peeks through a few broken windows but fails to enliven the decay.

I walk out into the sunshine and cross over to a smaller hut, its shell scarred black by some past fire. The hut consists of tiny cubicles. I walk in and out of them, touching the fragile walls and kicking away fallen timber. In the last cubicle I look out of the small window from where I can just glimpse the blue water of the lake. The earth outside is a dull orange. I light a cigarette and wonder what my father thought of this landscape when he first arrived. I recall the dark mountains that surround his village in Eastern Europe, the cool air that bites into the skin, the luscious green of the forests. I awake from my daydream: I thought I heard the whisper of a voice not speaking English.

Outside Barney wraps a firm arm around my shoulder. He kisses me and we walk around the huts and back towards the main road.

The old administration hall is as decrepit as the huts. Dry yellow grass grows wild and tall around it. The hut is locked and Barney tries unsuccessfully to break down the door. I'm too nervous to assist. The badly weathered mess hall marks one of the boundaries of the old camp, and now, across the road, there is a bright red-and-white-painted restaurant announcing specials on chicken and chips. As we walk around the back of the hall, where the grass grows even taller, I stamp on the ground with my boots to scare away the snakes. We walk back to the front and Barney films me as I walk up to the battered doors. I peer through the windows secured by wire mesh and try to see inside. But there's not enough light.

'Let's go,' I tell Barney. He keeps his camera on me. I wave my hands in front of my face and order him to stop. He keeps filming. I run around, my back to him, and he comes closer. When he has me in close-up I turn around quickly and yell into the lens, 'Wogs rule!' The words ring loudly around us; their echo bounces around the whole stinking town and finally is lost in the deep blue emptiness of the sky.

•

Barney insists on driving and I rest back in my seat, watching the scenery and listening to soul. He avoids the main highways and we drift east. Late in the afternoon, we drive along a crest that rises towards the sky and then drops us in front of the great sapphire span of the Pacific.

'Where we going?' I finally ask. The beauty before me makes me forget the forlorn fantasies my imagination had begun to spin back at Bonegilla.

Barney just smiles.

He pays for a night in a hotel in a coastal town just outside of Eden. I argue that he can't afford it but he shrugs off my concern. The hotel is small but comfortable and we have a room that overlooks the lazy port.

'Are you sure you've got money for this?'

Barney gives me a thumbs-up. 'Hey, I got well paid for the painting job I did with Harry.' He sits next to me on the bed and strokes my face. 'And, baby, it's your twenty-eighth birthday.'

He smiles slyly at me. 'Saturn return. Big cosmic year for you. Your karma is coming home to roost.'

I throw a pillow at him. 'I don't believe in that shit.'

He keeps grinning. 'It doesn't matter whether you believe in it or not. It happens.'

I jump up and start getting dressed. When we're both ready we scout the town looking for a seafood restaurant. On the way we stop at a payphone and I ring my parents. Mum wishes me a happy birthday and asks a rapid series of questions, but I'm anxious to talk to Dad. She finally goes to find him. The small screen on the payphone tells me I only have forty cents worth of time.

'Many happy returns.' My father sounds gruff and tired on the phone.

'Dad, Dad,' I say quickly, 'Barney and I stayed in Bonegilla last night.'

The old man laughs. 'What the hell you want to go to that shithole for?'

I'm disappointed in his response. 'I just wanted to see what it was like.'

He laughs again. 'Anything there?'

'Nah. Just a few sheds falling apart and the old administration centre.'

'They should burn the whole of it down. It was a hateful place.' We are both silent on the phone. Twenty cents left: the screen is flashing a warning.

'Wish Barney my best, will you? You know, with his old man and everything.' The phone goes dead.

That night Barney and I have a huge meal over two bottles of red wine. We talk about Bonegilla, about our fathers, about work and how to get it. We make plans to see the world, and laugh about our favourite episodes of *Gilligan's Island* and *Number 96*. We stumble back to the hotel, Barney singing snatches of mean-spirited punk, as we are silently cruised by a cop car.

In our room I take off Barney's clothes and he tells me he loves me over and over. I cradle him in my arms as he sits naked on the floor, his clammy skin tasting sour from alcohol. He is crying softly. There is nothing I can say or do to stop the tears.

We are going to Sydney to be with Barney's father when he dies. I haven't spent much time with Daniel but he is a remarkable man. For twenty years he has wandered the country, trying to find work as a musician, more often settling for any labouring work he could find. For a long time Barney and his mother followed the stray paths Dan chose to take them along, but eventually Sheila had had enough. Barney and his mother moved to Sydney and Dan continued to crisscross the desert to get to whatever was on the other side. His guitar remained faithful.

Barney doesn't know where his father picked up the virus and he thinks it is pointless to guess. There were plenty of opportunities. Drugs and sex did not dominate Dan's life like music did, but he wasn't averse to experimenting with them. He was as attentive to his son as his life allowed, but he knew that Sheila was a decent mother and probably did better with him not around. Barney can be damning of his old man, moaning about his laziness and his irresponsibility. But Barney detests normalcy too much not to have a grudging respect for the way Dan had chosen to live his life, for the things he had learned and the people he had got to know. Lining our kitchen wall back in Melbourne is a scrappy collage of photos that Barney has made of his father. Dan in Nepal; Dan and Sheila smoking a bong; Dan and an old girlfriend nude at ConFest; Dan playing guitar with a tiny Barney on his knees. And in pride of place, in luminous black and white, Dan beaming with his arm around Screamin' Jay Hawkins. Los Angeles, 1979.

•

Just before we arrive in Sydney's outer suburbs, Barney stops the car and asks if I mind driving. We change seats and I drive into the city. It is late morning and the closer to town we get the more the traffic hems us in.

Barney closes his eyes and lets out an infuriated groan. 'I hate this shithole.'

I don't. I'm excited to be back in this furious, massive city.

•

Dan opens the door and I can't hide my shock at how ill he looks. I stumble over my greeting. His hair has fallen out, his face has sunken in and his whole body seems to have shrunk. He sees my confusion and reaches out to hug me. I loop my arm carefully around his frail frame, fearful of hurting him, but I kiss him strongly on the neck. Barney is standing behind me with our bags. I move aside as the two men hold each other tight.

The house is a small terrace in Glebe. It smells of coconut, tobacco and frankincense. Dan ushers us through a blanket hung across a doorway and into the lounge. A glass sliding door separates the kitchen from the lounge room. The rooms feel warm and light. Big bright canvases fill the walls, and the kitchen is all white surfaces broken up by a collection of posters. Even though it is warm early autumn, a small heater is blowing out hot air.

Dan bends down slowly and clumsily turns it off. 'Sorry, boys, I feel the cold these days.'

Barney reaches down and turns it on again.

•

The first night is a party. Three friends of Dan's come over, with beer and Turkish takeaway. One of them is a tall man called Stanley. He wears faded clothes, has long thin hair, and proceeds to tell excellent stories about religion and magic. He looks a little like a warlock himself. He is dating Katerina, who is a huge Greek woman with a grand wave of hair, streaked in thick stripes of silver and black. A shy man our age arrived with them and he quietly sits in a corner rolling joints. Very soon Barney and his father are arguing politics with Stanley, and Katerina has put Bob Marley on the stereo and is dancing lazily by herself. I sit next to the young man, Richard, and take puffs from his joints. Soon his shyness lifts and he becomes garrulous.

My eyes keep returning to Barney and his father. With both of them animated and focused on their argument, I have time to study their faces.

Even though Dan is so very ill, you can still see the father in the son. They don't share the same features but their heads and bodies have the same shape. Barney sits in between his father's legs, one hand casually slung over a knee. Dan has one hand resting on his son's shoulder. As the argument continues he seems to grow tired and leans back into the sofa.

'Barney,' he suddenly barks, 'can you fetch your old man a glass of water?' He is wheezing. He leans across the sofa and picks up a black wooden box. Inside are assorted packets and jars of pills. He quickly sorts through them and swallows his selection in one gulp.

'Bedtime,' announces Stanley. There is rapid action in the room. Katerina starts clearing things away, Richard goes to wash dishes, and Stanley and Barney take Dan to bed. I help clean up. Barney and his father remain talking in Dan's bedroom and I'm the one to farewell the guests.

I get ready for bed. I feel like an intruder in the house. Taut, anxious—I am very conscious of the two men talking downstairs—I begin to wonder if it was a mistake to come along on this trip.

When Barney comes into our room he doesn't put the light on. I watch him undress; the fluorescent streetlight outside our window makes his skin golden. He slides into bed next to me and asks if I mind him smoking.

I have one as well; my first full cigarette for months.

'He looks really sick, doesn't he?'

I slowly nod my head.

'He's such a funny old geezer. You know what he wanted to talk to me about just now?' Barney sits up on one elbow. He looks handsome and so very cool in the half-light. Like a great jazz sleeve. 'He wanted to talk to me about George Jones. He wanted to make sure that they play George Jones at the funeral.'

'Will you?'

'Of course.' He lies flat on his back again, silently smoking, his body not touching mine. Then, mashing the butt of the cigarette into a teacup, he speaks. 'My mum still can't stand George Jones. Says it reminds her of too many years stuck in outback outhouses.' He mimics Sheila. '"For fuck's sake, Dan, can't you play something else? It's already enough like frigging Alabama here without having to listen to that redneck country and western crap."' He gives a deep sigh. 'I hated that shit too.'

There is a pause.

'I don't want to fight with him anymore. I'd like to think it's because I'm growing up but I think it's because he's dying.'

'He is, you know. He is dying.' My anxiety takes over and I blurt out the words.

Barney keeps talking, as if he has not heard me. 'He's not like your dad; he's not generous. Though Dan would call your father sacrificing. He was always a lot of fun but lousy on being there. Never sent enough money, never thought to ask if we had enough to eat.'

I remain silent. I've heard this before but tonight it sounds different: there is no bitterness, no anger.

'I told him that I'd be happy to stay.' Barney looks over at me, then quickly turns away. 'That we would both be happy to stay and look after him.'

'And? What did he say?' I try to keep apprehension out of my voice.

'He said he doesn't want that.' His chuckle surprises me. 'He said he'd hate to do that—to clean up someone's shit, to have to feed them and wash them. So he doesn't expect anyone to do it for him.'

Barney turns and looks at me. His eyes shine enormous in the dark. 'Do you love me?'

I'm surprised and answer instinctively. 'Of course. Why would you ask?'

'I don't know. Tonight I just want to hear you tell me it. Just tell me it.'

I hold him tight and tell him how much I love him, tell him how I want to always be with him, tell him how my gut, my heart, my cock all burn for him. The words come out easily. I can trust every single one of them.

•

Next morning we take Dan to hospital. It is St Vincent's, near the city, and we decide that the chunky Valiant will be too much of a bitch to park.

Dan rings a taxi. 'I can't be bothered with public transport anymore,' he explains.

'Go ahead, blow my inheritance,' his son answers drily.

While Dan is in hospital, Barney and I take a walk up to Oxford Street. It has been a few years since either of us has been in Sydney and Barney keeps exclaiming over the changes. Many pretty and fit young men walk past us, and I catch a few eyes. Barney ignores them all. We turn into Crown Street and he walks into a small Vietnamese coffee shop. 'Can we just get a coffee?' he asks the young guy behind the counter and the man nods yes.

We take a seat and I use a chopstick to sketch lines in the sugar bowl. 'Why come here?' I ask. 'The coffee will be crap.'

'To feel normal,' he almost shouts. He quietens down. 'Sorry, babe, this bloody town gets glitzier and more superficial every passing year. And whiter. Where have all the ethnics gone?'

I break out into a grin. 'You're just a sucker for wogs.'

'Definitely,' he agrees. He leans over and kisses me. We are interrupted by the waiter who serves our coffee. He looks indifferent.

'You reckon that was alright?' I ask when he leaves.

'What was alright?'

'Us kissing.'

Barney laughs. 'He works in Darlinghurst, mate. I'm sure he's seen worse.' He pauses and pours sugar into his coffee. 'What makes you think he's straight?'

The question embarrasses me. 'I just assumed it,' I admit. 'Why, what do you think he is?'

Barney shrugs his shoulders. 'How would I know?'

After coffee we take a walk around Surry Hills. Barney points out houses and shopfronts to me. This is where he played soccer. That's the house he lived in when he first came to Sydney. We pass a corner pub, its door wide open to welcome the breeze. Inside, a few old men are drinking beer, huddled around a cheerful barman. Across the street, a fancy café with discreetly angled table umbrellas is pulling in a younger, more stylish crowd. Barney stands precariously on one foot, his other raised inches off the ground. He is staring across at the café.

'That used to be . . . that used to be . . .' He puts his foot down firmly. 'Not a café. An old couple used to fix radios in that shop.' He turns around and enters the pub. 'Let's have a beer.'

•

Barney and I have never had much money. That makes a big difference; that's why we are still together. Money, as the song goes, does change everything. Who you know, what you know, how you know. Rich people don't mix with poor people, not necessarily out of conceit or malice, but maybe because they can't understand the anxiety that comes from worrying about money. I've noticed that you can never talk to a rich person about money, whether it's paying the rent or getting screwed at work. They get uncomfortable. No matter what they might say they believe, a rich person can never trust a poor person.

And vice versa. At some point, over some dumb argument, the rich person will utter the words: that's mine, I paid for it, I own it. And there's no fucking way the poor guy can compete. I don't have to explain any of this to Barney. He understands automatically.

In fact, he goes further. 'It's a different world, idiot,' he once screamed at me. 'I thought you understood that.' It was early in our relationship and I had bragged to some university friends about how Barney was selling sticks of dope. 'They're rich kids and they don't have to break the law. Don't ever trust them.'

Being poor means you have to break the law. That's how it works. They make laws about everything, to protect everything. It's breaking the law not to pay a fine; it's breaking the law not to pay back credit; it's even breaking the law to steal sugar sachets from a restaurant. If you're poor it's hard to live within the letter of the law and survive; even harder to do that and have a good time. It is impossible to do both. Barney never lets down his guard around the rich, not even when he was at uni, where he first met them.

'You and me,' he told me soon after we'd met, 'we got here because of our brains. The rest of them are here because mummy and daddy have got money.' His smile was radiant. 'That makes us better than them. And they know it.'

•

The next few days rush by. I cannot shake the feeling that I am intruding. The father and son spend hours together while I take long, solitary walks through the neighbourhood, check out the coffee shops and write stilted, distracted journal notes. I watch a lot of television. One evening we visit Sheila and I relax a little. Barney loosens up around his mother, loses the distilled intensity that he has with Dan. Sheila herself, loud, kind and abrupt, responds affectionately to her son, and he feels free to argue with her, to bait her. We arrive back at Dan's very drunk.

As soon as we open the door the heat hits us. The night outside is warm but the heater is whirring furiously and Dan has wrapped a blanket around himself. He is watching our Bonegilla footage.

'Dad, you should be in bed.'

The old man ignores him. 'What's this?'

Barney and I sit down and we watch the limpid colour of the video. Barney has framed me staring out of a broken windowpane. I'm unaware of the camera and my eyes seem huge, very bright.

'It's Bonegilla. My father was at the migrant camp there when he first arrived in Australia.'

'When was that?'

'Nineteen fifty-nine. The camp lasted into the late sixties, I think.'

Dan is racked by coughing. Barney fetches a glass of water. On the screen a sheaf of yellow grass obscures the gnarled timber wall of the Bonegilla administration hall.

'Never heard of the bloody place.' Dan shook his head slowly.

'I've been all over this country and no one ever told me about this place.'

'Let's get you ready for bed, old man.' Barney puts a gentle hand on his father's shoulder.

Dan yawns an agreement. The video images falter, the screen goes black and disintegrates into static.

As he gets up, Dan turns a wrinkled, mischievous face towards us. 'I saw the first part of the video. Afraid I did not find it very erotic.' He laughs as he shuffles towards his bedroom. For the first time in a long time I see Barney blush.

•

The days rush by but I am conscious of every passing minute. Between them Dan and Barney are making decisions, tying up loose ends. Dan does not own very much but what he has is going to his son. It's the music that matters most. To both of them.

Barney reacquaints himself with his old hometown as he completes chores, paying his father's final rent, organising the funeral. He remains warm and considerate of me, especially when we are alone, but his concentration is fully on his father. I understand—or rather, I try to understand—and step to the sidelines. On the eve of his father's death, Barney has a sleepless night, sitting very still on the balcony, watching the moon. I wake up four or five times during the night and each time see that he is lost in a place so unimaginably far away that I cannot be there with him. I fall quickly back to sleep. In my dreams I hear him praying.

From early morning the small house fills up with people. Men and women, some young, but mostly around Dan's age, come and go, bidding him farewell. The whole day Dan is beaming, drinking whisky and, for the first time since his immune system started to collapse, smoking the odd cigarette. Barney gets drunk quickly but he remains attentive to Dan; his main task is to keep the turntable spinning. A cornucopia of music is played this day. I keep registering favourite songs, and I recognise tunes and melodies I can't put a name to.

I am introduced to dozens of people but I am only aware of Barney. I watch him all day, watch how he interacts with Dan. Sheila arrives in the afternoon and she pours drink after drink for me. From time to time she breaks down and cries, and someone close will put their arm around her. The conversation is lively, many stories are exchanged about Dan, and every new arrival brings more to drink. At one point Dan puts the Bonegilla video on and I face the embarrassment of a roomful of strangers watching me ejaculate when he rewinds back too far. There are squeals of laughter. As the camp footage begins, Barney comes over and takes my hand. He is trembling. After it is over, people come up and ask about Bonegilla. I'm drunk enough to make it up as I go.

Dan catches me at it and hugs me spontaneously. 'You Greeks are like the friggin' Irish,' he raves loudly. 'Born bullshitters.' He drops his arm awkwardly then whispers close to my ear, so Barney can't hear: 'Look after my son. He's got too much of me and not enough of his mum in him.'

At night's fall the guests leave. All except for Sheila, Stanley and Katerina. Sheila and I cook a light dinner for everyone, and we eat our green salad and nachos sitting around in a circle. I want to remember a certain moment: Barney lying across Sheila's lap, his leg entwined in mine, Dan nodding along as Katerina plays African music on the stereo.

'I never did get to Soweto.' Dan taps his fingers to the music. Barney and I sit silent as the older people talk about the past, about what Surry Hills was like before the yuppies and the gays took over.

'Don't get me wrong, Stanley,' Dan says quickly, but looking over at me, 'there were always poofters around here, but they didn't used to have money.'

Katerina talks about coming to Australia, about the dullness of the conservative fashions, and how odd it seemed that people did not go out at night. Sheila nods and then moves the conversation on to Whitlam. Labor in government. Feminism. Dan butts in and soon there is a heated argument. Sheila calls him an irresponsible bludger and he calls her an ideologue. They curse expertly at each other, but again there is the weird absence of bitterness or anger. Tonight I can imagine them having once been in love.

After a break in conversation filled only by the bass-enhanced tribal rhythms bouncing from the speakers, Barney asks Dan to name his desert island discs.

Dan leans forward. 'How many can I choose?'

'Five.'

'Individual songs or albums?'

'Either.'

There is a pause. 'This is it, Danny Boy, the final list,' says Stanley quietly.

'*The White Album.*' This is said firmly. I find myself waiting eagerly for his next words.

'"Good Year for the Roses", the George Jones version.'

'Of course,' groans Sheila.

'*Highway 61 Revisited.*'

'Sixties child,' Barney teases.

'And proud of it,' responds Sheila.

'Shh,' interrupts Stanley. 'Go on, Dan.'

'"Runaround Sue", "Sweet Jane", the *Street Hassle* album, "God Bless the Child", "I've Been Loving You Too Long", "Solsbury Hill".' A whole chain of songs is rattled off. 'And that one rap song I like; you used to have it, Barney.' Dan starts chanting the rap.

'"The Message".' Barney shakes his head. 'Dad, you can only have five.'

'Never was good with limits,' chuckles Dan.

'How about films?' I interject. 'What about your desert island films?' All eyes are on me.

'That's easy. *The Godfather, Medium Cool, Paths of Glory, The Wild Bunch* and *Rosemary's Baby.*'

Barney laughs. 'Dad, that list hasn't changed for over twenty years.'

Dan yawns and the room goes very quiet. Stanley stands up and from his jacket pulls out a small paper bundle. An elastic band is folded around a paper bag and its contents. He leaves the bundle on the table. Katerina rises as well. She is crying. So is Sheila. Barney is looking down at his feet but I can tell he is frightened. So am I. Dan walks Stanley and Katerina out to the front verandah. The night has exhausted him: they both support him. Sheila opens the package on the table. There is a syringe and a small plastic bag of powder. Sheila lights a candle and begins to prepare a solution of the powder. I am holding my breath.

'You don't have to do that.' Dan stands in the doorway; Stanley has a thick arm around him. Dan looks tiny. He looks frightened as well. And—maybe because of the fear—he looks years younger.

Sheila smiles sadly. 'I don't mind. I can't believe I can still remember how to do this.' She looks up at Stanley.

'Best friend.' His voice cracks, falls into a sob.

Sheila has mixed the solution in a small glass bowl and she holds it over the candle a few moments. She pulls back the plunger and fills the syringe.

'Are you sure this is what you want?' Her tone is surprisingly matter-of-fact.

Dan nods his head.

She looks down at her son. 'Are you ready, baby?' she asks softly.

Barney gets to his feet. Dan hugs me, kisses me on the lips, and I watch the four of them walk down the corridor to Dan's bedroom. I remain standing in the doorway. The bedroom door shuts. The night is humming wildly in my ears. Time is suspended.

When the door finally opens again, Barney rushes out sobbing and falls on me. I hold him tight. It is not as if he is crying exactly; rather, sorrow is pouring out of him, from every heaving breath, from every lacerating tear. The warm lounge room is suddenly freezing and the only heat comes from the place where our bodies touch. I strengthen my hold on him. I'm scared that if I let go, not only the room, not only this city, but the whole world will go cold forever.

Genetic Material

I SAY, 'HI, DAD, HOW ARE you doing?'

His eyes snap in my direction, there is a sudden jerk of his body as he recoils from my voice, then he slumps back in his chair. There's nothing in his eyes: no light, no emotion, no recollection. 'Who are you?' he asks me, his voice listless.

I'm your son, Dad, I'm your fucking *son*.

But I don't say that, of course. My sister has instructed me—as is her way, not once but over and over—'You have to remind him of who you are, you have to give him a narrative that he can make sense of.'

'I am David. I'm your son. I'm Sophie's brother.'

The eyes looking up at me are still blank. I resent my sibling's use of the word *narrative*; I know she has gleaned it from the medicos and the social workers. I am irritated every time she uses the word, as if it contains a metallic core that whips against my ear as she says it. There's no *narrative* for this old man: no illumination I can offer him, no characters he can identify with, no descriptions to orientate him, no plot strands for him to follow. I feel useless. Much worse, I think he is useless.

'We're living too long.' Mick's father is eighty-seven. He has a walking frame, has had his right knee reconstructed, his hips replaced. It takes him an age to walk to the coffee shop on High Street where he has his coffee with his Maco mates.

Every morning he wakes up and says, 'Why didn't the damn night take me? Who wants this useless body? We're living too long.'

Mick's mother, Adriana, mocks him, shouts, 'Then why the bloody hell don't you take your shotgun and blow your brains out?' She is ten years younger than her husband, she is sprightly, still thin, will only ever eat half of the food on her plate, and rushes from the grocers to the supermarket to the butcher without having to stop for a rest or take a breath. At Sunday lunch she hovers over all of us, making sure we have enough food on our plates, and enough beer in our glasses.

Adriana is always on the go. 'I walk,' she admonishes her husband. 'I have always walked; I walked ten miles to school and back every day as a child and I still walk every evening. If you walked,' she yells at him in Macedonian, 'if you had walked instead of coming home and sitting in front of the bloody television, you wouldn't need a new hip, you wouldn't need a new knee.'

I stand next to her, helping dry the dishes, listening to her abuse her husband.

Then she will lower her voice, and whisper to me in English, 'But he's right. We are living too long.'

My father, who doesn't recognise me, who doesn't know where I fit into the story, because he has no story left beyond his nursing-home bed and the slow shuffle to the canteen where he eats, is purposefully ignoring me. If he looks at me the fear returns. So instead he sits staring out of the window to the stretch of even mown lawn beyond. The grass is such a vivid green it seems plastic, as do the beds of hydrangeas. He is dressed in striped blue and white pyjamas, like the people in Auschwitz, I cruelly think, or Mauthausen or Bergen-Belsen. My father doesn't recognise me and I think if only I had a shotgun I would put it on his lap. He'd take it and blow his brains out. That's what he'd want to do, that's how he'd want his *narrative* to end.

I place the newspaper on the bed. He glances up from his seat by the window and then quickly looks away. I know when I have left he will pick it up and turn straight to the sports section. The news of the world, the news from Australia, also scares him. But he remembers that he follows the Collingwood Football Club. He remembers that.

'I am your son David,' I repeat. 'I am Sophie's brother. And Sophie has just had another baby—you're a grandfather again. His name is Nicholas. Sophie has named him after you.'

The old man is still staring out the window. He won't look in my direction.

I wish Sophie was here, I wish my mother was here. My sister talks to our father as if he was another one of her children; my mother refuses to believe that her husband doesn't know who she is, that forty years of marriage and sharing a home and arguing and raising children and sleeping together and loving each other can be erased from memory. She tells him what their neighbours are doing, what their grandchildren are saying, what they do at school, where they went on their holiday. She stares at his vacant expression and refuses to see the panic it is masking; she doesn't see his struggle to resist the terror of this stranger invading his room, this woman who won't stop babbling at him. What she sees is the man she married; she sees the man she loves.

I usually make sure to visit when Sophie or my mother are there, when I can stand in the corner and watch them chatter away over him, adjust his bed, wash him, feed him. The times he gets angry, his moments of fury, when he screams at them, throws his tray across the room, shouts at them to fuck off, just fuck off, those are the times I can't help but feel vindicated. That's the father I remember, the father I know. He won't play your game, I want to tell them, he won't submit to being a child for you. He is a man; you women don't understand that this is all that matters to my father: that he be a man.

But now, alone with him in his room, I find myself prattling, treating him as I would my nephews, or Mick's godchild. 'Looks like the sun will come out, don't you think, Dad? Maybe we can take a walk outside.' The bitter look he throws my way reflects the contempt I feel for the empty words I am saying.

I walk over to the window. The trees along the edge of the car park are spindly and denuded of leaves; spring has yet to touch them. As I pass him I place a hand on his shoulder and he slaps it away. I catch the overpowering reek of urine. Sometime after his morning feed the old man has wet himself.

'Dad,' I say, my voice shaking so much it ends up slipping into a higher register, 'I am going to wash you; will that be okay?'

His head flicks towards me again but now there is relief. 'Are you the new nurse?'

I nod. 'Yes,' I answer, 'I'm the new nurse.'

•

All my life it was said of my father that he was a handsome man. And it was true: his was a ravishing beauty, accentuated by a virility that cleaved from it any hint of effeminacy. He was raised on the land, and even though he was only an adolescent when he came to the city to start his apprenticeship, he always made time to return to the bush. As youngsters every weekend would be spent out of Melbourne; we would follow him into steep ravines, walk for hours in the forests behind the Great Ocean Road. There were times when we walked so far, walked so long, that all I wanted was to sit down on a rock and weep. But I never did. I knew I had to be as tough as him, I knew he would never love me if I wasn't as strong as him. So I walked:

I walked with blisters on my feet, I walked in the burning sun; I walked in the drizzle, in the sleet and in the rain.

My mother, my sister and I had always lived in the shadow of his good looks. Not that my mother wasn't herself attractive, or that Sophie and I were ugly. Quite the contrary. However, my father was the kind of man who could walk into a crowded room and draw every set of eyes to him. Wherever he was, he would be the centre of attention. There were moments when I witnessed women literally draw in their breath at the sight of him. It was also his good fortune to be possessed of a disarming larrikin charm, a natural gift for telling stories and jokes, and a speaking voice that was both melodic and of a rich baritone timbre. He entered the room and everyone turned his way; everyone wanted to be close to him, to be captivated by him.

I wouldn't have been more than six or seven when I first became aware of the power of such beauty. It was in the middle of summer, a wretchedly hot day, and our parents had decided to take us to Mordialloc Beach. My father had taught us to swim when we were very young and one of my earliest memories was of giggling while he held me over gently lapping waves. He would often swim out far from shore, outdistancing the other swimmers, his strokes carrying him so far that my mother would rise from her beach towel and come to stand beside my sister and me to make sure that he had not completely disappeared from view, that she could still make out the faint speck of him on the horizon. A smile would spread across her face once she glimpsed him returning to us through the waves, his strokes measured and unforced, his outline slowly gaining shape and solidity. She would lie back on the sand, return to her book, and await the moment his shadow would fall across her, the sea water dripping onto her body as he stood over her towelling himself dry, his eyes ablaze with the pleasure of the swim. Sophie and I would look up to see him fall to his knees on the sand, kiss our mother's shoulder, put on his sunglasses and lie down beside her in the sun. It was one of the most comforting sights of my childhood.

On this particular day an unexpectedly dramatic wave had run up the beach, terrifying Sophie and demolishing the sandcastle we had so carefully been building. My sister started to wail and I, confused, had looked towards my parents for guidance. My mother was upright, peering over her sunglasses and calling for Sophie to come to her. My sister had run to my mother and been swept into her arms, and I followed slowly. I might have been fearful that I was going to be punished for my sister's distress. I was the older child, a position in the family that always felt laden with responsibility. But my father too had half risen from his towel, had taken off his sunglasses and was beckoning me to come over. He was smiling and I started to run towards him.

His right arm was raised, he was scratching the back of his head while the other hand was gently tousling Sophie's hair as she burrowed further into my mother's embrace. The hair under my father's arm seemed shockingly abundant, chestnut in colour, glistening from sea and from sweat: possibly the jolt of it, it seeming so animal, so untamed, was what was so tantalising. The summer had tinted his skin bronze, his green-grey eyes were alert and shining and full of love for me. I had no language then to name what I was experiencing. All I knew was that the shock of my father's underarm hair was blistering, that I felt knocked off my feet, that the sand and the sky and the sun were spiralling madly around me. So overwhelming were the emotions I was feeling, so ferocious this inexplicable need to touch him, to sink into him, to press myself against him, that there seemed only one thing I could do.

I walked up to my father and, mustering all the force I could, I punched him in the mouth.

The strike would have been wildly ineffectual, but there may have been a residue of fine sand on the underside of my palm, or the angle of my blow was such that a fingernail may have gone into my father's eye; for once I struck him he let out a curse, an almighty holler, and bent over with a hand cupped to his left eye. His outrage started my sister off again on another bout of crying. Frightened, and with no idea of what I was doing, I began to run. I ran and I ran, the sand unyielding under my feet, burning my soles; but I kept running. Within moments I was conscious of my father behind me, of his shadow looming, gaining ground on me, and then of his arms scooping me into the air, holding me tight against his chest, of my mouth on his wet skin. 'It's alright, Davey,' he was whispering, over and over, 'it's alright, son, I'm not angry.'

•

The hair on his chest is now white, and the brown knot of his belly button protrudes obscenely from his pink, fleshy belly. I strip him of his pyjama top and he steps out of his bottoms; I have to hold my breath from the stink of his piss and sweat. I fill the small basin with warm water, take the sponge and begin to soap down his body. I wash his neck, chest, shoulders, belly; I crouch down and wipe his thighs, his calves. He turns around and the soiled white underpants drop to his feet. His buttocks sag, pale as the moon. I wash him there, spread his arse cheeks and scrub vigorously between them. I run water to rinse the shit from the sponge and when I turn back he is facing me. The hair on his groin is white, sparse, as if he has gone bald down there. His testicles, bloated, almost purple in colour, hang low; his penis is wrinkled, speckles of white along the flesh of it. Carefully I lift his cock to wash under his scrotum: it feels limp and heavy in my hand, like a fillet of chicken thigh, like dead meat.

My father's cock stiffens at the touch of my hand.

'Alice, Alice,' he sighs. But there is laughter in his voice, a tone I haven't heard in years. 'Alice,' he repeats as he exhales, his bright eyes staring straight into mine, 'we shouldn't do this.'

Alice is not my mother's name. I don't know an Alice. But my own cock has swelled, pressing so hard against the denim of my jeans that it hurts. My hand tightens around him.

'Do you want me to stop?' My voice is hoarse, my skin is

flushed. I am looking at my father, I am looking him straight in the eye and he is smiling; there is strength there again.

'You crazy bitch,' he whispers back to me, 'of course I don't want you to stop.'

My fist is sliding up and down, up and down. I know the door to the room could open any moment, I know we might be caught. But I don't stop. My father's eyes are closed but the smile still plays at the corner of his lips. He shudders, there is a groan, his jaw trembles; a thin liquid dribbles over my hand.

I grab the sponge again and wipe him clean. He is sheepish, embarrassed, the underpants still around his feet. I open a drawer in the dressing table next to his bed.

'Lift your foot,' I order. Obediently he lifts his right leg, then his left, and I put a clean pair of jocks on him. He lets me dress him in freshly ironed pyjamas.

When I am finished he takes his seat and watches me rinse out the sponge. 'How's Jimmy?' he asks tenderly. 'How are the kids?'

'They're fine, mate, they're fine.' I am thinking that he's never asked after Mick with such affection, never inquired into my life with such warmth.

He starts speaking. I sit on the bed and listen to him as he starts talking about the time we were neighbours in Coburg, the house in which his son was born but which they had moved out of before Davey started to walk. He tells me how he has never found neighbours as good as Jimmy and me, how he misses the

Sunday mornings he and Jimmy would go out to the bay to fish, the weekends we'd go shooting rabbits in Dandenong.

'You know I loved Jimmy,' he tells me.

'He loved you too,' I answer.

Then there is a knock on the door and a young nurse enters, all cheer and beaming smile, a small plastic container of apple juice in her hand. 'How are you doing, Nick?'

The cheer has vanished from my father's face. Unperturbed, she places the juice on a tray and motions for me to get off the bed. I obey and watch her strip the sheets.

'We'll change your bedding, Nick, you'll have lovely clean sheets for tonight. You'll like that, won't you?'

Sullen, my father turns away from her.

'I see your son has given you a wash, Nick, and changed your pyjamas. You're very lucky to have a son like that.'

My father is looking out of the window, at the too-perfect lawn, the ugly red-brick buildings beyond, the grey sky above.

At the doorway to his room, I look back. 'Bye, Dad.'

He offers no reply, he doesn't look my way. The nurse calls out a farewell but I don't answer.

Walking down the corridor, I glance through a window to the common room. An old woman sitting in a wheelchair is rocking back and forth, back and forth. Her right arm is raised and it shakes uncontrollably. She is mouthing words but I can't hear them. Two other women, one in a pink nightgown, the other in a lemon-coloured robe, are sitting on chairs in front of the television, studiously ignoring the woman in the wheelchair.

I find the men's toilets and walk in. I lock the door. I stand before the mirror and raise my hand. I can smell my father on me, the sour fish-sauce smell of semen. A small streak of it is drying, claggy and white, on my index finger. I bring it to my mouth, I lick at it. I taste of my father. My father tastes of me. I wash my hands in the basin, I wash my dad off me.

•

It's alright, Davey, I'm not angry with you, son, it's alright.

Holding me tight against his chest, my arms wrapped around his broad shoulders, walking past the couples and families sprawled on the beach towels on the sand, curious children peering at us, my howls seemingly unstoppable, my tears still falling, my father carries me back to my mother and sister on the beach. Gently he puts me down.

My mother is about to say something, to scold me, but my father motions for her to be quiet. She shrugs and takes up her book.

He is looking down at me. The wide black lenses of his sunglasses hide his eyes. I see a little boy reflected in each lens, pale and skinny and frightened.

I muster all the strength I have, I take in a breath and hold it, I force myself not to cry; I need not to cry, I have to show my father that I can not cry.

My father, a colossus soaring over me, a hero, a god, proffers me a dazzling smile and points out to the sea. 'Go and play, David,' he says. 'Just go out there and have fun.'

At the water's edge, the waves rushing at my feet, the gulls screaming above me, the sun beating down on me, I build myself another sandcastle.

Jessica Lange in *Frances*

THERE'S NOT MUCH HAPPENING OUTSIDE THE window. There is just sound and violence. I'm looking down on cars slowly inching their way up the street, stalled by the trams. People are shopping. It's a mid-afternoon, midweek crowd. The sun is still high in the sky, a thick sheet of heat.

The cat is asleep, sprawled across my lap. I'm touching my lips to the cool glass of my water, sniffing the drops of lemon I've squeezed into it. A drunk girl is cursing the world, stamping through the crowd below. She's fat: her oversized Adidas shirt can't hide the flab. I'm stroking the cat, drinking the water.

I can see Dirty Harry; he's knocking into people, they're

cursing him. He's eating paper. He tears it into strips, then sucks on it, chews it, swallows it all up.

'Why do you do that?' I asked him once. Drunk.

'I like it.' He asked me for another drink. 'It lines my stomach,' he slurred, 'slows down the effect of the booze.' He was scratching at a soaked beer coaster, scraping off the cardboard and rolling the scraps along his tongue. Washing it down with a whisky.

The telephone rings and I push the cat off my lap. She lands expertly on the floor, licks at a paw and then wags her bum disdainfully at me. I grab the receiver.

'It's me.'

I'm silent.

'Aren't you walking over?'

'Maybe.' I give in, I can feel a smile breaking through.

He senses it, the bastard can always sense it. 'You glad I called?'

'Where were you?' I'm not giving in, not straight away.

'Got pissed.'

'I figured that.'

'Oh, don't start with that shit.'

My smile is gone. 'I waited up.'

'I said I'm sorry.'

'No, you didn't.'

'I just did.'

The cat has jumped up on the coffee table and nudges herself into the fruit bowl. I'm lighting a cigarette, silent.

'You're smoking?'

I inhale.

'It sure sounds sexy.' Low, low voice. Late-night movie and joint voice. I exhale. Forgiving him.

•

The party was loud, crashing percussion on the stereo. There were bodies pressed against bodies in every room, the atmosphere thick and wet. Drunk people dancing, drunk people shouting, drunk people slumped in armchairs and couches. I turned up late, after a midnight session at the pictures. Sober. I weaved through the couples in the narrow hallway, made my way to the bathroom and tried to find a beer, but I was out of luck. There were only empty cans and cigarette butts in the icy bathtub slush.

'Looking for piss?' He held out his stubby to me.

I hesitated.

'G'on,' he urged, 'take a swig.'

I took one.

He stumbled over to the toilet bowl and unzipped. I took another sip and watched him. His jeans were baggy, so I couldn't make out the shape of his arse, but his black T-shirt stretched tight across his hefty shoulders. He started pissing and turned around to look at me. He held out his hand. I walked over and handed him the stubby and, still pissing, he took a swig before handing it back. We smiled, together.

'Finish it,' he said. The stream of urine slowed down to a trickle. He shook out the last drops, zipped up and left without washing his hands. I noticed that. I can't piss without washing up afterwards. The habit of a lifetime.

I found Leah in one of the bedrooms, sharing a joint with some of her friends from college. I sat down next to her, put my arm around her and kissed her neck.

'How was the movie?'

'Good,' I answered. 'Fun.'

The man from the bathroom was now standing in the doorway, stroking the face of a very beautiful neo-hippie girl. She had glitter on her cheeks and he was tracing the stardust.

I looked away, pretending to ignore him.

He was pretending to ignore me.

•

A grape has fallen into the cat's water bowl. Black hairs are swimming around in it. I pour out a dish of dry food for her and wash the bowl in the sink. The grape falls into the plug-hole and I squash it down with my thumb, watch the flesh drop through the grille. Some nights, especially when it's rained, slugs swarm around her bowl, getting into the meat, drowning in her water. I pick them up with toilet paper. I hate touching them, hate the sticky residue they leave on my fingers. He doesn't mind at all, picks them up and chucks them straight back into the garden, wipes his fingers across his jeans, leaving silver streaks.

The cat sniffs at the dry biscuits, eats a few, turns away. I close the laundry door, walk through the garden and go out the back gate. The kitchen hand from the Vietnamese restaurant next door is sitting on a milk crate, smoking a cigarette.

'How you going?' I ask him.

'Alright.' He drops his voice and points to the terrace behind us. 'But I wish I wasn't working in this fucking dump.' A strong wind is blowing stale hot air hard onto my face. I smell the greasy stink from the kitchen.

It takes forty minutes to walk to his place. I arrive hot, sweating and in a bad temper. He is out in the back garden, a wet cloth draped over his head, empty beer cans around his feet. He's wearing his underpants, nothing else. His white underpants, his very brown skin.

He looks up at me, squints, grinning. 'How are ya?' He doesn't wait for a reply. 'Feel like going to the pub, mate? I'm all out of piss.'

•

They had put chairs and a few cushions out in the backyard. Scented candles were melting over a small coffee table. I left Leah, her friends and their boring conversation about school and exams and gossip. I was stoned. There was no one else in the yard, the party had thinned out and I was enjoying the solitude. It wasn't much of a garden, a few patches of green. I lay down on a cushion, looking at the stars. A half-moon.

'Had enough, eh, mate?'

He sat down next to me and passed me the joint. We sat in silence for minutes, listening to the music, trance reggae.

We smoked the joint and I sat up. His eyes—black eyes, not brown—were shining bright, mirroring the candlelight. There was stubble on his baby face. It suited him.

He was looking hard at me.

'Enjoying the party?' It was an inane question, but I wanted to break the tension. This silence was getting uncomfortable.

'Where you from?'

I didn't expect that question. He kept on looking into me. 'Melbourne.'

'No, I mean where your parents from?'

And you, where are you from? That's what I was wondering.

'Jordan,' I answered. 'My father's from Jordan and my mother was born in Egypt.'

He whistled. 'Jordanian-Egyptian. Very sexy.'

I laughed. 'I'm a mongrel. Mum's half-French and half-Greek. I'm a genetic soup.'

'That's why you're so good-looking.' He said it softly. But every word was clear.

I got scared. But I liked him calling me good-looking.

'Are you going to come home with me?'

I wanted a cigarette. I started fumbling through my pockets. My pack was squashed. He offered me one of his. I took it, slowly, careful not to touch his hand.

'Are you going to come home with me?' Again, soft. The same steady insistence.

I pointed towards the house, to the party. 'That's my girl-friend in there.'

That's when he looked away, pulled his knees up to his chest and rested his head on them. He said something, said it to a place deep down inside himself.

'I can't hear you.' I wanted him to look up, to not be sad. I wanted him to look at me again.

He lifted his face. A wide, wicked grin. 'You still haven't answered my question.'

•

'Fuck you!' I scream it, stressing both words. I'm pacing up and down his concrete shithole of a backyard.

'I'm out of money, alright! All I did was fucking ask you to shout me some cans. You don't want to do it, fine. Just leave it.'

'It's the way you ask me. No hellos, no how are you, no nothing. I'm sick of it.'

'You want a kiss, baby?' Sarcastic tone, spat out in a faggot voice.

'You're a prick.'

A grunt.

'You're a prick!' I scream it out.

'Enough!' I can tell he's angry now, really angry. I shouldn't push it. But it's hot, too hot, I'm tired, and yeah, fuck him, I could do with some affection.

'You're nothing but a drunk.'

He stands up, abrupt. Automatically, his hand becomes a fist. I jump back. And he laughs.

'Come on, come on.' He leans over, kisses my lips. I lick his, we touch tongues and he pulls away. 'I'll cook you dinner.'

'You serious?' I'm dubious.

'Oath.' He crosses himself.

I go down the road, get him his beer.

•

I told Leah I was tired, felt a bit sick. She was having a good time, was talking about going dancing, and after a few moments of her stroking my face and holding my hand, we kissed goodbye. She asked no questions about him; she thought nothing of him walking out with me.

We walked through parkland. There were possums everywhere and he stopped in front of one, crouched, and whispered quietly to it. It looked at him, transfixed, but he overbalanced, fell, and the possum ran fast up a tree. I put a hand on his shoulder to steady him, and he took it and helped himself up. He didn't let go.

I looked around, nervous, feeling spied upon. His hand felt rough, enormous, so different to Leah's light touch. I took my hand away.

He grabbed it back, his grip tight. Then, letting go, he threw his arm over my shoulder, bringing me in closer to him. I felt safer. I noticed the thick hair on his arms, was aware of the heaviness of his body. We kept walking, his arm around my shoulder, staggering, mostly silent all the way to his house, except for when he asked me what football team I barracked for.

'Essendon.'

He nodded.

'And you?'

'Carlton.'

And that was it. We kept walking, through the park, down back alleys, all the way to his house. He was humming tunes I recognised.

When we got to his house he put his finger to his lips, opened the door and navigated me quietly to his bedroom. The light, when he switched it on, was far too bright. A naked globe hung low from the ceiling. He sat on the unmade mattress. I remained standing, wanting to be there and not wanting to be there, looking around at the bedroom walls. There were a few snapshots, a poster of *Taxi Driver*, and old record sleeves, Lou Reed's *Transformer*, Hunters and Collectors' *Human Frailty*. I looked everywhere but at him. Until he started stripping.

His body was firm but not tight. He took off his T-shirt and I looked at his chest, almost hairless, the long nipples, the three small folds of his belly. I felt a locker-room shyness, as if caught stealing illicit glances.

He dropped to his knees.

I looked away to a picture on the wall opposite me, a page torn out of a magazine. The edges were ragged. Jessica Lange, her gaze intense, straight into the camera. He was unzipping my trousers, kissing my cock through my briefs. My cock remained flaccid and I was blushing.

'Good movie,' I said, making conversation. He stopped kissing.

He looked over his shoulder and up at the picture. 'Yeah, ace movie. A fucking classic. What they did to her, you know, Frances Farmer, that's the worst thing you can do to someone, take away their soul.'

I was looking down at him. His hair was limp and fine. I was feeling tenderness: the footballer's shoulders and inside them the little boy. I stroked his hair, his face, and

we were kissing and

his mouth was harsh, not a girl's mouth, and his body was hard as it pressed against

me, covering me, but the skin was just so soft, like touching the underneath of bark

and I thought a few times, as we were making love, that

fuck, it's a man, this is a man

but our bodies worked together, and I liked him coming all over me, groaning and swearing loudly,

repeating

oh man oh man oh man

and as I was coming I had my eyes closed but I was digging my mouth into his neck and

I had to stop myself screaming, so I bit into him, because what I wanted to scream was something about love. Which is terror, which made me want to hit him, kick him. And then I came, the tremors stopped and I could finally breathe out.

He got up, switched off the light, grabbed his T-shirt and wiped the cum off me. I lay there, still. From the street I could hear cars, the screech of cats fighting. He held me, his arm wrapped around my chest. The sharp odour of his perspiration, overwhelming, nothing of sweetness in it. I kissed his skin just to have the taste of it.

'Are you going to tell your girlfriend?'

'No.' The streetlight was making ghosts of the pictures on his wall.

'Is this the first time you've slept with a guy?'

I nodded.

'Me too. I mean, I've had sex with guys before. But you're the first guy I've brought home.'

I was aware of the pressure of his thigh on mine, coarse hair digging into my skin.

'You believe me, don't ya?'

'It doesn't matter.' I remember thinking, women taste of nectar, men smell like citrus.

'Of course it fucking matters.' He whispered it. 'Of course it matters.'

I fell asleep in his arms, watching Jessica's hair dance silver.

•

It's ten o'clock and my stomach is rumbling. He's back from another trip to the pub. There's an English cop show on television but I'm not taking it in. He's lying on the couch drinking. I notice his belly's got bigger.

'You're getting fat.'

He pats his stomach and lets out a Tarzan yodel.

'I'm hungry.'

'Order some pizza.'

'I'm tired of pizza. You said you'd cook.'

'Can't be bothered. Order a pizza.'

'Who's going to pay?' Fucking user. I don't say that. I don't want to believe it.

I get up off the floor and walk into the kitchen. There's dry bread in the cupboard. Two tomatoes, a lettuce, a jar of mustard and some tinnies in the fridge. That's it. I walk back into the lounge room and position myself in front of the TV screen.

'Let's go out. Get something to eat.'

'Get out of the frigging way.'

I don't move.

'What the fuck is up with you?'

'I'm hungry.'

'Well, go out and get something to eat.' He opens another can of beer.

'Come with me.'

'Look, mate, I just want to watch some teev. I'm not in a mood to go out.'

'You were last night.' Without me. I've not forgiven him.

'Last night was different. Now get out of the way and let me watch the show.'

'You're a drunk.'

He takes a long sip, he's silent, watching me.

'You're also a pig.'

He finishes the can in two long gulps, throwing the liquid down his throat.

'You always stink of piss.'

'That's enough.'

I sense the outrage in his voice. I don't move. I keep going. 'And you're dumb. Dumb as dogshit.'

'I said, enough!'

I keep taunting him. Call him more names, give in to my anger, call him a poofter, call him a loser, call him a bore, I keep yelling until he bolts up and it happens so fast that I don't have time to run, not even time to plead, though I hear myself screaming something before he's hurtling into me and I'm kicking but he's stronger and bigger and tougher and knows how to fight and he cracks me sharp across my face and as I fall his knee crashes into my stomach and that's it, I'm crying, flat on my arse and it's not even that it hurts very much until he punches me in the middle of the mouth so my teeth bite on my tongue, I'm tasting blood, and he turns me over and twists my arm up my back and with his free hand he pulls at my hair, banging my head on the carpet until he hears something break and he lets go and I slump on the floor.

Then he pulls my shorts down to my knees and sticks his fingers up my arse, so hard it's like a punch going right up me, in me, through me, and he tries to push his cock in and I'm struggling, squirming, screaming so he bangs my head down on the carpet again and again until I've shut up.

The first five thrusts,

I'm counting them because they're slicing through my gut,

it feels like a blade has torn through my bowels and up into my stomach.

All I do is grunt like a pig and then the thrusts become a pounding.

And I prefer the hammer to the blade because the pain is duller and I'm waiting for it to finish, the television is on and a cop is running after some white kid who's been dealing drugs on a housing estate, out of nowhere I'm hearing a shit Bryan Adams song in my head, and as the thrusts become more rapid he is throwing himself deeper into me and all I'm thinking is please god, don't let me shit, oh please god please don't let me shit please god don't let me shit.

He comes, goes soft inside me, and falls heavily onto me. There is wetness on the back of my neck, maybe his tears, but probably just spit.

The cop gets the white kid.

•

Neither of us makes a sound. I'd be sick if he tried to talk to me. There's not a word. All I'm aware of is the acrid stink of the alcohol. There's blood in my mouth. I spit it out.

I watch the television, watch the red dial on the video recorder clock count down the time to midnight. He's falling asleep. I won't move till I'm sure it's deep sleep. I'm fixed on the red digits. I hear the muffled snores, they shudder along my neck.

Slowly, carefully, I shift from under him; though he stirs, he rolls over and is back to sleep. I'm dripping blood all over the carpet, over him.

I get up and wash my face in the bathroom sink. In the mirror my face is bloated, bloody. I move quickly through the house, taking the alarm clock I lent him, grabbing the book I'm reading, taking my shirts, my socks, my underwear. I'm erasing myself from this house.

I pause at the three strips of photos pinned to the bedroom mirror. Black-and-whites from a photo booth. I take one strip, shove everything into a plastic bag and leave the bedroom. But then I turn and go back, to take the picture of Jessica Lange. I'm making it mine.

The television is playing the news. Trade conference in Asia. He's still asleep, heavy, congested drunk snoring. I lean over him. His black hair is sweat-plastered to his forehead. I can still see it, still fucking see it: his face is sweet. I lean closer, trying to get through and back to him. I try to smell him but I can only make out the alcohol, the mouldy yeast of beer. I am, finally, repelled.

•

The first taxi driver takes one look at me and speeds off. The second takes me, but won't talk to me. I don't mind. I sit in the back, hugging myself tight to stop the shivering.

The cat is crying for food. I feed her fish and notice the slugs. One monster in particular. Its thick slimy body has climbed over the rim and sits inside the bowl oozing filth. I grab a tissue, pick it up, holding it far away from me. The cat ignores me, she's lapping up her food. I take the slug, wrapped in tissue, into the loo and throw it in the toilet bowl. I piss and I make sure I aim my stream directly at the slug, torch it with my urine. When I'm finished I flush, watch the water, the tissue, the slug spin round, round, round. Then all of it, abruptly, is gone.

The upstairs room is hot and I open the window. The street comes rushing in: dance music from across the road, the squeals and horns of cars, a crazy man is yelling out obscenities, teenagers are laughing. My mouth is hurting, swelling. My gut, my arse, they are fire.

I retrieve the picture of Jessica Lange from the plastic bag. I run my thumb over its shredded edges. Shaking, I light a cigarette and put the smouldering tip through the picture. I watch the hole expand, burning her mouth, her chin, her angry eyes. As the picture becomes flame I throw it in an ashtray, mash it up, turn it to ash, to dust.

I sit and watch the traffic flow. The night is warm, but a breeze is blowing in from the south, off the ocean. I lean out the window. I'm still fire. I pack ice into a glass, fill it up with water. Again. It's no good. Nothing helps to cool me down.

The Disco at the End of Communism

IT WAS SAVERIO'S WEEK TO DO the shopping. Trying to fit the key into the front door lock, both hands laden with supermarket bags, he noticed the shadowy form of his wife coming towards him in the cloudy beer-bottle glass of the door pane, rushing to open it for him. He was about to kiss her, to ask her to help him unload the other bags from the car, but froze when he saw her expression. He didn't drop the bags or cry out, but he could not speak for fear of what she was about to say.

'It's not the kids—they're fine.' Rachel grabbed some bags from him and ushered him into the house, leading him by the hand. When they got to the kitchen, she put down her bags and took his hands. 'Julian rang while you were at the market. I'm so sorry,' she said, her voice quavering. 'It's Leo. He had a stroke this morning. He's dead.' She gently shook her head. 'There's nothing anyone could have done, Sav. It must have been quick, he wouldn't have suffered.'

His first thought was to protect her, to banish the fear and confusion from her eyes. He did so by gripping her hands tighter. She started to cry. Instantly he envied her ability to exhibit all the appropriate signs of grief. It had been well over a decade since she had last seen Leo.

'Julian's left a mobile number. He wants you to call him back straight away.'

'I'll unpack the groceries.'

She shook her head again. 'I'll do that, baby. You call Julian.'

Julian answered on the first ring, his voice surprisingly youthful and clear. Saverio had always liked Julian, had considered him good for Leo and had been distressed when he'd heard that they had split up. But Julian had remained loyal to the friendship, and Saverio was not surprised that he'd been the one there at Leo's end. Julian was assuming all the responsibilities that, in the normal course of events, should now be Saverio's. But Leo had never been one for the normal course of events.

'Thank you.'

'What for?' Julian sounded astonished.

'For being there.'

There was silence, then a rapidly muttered, 'That's okay.'

'Rachel said that it was immediate, thank God.'

'Yes.' He could hear a match being struck, the long inhalation of smoke. 'He's been pretty crook, his liver has been giving him trouble for some time now.' Julian hesitated, then said quickly, 'I might as well be straight with you, Sav. He was pretty drunk when it happened—he was shooting up amphetamines.'

Saverio watched as Rachel methodically stacked the groceries on the kitchen table: toiletries for the bathroom, food and drinks for the kitchen and pantry, cat food and detergents for the laundry. Every now and then she would throw a quick glance over at him. Her eyes were still swollen and red.

He died shooting up speed, Rachel, he wanted to mouth at her. The dickhead was shooting up speed at fifty-two. The stupid, stupid fool.

'When did it happen?'

'Sometime last night.'

'Who found him?'

'There's a woman close by who keeps an eye on him. She's a good soul. She rang the police and then she rang me.'

'Are you there already?'

'Nah, nah, mate, I'm still in Sydney. I'm flying up tomorrow morning.'

'Does the coroner have to deal with it?'

'No. I've talked to the local cops and they say it's all straightforward.'

That was it. Saverio was out of questions.

Julian cleared his throat. 'I'll arrange the funeral from Demons Creek. I've already got a copy of Leo's will, he wants to be buried up there. Sav, I want you to come up for it.'

Rachel wasn't concentrating. The dishwashing liquid was in the pile with the laundry stuff.

'Of course I'll come.'

Saverio caught the relief in her eyes, and felt it as well in Julian's affectionate farewell. He hung up, wanting to slam the phone against the wall, wanting to explode in anger like a child.

At that moment, shirtless, with his pyjama bottoms hanging half off his arse, Matthew shuffled into the kitchen, greeting his parents with a muffled grunt. Saverio checked the clock. It was just past noon. The useless prick had been clubbing all night, wasting his money, probably doing the same stupid drugs that had just killed Leo.

'*Cazzo!* This is not a civilised hour to crawl out of bed, you lazy shit!'

Rachel's eyebrows arched and her mouth fell open, but she said nothing.

Matthew, who was peering into the fridge, swung around. 'What the fuck's wrong with you?'

Rachel came and stood beside Saverio, placing her hand on his shoulder. He wanted to shrug it off.

'Matty, we've just heard that your uncle Leo has died.'

There was a moment of incomprehension and then Matthew sheepishly hung his head. 'I'm sorry, Dad.'

Saverio couldn't speak. He felt wretched. He wasn't sorry that his brother was dead, he could only feel relief.

It was over.

•

In the end Rachel did not fly up north with him. She had been on higher duties since the beginning of the year, taking over the management of her unit from Gloria, who was on long-service leave. The extra money had been useful, allowed them to pay Matthew's university fees upfront, but it had meant Rachel working longer hours, bringing work home on the weekends and having to fly regularly to Canberra to assist the minister while parliament was sitting. Saverio felt as if he had hardly seen her over the last month; she had worked late every night organising an international conference on industrial relations. In response to his complaints she had booked a four-day retreat for them at Mount Hotham after the conference. Saverio was a keen skier but it was years since they had visited the snow. On the night they'd heard the news about Leo, she had come into the bedroom and announced that she was going to cancel the retreat.

'Why?'

'I'm sorry, darling, I can't go to both Leo's funeral and the snow. I just don't have the time.'

'I want to go to Mount Hotham with you.' He beckoned her over and pulled her onto the bed. Her hand was greasy with the lotion she'd been rubbing into her arms. 'I really want this holiday. You don't have to come to the funeral.

I just want to bury him, say my goodbyes and that's it. I'd rather go alone.'

Her eyes were searching his face. She didn't believe him. Or didn't want to believe him. 'I think I should be there.'

'Oh, for God's sake,' he groaned. 'As if Leo would have given a fuck if you were there or not.'

Her hand slipped out of his. Her eyes were cold, distant.

'More than anything,' he continued, lowering his voice, introducing a note of pleading, 'I want to be away with you, just you. That's what I'm going to need after the funeral.'

She gave no answer, just kissed him on the forehead and went back into the ensuite. In the mirror he watched her finish applying her creams, watched her floss and brush her teeth, grinned as she slid the door shut to take a pee, enjoying as he always did the fact that even after so many years she could still be shy with him. He'd also caught the hint of relief in her expression. She would have willingly come to say her farewell to Leo. He had always made her laugh. But Saverio knew she would have been dreading the idea of spending time with any of Leo's old friends.

•

As the plane began its descent into Coolangatta, Saverio took out his earphones and looked down at the splendour of the Pacific and the ugly town thrusting out of the lush green landscape.

Matthew had been rendered almost dumb by the news of his uncle's death; not from any personal shock or grief, for he had very few memories of Leo, but rather out of fear of having to communicate somehow with a supposedly mourning father. He had created a playlist on Saverio's MP3 player filled with uncomplicated rock-and-roll from the late seventies and early eighties. A tinny whisper of 'Brass in Pocket' still seeped softly from the earphones as an unsmiling stewardess leaned over to scold him. 'Please turn it off, sir, we are about to land.'

Saverio settled back in his seat. He did appreciate Matty's clumsy effort at sympathy; it was a loving, masculine gesture. Words would have been impossible between them. Saverio didn't dare confess to his son his ambivalence about Leo's death. He had always been more comfortable with his daughter. On hearing the news, Adelaide had rushed to him and clutched him tight, whispering, *I know it's difficult, I know it must be.* It had been exactly the right thing to say. He had marvelled at her innate wisdom: only two years older than her brother and, no matter how much Saverio still tried to deny it, undoubtedly an adult.

He gritted his teeth and held tight to the armrests as the aeroplane surged. In a few seconds the wheels would touch earth, the moment he always feared, the point where the hubris of this mass of steel and wire defying gravity would end in calamity for all on board. The bronzed gentleman farmer sitting next to him, with the open-necked polo shirt and the clearly expensive Italian loafers, stifled a yawn. The wheels of the craft touched asphalt, the plane pogoed, swayed from side to side, then righted itself and screeched forward on the runway. They were safe.

The drive from Coolangatta to Mullumbimby cut through some of the loveliest forest in the country. Saverio could see that if one believed in deities, one could call it God's country, could imagine that the hills and coves and vast open space were the garden and sky of Eden. From time to time, as the rental car climbed into the hinterland, he would catch sight of the ocean sparkling in the rear-view mirror, the silvery light of the sky touching the glimmer of the sea. It was beautiful. No wonder his brother had made this part of the world home. But as he veered off the highway onto Demons Creek Road, Saverio felt a knotting in his stomach. He tightened his grip on the wheel.

Money had clearly been put into the communities that dotted the verdant hills. Eleven years ago the road had still been gravel. Now it was shiny black bitumen. Architect-designed houses jutted out of the greenery, all with prominent verandahs overlooking the sea.

When Leo had first moved there in the early nineties there still existed the remnants of a commune, the property itself owned by a septet of academics who had been radicalised as students at universities in Sydney and Melbourne. The commune had disbanded soon after Leo had moved there with Julian but, nostalgically loyal to their old politics, the landlords had all agreed that Leo could live and paint there rent-free. Saverio and Rachel had urged him to buy some land when it was still going cheap, but Leo had scoffed at their capitalist avarice. To the end he had refused any of the money left to him by his parents.

'I don't believe in inheritance,' he had said brutally to Rachel when she phoned after his father had finally died and they needed to know what to do with the portion of the estate left to Leo.

'But what do you want to do with the money?' she persisted.

The answer had come a week later in the form of a letter. Half of the money, it stated, was to go to the Aboriginal community centre in Redfern, the rest to an outreach centre in Kings Cross.

The lawyer had raised her eyebrows on reading the letter and whistled out loud. 'Are you sure your brother is fully cognisant of his responsibilities?' It was intended as a joke but they did not miss the appeal in her question.

'Just do whatever he says,' Saverio had replied. 'Just as long as I don't have to speak to the prick.'

The car nosed its way up the dirt drive to the cottage. Eleven years before there had been an immaculately maintained herb garden, a fig tree, and lime and lemon trees. The garden was now overrun by weeds, and rotting fruit covered the ground underneath the untamed foliage of the trees. Saverio wasn't surprised. The garden had been Julian's project and once he'd gone Leo wouldn't have had the gumption to keep it together.

The chassis of the car scraped along the ground as the front left wheel sank into a pothole. Frigging Leo, Saverio thought, he couldn't look after anything. Five or six cars were already parked haphazardly across the yard.

There was music coming from the cottage and Saverio could see people standing and sitting on the wide verandah. He felt as though every eye was on him, and his hand trembled as he turned off the ignition. The sun was setting behind the mountain and the crowd on the verandah was in shade. He was dreading the small talk, the hours to come. For a moment he contemplated simply turning back, weaving down the mountain back to the coast, to get the last plane home to Melbourne. The seatbelt was still buckled up, his foot still rested on the accelerator.

He started at a tap on the window. Julian's cheery tanned face was smiling down at him—some grey stubble on the chin, the buzz-cut hair speckled salt-white at the temples, but his skin still smooth and his shining eyes still youthful.

Julian opened the door and the two men hugged awkwardly. Saverio couldn't help thinking, what are we to each other? Not really friends; ex in-laws? Was there a new language, as yet undiscovered by himself and Rachel, that covered such relationships? He was relieved when Julian stepped back.

•

Within the first half-hour Saverio was deeply regretting coming up north. He was sure he wasn't imagining the suspicion and disapproval directed towards him. He wished that Julian could have been the only one there; he alone seemed to bear Saverio no ill-will.

The others he had not seen for decades. Hannah Wiszler, who used to wear workers' overalls and shave her head, was now a journalist at the ABC; Siobhan F, who had dropped all but the first letter of her surname in the late seventies when she was sixteen and playing electric guitar in a three-piece called Penis Envy, was now a doctor with Médecins Sans Frontières. Dimitri Alexandropoulos he knew of, a playwright and scriptwriter; Ben Franks was a noted visual artist; Dawn Sallford was a parliamentary secretary; and Tom Jords was still a poet and still a drunk. They all had to be reminded of his name, and none of them were the slightest bit interested in him or his life.

Saverio took the wine offered to him by Julian and sat on the top step of the verandah listening in to their conversation, their reminiscences of Leo. Leo at university, Leo at protests, Leo as an artist, Leo's jokes, Leo's feuds, Leo's insults.

'Wasn't he fabulous?' That was Dawn Sallford, her voice a rasp from the cigarettes she still chain-smoked.

You'll be dead soon as well, Saverio couldn't help thinking. He hated himself for descending into the pettiness of the past, instantly transforming back into the unconfident, awkward older brother who never knew the right books to read, the right films to quote, the right music to have in his collection. They had all been so erudite, so opinionated, so intelligent. Even his father, who had despised the effeminacy and pretension of Leo's university friends, had reluctantly granted them that. 'They're smart,' he used to spit out. 'That's all they are.'

Dawn was launching into another story about Leo, some political meeting which had bored them both and in which she had dared him to strip naked. It seemed Leo had taken the dare, had stood up in the middle of the room and begun to undress.

The rollie in Dawn's hand swung wildly as the tale unfolded. 'And I'm going, Dah-dah-DAH dah-dah-DAH dah-dah-dah-DAH—you know, that frigging strippers' music—and Leo is down to his jocks and he pulls them off and throws them at the facilitator, who was this dumb-fuck po-faced Stalinist who bored you shitless with quotes from Lenin and deadshits like that.'

Except for Saverio, everyone was laughing, Dawn so hard that she couldn't continue.

'And then? What else happened?' Julian's face was eager, expectant.

For Christ's sake, Saverio thought, he must have heard this story, must have been bored by it a hundred times already. But no, he was like a child anticipating his favourite moment from a well-loved storybook. He was so young compared to them all, at least ten years younger than Leo.

'Come on, Dawn,' said Julian, 'tell us. What was so funny?'

Dawn straightened up, sniffed, took a breath. 'Now, what was that prick's name? Nick? Nick Tate? No, that was the actor.' She looked triumphant. 'Nick Simmonds. Anyway, Leo's white jocks are flung over Nick's face, everyone is looking at him, so shocked, Leo's standing starkers in the middle of the circle—getting a stiffie I might add . . .'

'Always the fucking exhibitionist!' shrieked Tom Jords.

Dawn was coughing and chuckling again. 'He loved getting his bloody cock out, the silly old poof.' She took a swig of wine, finished the last puff from her cigarette, flicked it into the ashtray precariously perched on the bannister. 'So there's this silence and everyone is shocked and open-mouthed and I'm looking over at Nick and there's this big pair of white Y-fronts covering his head. So Leo, starkers, turns to me and announces, "Dawn, I think we're going to get purged."' Dawn again collapsed into spasms of mirth.

They all did, except Saverio. He threw back his wine and rose to his feet. 'Where am I sleeping?'

They were laughing so hard they couldn't hear him.

He cleared his throat and repeated the question.

Julian, still chuckling, smiled up at him. He pointed inside. 'You've got the main bedroom.'

'Thanks.' Saverio grabbed his bag off the verandah and walked into the house. They had all fallen back into laughter. He knew it was foolish, that it was not at all the case, but it felt like they were laughing at him.

•

'You think that's something to be proud of, do you? It's not. You should be fucking ashamed.'

It was at Leo's twenty-first birthday party and it had been Dawn who'd said it to him.

Saverio had recently completed his engineering degree and that morning had received the call to say he'd been accepted as a graduate by Shell. He was just about to turn twenty-three and was excited at the prospect of his first professional job.

Leo's birthday had been held in rooms above a popular vegetarian North Indian restaurant in Carlton. It attracted students and it was said that if you knew the staff they would let you onto the roof to smoke joints while looking over the skyline of Melbourne. Not that there had been much of a skyline to Melbourne back then. Just the forlorn apocalyptic Bauhaus towers of the housing commission.

Saverio couldn't wait to tell his brother about the job. Leo had already been living out of home for two years, having walked out after a final argument with their old man that had ended, as they usually did, with their father lashing out at Leo; but this time Leo had punched back.

It was the night Leo had told them all that he was homosexual.

'*Finocchio*,' their father kept repeating, confused. '*No, non lo sei!*'

'I am!'

'*No, no, no. Finocchio no!*' Saverio remembered the finality in his father's tone, the distaste and denial firmly set on his face. He would not accept it. He would not have it.

'You know, Dad,' Leo had shouted, 'you would have benefited from a good cock up your arse. It would have made you a better man. It would have made you a better husband.'

Saverio had not believed that his brother could say such things to their father. With a roar, their father had rushed over to Leo and started pummelling him with both fists. Saverio had been ready to leap up and defend his brother when Leo had raised a fist and struck back. It had been an ineffectual, weak hit, Saverio had thought, so fucking pansy, but it was enough to stop their father cold. A son had dared to strike back.

'Go.' Their father had pointed at the door. 'You don't live here no more.'

Leo had smiled, a cruel, gloating smile that had been directly passed down to him from their father. 'I'm already gone, you ignorant shit. I've been gone for years.'

That, of course, had been Leo all over: throw a bomb, walk away and let someone else clean up the mess. It had always been that way; Leo and their father seemed to be born to battle. Leo refused to learn Italian, Leo wasn't interested in anything to do with soccer, all Leo wanted to do was get lost in books.

At first it had been their mother who intervened, protecting Leo from her husband's violence but also pleading, remonstrating, coaxing Leo into making his apologies. Then the cancer struck and she was dead within a year. Saverio had been fourteen and Leo just about to start high school. The younger boy disappeared deeper into his world of books and imagination, and Saverio had become the go-between, even years later, after Leo had left home and immersed himself in the stimulating intellectual and political life of university, discovering the pleasures of drugs and sex.

'Why can't you say something to him?' his father would roar. 'What kind of older brother are you?'

Ashamed, Saverio would try to broker peace.

It would then be Leo's turn to scream at him. 'I don't have to apologise to that patriarchal fascist shit!'

'You think that's something to be proud of, do you? It's not.

You should be fucking ashamed!' Dawn's voice had been brutal and disapproving.

Saverio had looked over to his brother, wanting Leo to save him from the ferocity of her contempt, but Leo had made no reply. It was a ghastly moment, one of those times when all other conversation had ceased and everyone seemed to be turned towards him. That could just be memory playing a trick, of course; probably no one else at the party really gave a damn. But he did not make up Leo's silence. Leo had not defended him.

'Dawn, I've been looking for work for ages, since completing my degree—'

She hadn't let him finish. That was what he remembered most about Leo's friends: the surety of their beliefs, the passion and the hostility. 'Shell supports the apartheid state in South Africa. You want to be part of that?'

No, I want a job. They interviewed me, have given me a graduate position, I've been trying for months. But that wouldn't do for Dawn, so he had said nothing.

She had stepped closer to him, and the vehemence in her eyes had startled him. She felt it so strongly. She wasn't even black. 'Don't take the job.'

'What?' He had been astounded. 'Of course I'm taking the job.'

He had thought she was going to spit on him but instead she had turned around and dismissed him with a guttural, vicious grunt of disgust.

From Leo there had been no word of congratulations, no questions about the job, what he would be doing, when he would be starting.

'She's right. You shouldn't take the job.' Then Leo had walked off to whisper and laugh and joke with his friends.

•

Saverio slammed his suitcase onto the bed. That night was over thirty years ago, but the recollection of it still rankled, still filled him with impotent fury.

He stared around the room. Every spare inch of wall was filled with canvases or photographs: Polaroids, cheap travel shots in florid colours, artistic black and white prints. Framed photos were crammed onto the bureau and bedside table. A stack of Leo's paintings was resting against the far wall, under a framed Aboriginal Land Rights poster that Saverio remembered from the early eighties. The photographs were of Leo and his friends. Leo in Hanoi and Paris and Mexico City. Leo and Dawn in Cuba. Leo and Tom Jords wearing pink T-shirts emblazoned with a black Women's Liberation fist at Mardi Gras.

On the small table was an old framed black and white photograph of their mother, taken when she was a young girl in Rome, her face sullen as she braved the camera. Of Saverio and their father there was nothing at all, not one snapshot.

He shouldn't have come. Leo's true family had been the men and women who were laughing and swapping reminiscences on the verandah.

There was a muffled 'Can I come in?', and Saverio swung around. Julian was holding out a glass of wine with an apologetic smile.

Saverio took it and gestured for Julian to enter. 'You should be the one sleeping in here,' Saverio said quietly.

Julian laughed and shook his head. 'It's fine. The old gang are going to sleep on mattresses and sleeping bags on the living-room floor. We'll probably keep you awake with our drunken raves.' Julian's brow suddenly squashed into a frown. 'Unless you prefer not to sleep in . . .'

'No, no, that's fine. Thanks, it's kind of you.'

Saverio was not frightened of Leo's ghost. They had that in common, brothers in their rationalism and atheism, their father's sons.

Julian walked around the bed and started flicking through the canvases against the wall. 'I'll have to sort through all of these before I head back to Sydney. Leo's named me executor of his estate.' Julian's voice had dropped to an anxious whisper.

'That's how it should be.'

Saverio glimpsed a corner of a painting, the strokes thick, the colours warm, fiery. A lavender-veined penis pushing through a glory hole. Julian let the canvases drop. He seemed to be searching the walls of the room and his gaze lighted on a small, vividly coloured Polaroid. It was of a beaming Filipina woman holding a chuckling naked boy. Julian's features, his smile, his mischievous eyes, were unmistakable. Julian unpinned the Polaroid and put it in his shirt pocket. 'Leo was always meant to give that back. It's the only photo I have of me and Mum back in Manila.'

Saverio felt as if he were sinking. He had hoped that it would be cooler up in the hills but he had forgotten that it was impossible to escape the humidity in this part of the world. He wanted to be back in Melbourne, in less intense light, where he didn't feel that every corner and spare inch of space was illuminated. He didn't want to be sipping red wine. He wanted a beer. He didn't know how to make conversation with these people, even Julian who had always been kind to him and Rachel.

There was the sound of smashing glass on the verandah and peals of laughter.

'It's probably going to be like this all night.'

Saverio searched his pockets, clasped the car keys. 'I'm going to go into town. Do we need anything?'

Julian, surprised, shook his head.

'I'll see you in an hour or two.'

'Sav, will you deliver a eulogy tomorrow?'

He felt snookered. No, he did not want to deliver a eulogy. There was absolutely nothing to say.

With a toss of his chin, Julian indicated the world outside. 'We'd all appreciate it.'

I thought you didn't believe in family. I thought you believed it was a patriarchal capitalist construct. But maybe they did now. Maybe now they believed in family and shares and television and parliamentary democracy. He just wanted to leave the room, the house, the unbearable heat.

He nodded and Julian smiled.

An old lime Volkswagen Beetle was coming up the drive. There was a noisy crunching of gears, and then a small shudder before it came to a halt. Saverio looked through the flyscreen door to see everyone leave the verandah and cluster around the white-haired woman who got out of the car. She wore faded bermuda shorts and a yellow singlet.

A much younger woman stepped out from the driver's side. She looked as though she was still shedding adolescence. She was wearing a pink see-through shirt and even from behind the screen Saverio could see the outline of the black bra beneath.

Julian pushed past him through the door and Saverio almost fell out onto the verandah.

Everyone was talking, calling out, hugging and kissing the older woman. Only the young woman looked up and smiled ruefully, as if to acknowledge him. She was not dressed for the weather at all. She had on a tight black miniskirt with embroidered white stockings. Her thick-soled black boots laced up past her ankles. Her hair was dyed a platinum blonde, set in curls that fell to her shoulders, and her face was heavily made-up with rouge, thick black eyeliner and scarlet lipstick. She reminded him of a young Marilyn Monroe. She seemed to know everyone, greeting them with kisses. Julian had placed a protective arm around her and was beckoning Saverio to come down.

The older woman looked up as he descended the steps. He recognised her face: Margaret Cannon was a well-regarded fiction writer; Rachel had read all her books. Saverio had no recollection of meeting her before. But her smile was warm, inviting, and her grip firm as she shook his hand. 'It's Stephen, isn't it?'

'Saverio.'

'My apologies. That's a much better name.' She turned to the younger woman. 'This is Leo's brother, Saverio. And this is Anna, my daughter and Leo's goddaughter.'

The young woman's hand was moist. She winced apologetically. 'I'm sorry. I'm so sweaty.'

'Of course you are, Anna. Look at what you're wearing.'

Anna's laugh was loud and deep-throated. 'You're a bitch, Dawn.'

'Yeah, shut up.' Julian's arm tightened around Anna's shoulders. 'I think you look gorgeous.'

'Thank you, Jules, so do you.'

Saverio now found himself at the edge of the circle. He jiggled the car keys in his pocket. 'I'm going into town. Anyone need anything?'

'Do we need more grog?'

'There's plenty. Even for us.'

Dawn wasn't satisfied. 'Is there whisky?'

Julian rubbed at his chin. 'I can go and have a look . . .'

'Get us a bottle of Scotch,' she interrupted.

Give us some money, thought Saverio sourly.

But it was Anna who answered. 'Jesus, Dawn, what did your last slave die of?'

Dawn didn't miss a beat. 'Laziness.'

He couldn't help it, even he had to laugh. They were so fast, so sophisticated, so smart. He nodded and moved towards his car. He was surprised to find Anna following him.

She turned back to her mother. 'I'm going into town as well.'

'We just got here!'

Anna ignored her. She was waiting for Saverio to unlock the doors. She smiled across at him. 'It's alright with you, isn't it?'

'Of course.'

As they turned onto the Pacific Highway, Anna let out a sigh of relief. 'Thank you. That was a bit too much.'

'What was?'

'Seeing everyone en masse. You know, that old libertarian femo crowd. They're lovely but it will be all the same stories: who slept with Germaine Greer, who sucked off Robert Hughes while they were all on acid.'

She reminded Saverio of Adelaide, the affectation in her outburst. They were both young women, trying out accents, tones, registers. He wasn't at all shocked by her language. It just reminded him of how young she was.

'Tom looks awful.'

He didn't reply.

She shrugged her shoulders. 'I guess that's because of all the antiretroviral drugs he's on. And because he's a drunk.'

'He's always been an alcoholic.'

He felt her gaze fix on him. 'I didn't know Leo had a brother.'

'I didn't know he had a godchild.'

'He's got two. But Danny is in England or Poland or somewhere like that.'

They fell into silence. But something she'd said had made him curious. He couldn't help it. He felt a little embarrassed asking but ask he did. 'Who *did* Germaine Greer fuck?'

Anna grinned mischievously. 'Probably all of them.' She was searching through the glove box and underneath her seat. 'Do you have any music?'

'No. It's a hire car.'

She was examining the stereo unit. 'I should have brought along my iPod. There's a jack.' She turned to him eagerly. 'Do you have one?'

So that was what that attachment on the stereo was for. She, like his own kids, seemed to have a second sense for technology. He shook his head. 'I'm sorry, I left mine back at the house.'

Disappointed, she turned the radio on instead. She kept punching buttons, rapid sprays of music, country and western, pop, snatches of talkback. She settled on a familiar strained melancholic voice singing above a jangling melodious electric guitar.

'Do you like U2?'

They were a favourite, one of the few passions he shared with Matthew. 'I think I have every album,' he announced proudly.

'They're alright.' She sounded uncertain. Then with a derisive sniff, 'But that Bono is a sanctimonious cunt. He makes me want to hate them.' She was flicking through her purse and she placed a cigarette to her lips.

'This is a non-smoking car.'

'I thought you lot were all anarchists?'

'I'm not part of that lot and I don't want you to smoke in the car.'

She made a face, but returned the cigarette to its packet. Her fingers started tapping on the dashboard. 'How come I've never met you before?'

'Leo and I haven't seen each other for a while.'

'What's a while?'

'Eleven years.'

'Fuck!' There was awe as well as shock in her exclamation. 'You must be feeling awful.'

She was right. Probably not in the way she thought, but she was right nonetheless. He did feel awful. He was furious at himself. He had been cold and unfeeling for days and this was not the moment to experience the sting of tears in his eyes. He did not dare look at her.

'I'm sorry.' For the first time her voice had lost its brazen inflection. It sounded young and frightened.

He did turn to her. She was looking out of the window at the lush landscape falling away from them. She continued to speak in that shy, childlike tone. 'I loved Leo. He was amazing, wonderful. But he could be so mean.'

She followed him confidently into the pub, as if they had known each other for years. The Demons Creek Hotel was a three-storey Victorian building with an ugly, box-like extension attached to the side of it which functioned as a bottleshop. It was blessedly cool inside the double-bricked walls of the building.

All heads turned to look at them as they walked into the bar, then just as quickly everyone went back to contemplating their drinks. It was far from crowded. A few tradesmen who'd just knocked off work, two ferals with dreads, some elderly National Party types propped up on stools at the bar. The pub catered with egalitarian ease to the long-established farmers, to the hippies and children of hippies who had laid claim to the hills over the past three decades, and also to the constant stream of local and international tourists who passed through on their way south to Byron Bay. The locals obviously assumed that Anna and Saverio were part of the latter group. No eyebrow was raised at Anna's aggressively urban attire. Saverio was conscious that if their entry had aroused any suspicions, they would have had to do with what a middle-aged man like him was doing in the company of such a young woman. She's my brother's goddaughter, he wanted to call out. She's got nothing to do with me. Instead he asked her if she wanted a beer and she said yes.

The three elderly blokes at the bar fell silent as he approached. He nodded to them and received a gruff 'g'day' in response. They all had wrinkled ruddy skin and thin wisps of silver-yellow hair, and all wore open-necked white shirts that accentuated the burnt V of their necks.

Saverio looked around the bar as he waited for the beers. He wondered if his brother had spent much time there; he couldn't really imagine Leo discussing Marxism with the farmers or anonymous gay sex with the hippies. He took a glass in each hand, nodded again to the old men, and found Anna at the rear of the pub.

As part of the extensions a small square dance area had been constructed against the back wall. On three sides mirrors ran from floor to ceiling reflecting the bar beyond. Anna was gazing at her reflection. A mirror ball hung from the ceiling. Some of the shingles of glass were missing.

'I guess this is where you come if you want to go clubbing.' She laughed again, a deep resonant sound that came all the way up from her belly. 'I can see Leo here, he loved a bit of a dance.' She put on an accent, Leo at his most queenie, cruelly caricaturing other gay men. 'They're playing "I Will Survive", Brooce! They're playing "I Will Survive"!' She was wiggling in such a close approximation of Leo's stilted dancing style that Saverio couldn't help laughing.

Anna took the beer and indicated a door with a handwritten sign taped to it: *To the beer garden*. 'Am I allowed to smoke out there?'

I'm not your father, he almost snapped at her. Instead he opened the door for her and followed her out to the courtyard.

It was a stunning view. The gently sloping yard was immaculately mowed, with tall grey-limbed gum trees throwing shade over the tables and chairs set around the lawn. There were no fences and the ground disappeared abruptly to give way to the jutting tops of thick forest trees. Beyond the greenery and as far as the eye could see was the curve of the mighty Pacific Ocean.

The garden was empty except for a blonde woman sitting on a bench at the end of the lawn, looking out over the view. She did not turn at the sound of their voices.

'So why did you and Leo stop talking to each other?'

He wished he had said nothing to her in the car. Tomorrow was the funeral and after that he would return to Melbourne. Then it would all be over.

He took a mouthful of beer. 'It really doesn't matter now.'

She was searching his face again, her eyes inquisitive and excited. She drew ravenously on her cigarette. 'Your father was a fascist, wasn't he?'

He banged the beer glass on the table. 'That's nonsense. Did Leo tell you that?'

Anna was not at all perturbed. 'Yep. He said that your father supported Mussolini . . .'

'My father did not support Mussolini!' Saverio drew breath and looked out at the view. She was a child; she wasn't to blame. 'My father hated the Blackshirts, thought them thugs and criminals, but he respected some of what Mussolini was able to achieve for Italy and for poor people in Italy. He was not alone in that. Millions of Italian peasants were in agreement.'

'He did beat your mother, though, didn't he?'

And how the fuck is that your business? Saverio looked out to the horizon again. The sky and sea offered no assistance. The setting sun still had heat in it and he wished he had remembered his sunglasses.

'I think Leo might have exaggerated some of what occurred.' It was impossible to explain further. Yes, their father had hit their mother, not very often, never bashed her; but yes, he had hit her, three, possibly four times that Saverio could recall, in front of him and Leo, smacks and slaps, always out of exasperation, driven almost unhinged by her whining, her hypochondria, her almost bovine passivity. How to explain any of this to a young woman coming into adulthood at the dawn of this digital century? How to explain the behaviour of men and women from the end of a feudal millennium?

'If he wasn't so bad, why did Leo hate him so much?'

That question was so childish; as if there were any easy answers to it. Because Leo was unforgiving. Because Leo was stubborn. Because Leo was selfish. Because Leo relied upon their mother's support and when she died he felt betrayed. Because mothers always favoured the gay son. All of this was true, but to say any of it was to lead into an argument.

He wished she hadn't come with him. He had wanted to forget Leo for a few hours, and her presence and her questions couldn't help but remind him of the duties he faced the following day. He couldn't do it; he just wasn't up to it. He would say so to Julian, and Julian would understand. I can't give a eulogy. I have nothing to say. I can't say what I want to say. I can't say that Leo was the kind of man who wouldn't go and visit his dying father, the kind of man who didn't have it in him to ask after his niece and nephew. The rage seemed to flood through him, threatened to drown him. The heat, the humidity, the thickness of it, like a blanket over the world, was exhausting.

'Are you okay?' She was concerned now, biting her bottom lip. Her incisors were long and crooked. He wanted her to shut her mouth; the exposed teeth made her look crude, ugly.

'I have to go to the bathroom.'

It was blissful to be inside the cool anteroom of the toilets. They were part of the original hotel and the thick tiled walls were effective insulation against the heat. He was the only occupant of the men's toilets and he unbuttoned his shirt to the navel and splashed water on his face, his neck, under his arms. He used his handkerchief to wipe himself dry.

He examined his face critically in the mirror. He hadn't shaved that morning, and across his chin and along his upper lip there had already formed a soft shadow of alternating white and black stubby bristles. He wished he'd had time for a haircut. His smoky grey hair was shapeless, and the harsh fluorescent light in the toilets seemed to shine directly above where his hair was thinnest.

You idiot, he hissed to himself. You vain, stupid fuck, you want to impress that young girl.

The colourless scar above his left eyebrow was almost invisible. He should point that out to Anna. This is where my brother hit me with a hammer when I was ten. The reason for the argument was long forgotten. All he could remember was trying to squeeze the life out of Leo, his hands around his brother's neck, and how Leo would not submit, how he kicked and struck and scratched like a wild animal. The argument had started in their bedroom. They had punched and kicked each other into the kitchen and rolled into the laundry where Saverio's hands were around his brother's throat and Leo's hand had landed on a hammer and it was in raising this hammer to Saverio's face that the battle had ended. He had blood in his mouth and had fallen across the laundry door and Leo was on top of him, the hammer raised, ready to strike another blow.

'Don't!' Saverio had screamed. 'Don't!'

Leo had dropped the hammer. His lips were trembling. 'You're bleeding.' He started to whimper.

'It's okay, I'm alright.' His own anger, his brother's anger, had disappeared in an instant.

When he got back to the table, the woman who had been at the end of the beer garden was sitting across from Anna. They were both smoking and looked up, smiling, as his shadow fell across them.

'Saverio, this is Melanie.'

'Call me Mel,' the woman said. Her voice was shockingly nasal and broad, almost a take-off of a rural Australian accent. Her grip was tight, firm. She wore sunglasses with big round lenses so he couldn't see her eyes but he guessed she was in her mid-forties. The skin around her mouth was wrinkled, her lips were thin, and her hair was dyed a chemical yellow. She wore a black T-shirt a size too small for her full breasts and pot belly, and black jeans too small for her expanding arse and thick thighs.

She was obviously what Matty and Adelaide would derisively call a bogan, and what his parents, with equal derision, would have called an *Australiana*. She was a woman who could not take root anywhere else but in this enormous infinite landscape. Unabashed, unashamed.

'He's better-looking than Leo.'

'Mel knew Leo,' Anna rushed to explain.

'Yeah, he was a good bloke, your brother.' Mel stubbed out her cigarette. 'I'm really sorry for your loss.'

It was the expected phrase, it came from a stranger, but she said it with unforced sincerity and they were the first words since he'd heard of Leo's death that brought home the finality of the event. His brother was no more. From now on there would only be past.

'Thank you.'

'When I first left Brendan and began seeing Suzanne, Leo was the only one I could talk to about things.' Mel was continuing a conversation she had begun with Anna while he was in the toilet. 'Small towns are fucked. Everyone knows you, and Brendan's really popular with everyone. He's done work on most people's pipes or plumbing so you can imagine what they thought of me when I took off with a woman.' Mel was shaking her head. 'I thought they were going to kill me. Kill both of us. Leo's was always a safe house; he'd let us come and stay, sleep over. Talk to us about gay rights and shit. Suzanne loved him. She's devastated he's gone.'

Saverio was horrified. Mel had started to cry.

'Fucking bitch, I hate her!'

Anna wrapped her fingers around Mel's hand. Saverio, confused, looked away. A line of surfers, black and grey and silver strokes, was visible against the vast blue of the ocean. Mel blew her nose into a tissue one more time then glanced down guiltily at Anna's cigarettes.

Anna nodded.

'I shouldn't.'

'Today doesn't count.'

Mel laughed. 'Yeah, that's right.'

She was looking at Saverio. He couldn't smile, he didn't know what she wanted from him. All he could think was what an unlikely lesbian she seemed. He had thought she was a bikie's moll, an ex-stripper, a small-town mum. Of course it was possible she was all of those things, and a lesbian to boot. Though Dawn wouldn't find much communion with her. Just like him, Dawn wouldn't know what to say to Mel.

The woman was standing up. 'Thank you for the smokes.'

Anna jumped to her feet and hugged her. 'You'll look after yourself?'

'Of course.' Mel seemed embarrassed by the spontaneous affection. She slipped out of Anna's embrace and held out her hand to Saverio, who had also risen. 'Mate, again, I'm really sorry. Your brother was a real good man.'

He couldn't speak. They watched in silence as Mel walked back into the pub. She was shaky on her feet.

'She shouldn't drive,' he said gruffly.

'I know, but her girlfriend's just left her for a younger woman so of course she's just going to do whatever she likes tonight. We'd all do that.' Anna pointed to the empty glasses. 'Another round?'

'One more.' He pointed to her empty chair. 'But you sit. I'm buying.'

'You bought the last round.'

'I work. I'm a corporate cocksucker, as my brother used to so fondly put it. You're young and a student. I'm paying.'

Anna looked as if she was about to protest again. Then, suddenly, she beamed. 'Sure. Thank you.'

At the bar, Mel was arguing with two men, one of them in a khaki uniform with an orange and yellow National Parks and Wildlife insignia stitched on the pocket, the other in football shorts, a paint-splattered work singlet and Blundstones. She winked at him as he walked past. Saverio noticed that the painter had his right hand sitting flat against her wide buttocks.

'I hope our friend is alright in there,' he said to Anna as he delivered the new beer.

Anna shrugged and drank greedily. 'She looks like she can take care of herself.'

That was not his impression. She looked tough but Mel hadn't struck him as being tough.

The dying afternoon sun was still strong, but finally a breeze was coming off the darkening water.

'She really liked Leo.'

'Yes.' He would keep his answers short, non-committal, give nothing away.

'It's good to be reminded of what a wonderful man he could be. You could always talk to Leo about anything. He'd always listen.'

He sipped at his beer slowly.

'One of the things I loved about him was that he would never give you the standard adult answer, he'd always take you a little by surprise. When I was ten I found a stash of Julian's pornos in the house and wanted to read them, but Leo asked me if I had started masturbating. I said no and he wouldn't let me have them, said it might dull my imagination. That was so unlike him, usually he let us watch and read anything we liked, no censorship whatsoever. Not this time. But he was right.' Anna sniggered. ''Course, once I started doing the old five-finger dance he let me have them.' She winked at Saverio. 'He was such a character. Was he always like that?'

'I guess so.'

Anna was frowning. For Christ's sake, what did she want from him? She lit a cigarette, sat back in her chair and crossed her arms. 'Saverio, I think you should forgive him.'

Sin, confession, absolution. These children of communists and feminists and true believers were just as moralistic as the old believers.

'Anna, I'm sorry, but you're a child. You don't know what the fuck you're talking about.'

He had humiliated her. He could see that she was holding back tears and felt immediate regret. Again, she so reminded him of Adelaide. She was young, she had yet to learn how to hide her emotions from the world. He knew he should apologise but he was enjoying the relief of being harsh and uncompromising. There was a thrill to punishment, he had learned that raising his own children; the thrill of deflating them, confronting them with their own limitations, ignorance, powerlessness, foolishness, inadequacy. What did she know about him and Leo? She should just keep her fucking mouth shut.

Don't cry, please don't cry.

She wasn't crying. She was looking out to sea.

'Four years ago, for my seventeenth birthday, I came to stay here with Rowan, who was my boyfriend. I thought Rowan was going to be the love of my life. He was two years older, he played guitar in a band, he was at university, his mother was a feminist academic and his father was an actor. I thought he was so cool and so handsome and so wonderful and that I was going to be in love with him forever. I wanted Row to meet Leo and I wanted Leo to meet Row. I thought they were both the most fabulous men in the world and I wanted them to know each other.'

Her voice was detached, she stumbled a little over her words, but she sounded confident and deliberate. He was aware that a large part of it was a pose, that there was something theatrical in her delivery. She kept her eyes out to the horizon of sea and sky, but he knew that she was fully conscious of his stare.

'Rowan took to Leo immediately. He loved how funny he was and he loved all the gossip. We stayed up all that first night smoking ice while Leo told him the Germaine Greer story and the Sasha Soldatow story and the Jim Sharman story and who fucked who and who blasted heroin and who really should have taken the credit for what, and of course Row was like a grateful child, just lapping it all up.'

Anna took a big breath. 'Do you want to hear all this?'

She was hesitating for effect. She would be crushed if he said no. He wanted to say no, that there was nothing that he could hear about Leo that would make his own heart feel any lighter.

'We all fall asleep at dawn, all in the big bed, and I wake a few hours later and decide to take a walk in the forest. It's a beautiful day and I'm still feeling fantastic because of the drugs and I walk all the way to town to the bakery and pick up some croissants and rolls and I walk all the way back to Leo's. I get there and Leo is cooking in the kitchen and Rowan is playing his guitar on the porch and when I come up the steps and I'm smiling he looks at me and bursts into tears. He just keeps saying, "We had sex, Anna, we fucked, Anna, I'm so sorry." I drop the bag of croissants and rolls and look up at the door where Leo is standing, a stupid apron on, a fork in one hand, and he just says, "Rowan wanted to tell you, I didn't. But he's still young and foolish. I told him you didn't have to know." Then he goes back into the kitchen and continues making us breakfast.'

Saverio couldn't believe that the bowerbirds continued their whispering song in the trees above, that the drumroll of the waves echoed off the coast below. He could barely control his voice as he asked, 'What did you do?'

'I cried and I asked them both how they could do it to me and Row was crying as well and he kept saying, "I'm sorry, I'm sorry, I'm sorry," and I ran after Leo and said, "Are you going to apologise, are you going to say you're sorry?" and he just said, "Anna, you know I am an anarchist and a libertarian. You don't possess Rowan and he doesn't possess you. There is nothing I have to apologise for."'

There was a burst of laughter. Mel and the two men had crashed through the door into the beer garden, cigarettes in their mouths. Mel called out to them as they sat around a table but Saverio did not register the names of the men as they were introduced. He heard Mel whisper loudly to the man in the singlet, 'That's Leo's brother.'

'What did you say to him?'

Anna turned back to him, her face now unsmiling. 'I hit him. I hit him so hard, I wanted to break him.'

'What did he do?'

'He kicked me out. He said he couldn't abide violence, that he had grown up in a violent house and he would not have it in a house of his own. He kicked me out, and Row and I drove back to Sydney, both of us crying all the way.' Anna shrugged her shoulders. 'Man, it was a miracle we weren't killed.'

Saverio stumbled out of his chair, across the lawn, bashed through the door, almost ran into the toilets. He wanted to put his fist through the mirror, kick down a cubicle door. If someone said the wrong word, offered the wrong look, made a move to stop him, he would gladly bring them down. He would gladly break their necks. But once again the toilets were empty. He breathed in deeply. Thankfully the toilets were empty.

•

'Do you think she'll be okay?'

He had been silent when he returned to the beer garden, had said nothing as they walked to the car, had been quiet for most of the drive. Anna, too, had said little.

As they'd been about to leave the pub, Mel had rushed after them, taken Anna's arm and tried to lead her onto the dance floor.

'I can't, we have to go.'

'Come on, just one dance, I love this song.'

The pub had begun to fill. The music was steak-and-three-veg Australian rock-and-roll, 'Cheap Wine' by Cold Chisel.

Anna pulled away from Mel. 'I can't dance to this.'

Mel, pouting, flung herself onto the dance floor. She danced on her own, claiming all of the small space, throwing herself into ugly jerks and spasms, singing along to the lyrics at the top of her lungs.

Uncertain, Anna looked around the pub, at the tables of men laughing at the dancing woman. 'Maybe we should stay a little while longer?'

Saverio ignored her and walked outside. She could stay if she wanted. Mel was obviously going to be a messy drunk and he did not want the responsibility of looking after her. Anna would learn that life lesson soon enough. But Anna was running after him. Without a word they got into the car.

'She won't be okay. We should have stayed.'

He grunted again.

Anna crossed her arms. 'Why are you so angry?'

Maybe he should drive the car off the road, end it all in screeching tyres, smoke and fire and melting metal.

'Aren't you going to say a thing?'

His reply was to switch on the radio.

She turned it off immediately. 'If I have forgiven him, so can you.'

The petulant spoilt child. This broke his silence.

'You have not forgiven him. How could you forgive him?'

'I have. I really have.' Her tone was urgent, pleading. But he didn't believe her. His brother did not deserve forgiveness.

'What you told me just confirms that he was indeed an animal.'

'That's not true.' She was fumbling for the right words. 'He was just, you know . . . uncompromising . . .'

'For fuck's sake, Anna, he was a cunt. I'm glad he's dead.'

The words appeared to strike her with the force of a punch. Her body shrank into itself. When she spoke next, she was timid, barely audible. 'Leo never lied. He loved sex. Sex was his politics. I always knew that about him.'

Politics? This wasn't politics, this was delusion. Thank God it was over, thank God what they called politics—Leo, Dawn,

Tom, the whole damn lot of them—thank God the world no longer listened to such rubbish. Thank God it was all going to die with them.

'Nothing can excuse what he did to you.'

'You're so hard. Just like him, just like all of them. Why the fuck is your generation so hard?'

His foot slammed on the brake and the car swerved onto the side of the road. Anna jolted forward. She screamed.

He turned on her. 'I am not like them. I'm not anything like them. Do you understand?'

She was terrified now. He was mortified. It didn't matter that Leo was dead. He'd always do this to him, always lay bare a rage he had thought long buried. Alive or dead, the memories and scars wrought on him by Leo were there forever.

She had just seen it, that childish selfish annihilating hate. She cowered away from him.

'I'm sorry. I didn't mean to scare you.'

'What the fuck did Leo do to you?'

He tried to explain. He told her about their father's cancer, how it began in the stomach, then spread to the pancreas and reached the lungs, how the old man, a skeleton in his bed, the folds of flesh hanging off his bones, how he had succumbed to a delirium in which the past and the present were one. Where is my son? Saverio, where is your brother? Has he forgiven me?

He told her about his countless calls to Leo, pleading with him, begging him to come home one last time. He told her what

Leo had said to him: 'Good, the old bastard deserves to die in pain, he deserves to suffer.'

'You can't mean that, Leo.'

'Don't you get it, Sav? That man means nothing to me.'

He then told her how the fury had gripped him, how he had organised the plane ticket and flown to Coolangatta and hired the car and driven down the coast and up through the hills to force Leo to return. He told her how they had screamed at one another, slapped and punched one another, how he had gripped Leo's hair and pulled him onto the porch, down the steps, dragged him through the gravel, Leo shrieking, biting him, scratching him, how it was only Julian who stilled their frenzy, Julian crying, howling at them to stop. *Don't, please, don't.* They were the words that had broken him.

He'd left Leo in the dirt and walked back to the car. 'Fuck off!' he'd roared, as he'd walked away, and Leo had screamed back, 'You're just like him!' And to this day, he explained to Anna, he did not know if they had been Leo's last words to him or his last words to Leo.

By the time he'd finished speaking, Anna was sobbing. Saverio, his eyes dry, his hands steady, eased the car back onto the road and drove them back to the house.

It was dusk when they arrived. The party was still in full swing on the verandah.

'Have you got my bloody whisky?' Dawn called out to them.

'We forgot,' Anna yelled back. She was looking at her face

in the rear-view mirror. She took a compact from her purse and applied powder to her face. 'How do I look?'

Like a child, he wanted to answer, you look like a child. 'You look fine.'

He didn't acknowledge anyone on his way to the bedroom. He closed the door behind him, shutting out the laughter and jokes and talk.

On the bed lay a small square canvas. It was a painting of his own children when they were toddlers on the beach. Matty was naked, plonked down in the sand, Adelaide standing next to her brother in pink undies. The colours were intense, garish blues and greens, flaming reds and yellows. His children's faces were elongated, distorted, but recognisable nevertheless. Adelaide looked bored, impatient. Matty's dough-like baby face stared blankly out at him.

Leo had painted them the first year that he and Julian had moved up to the coast. Saverio, Rachel and the kids had spent a week with them over the summer holidays, a week in which Leo had cooked for them every night and entertained Rachel with his wild stories, the gossip and slander from the past, extravagant narratives of sexual escapades and orgies. During the day, Leo and Julian would take the kids swimming or into town while Rachel and Saverio took long walks in the bushland, found near-empty coves to swim in, read books, had sex and did crosswords.

There was a knock on the door and Julian entered. 'Dawn's all good. I found a bottle of Jameson's in one of the kitchen cupboards.' He looked at the canvas in Saverio's hands. 'I thought you might want to keep it.'

Saverio wanted to say, I don't want to talk tomorrow, there is nothing I can say. 'Thank you.'

'Come out for a drink. Our bark is worse than our bite.'

Saverio shook his head. 'Nah, I want to ring Rachel, I want to check on things at home.'

•

The service began with a recording of Maria Callas singing an aria from *Tosca*, and then it was Dawn who first stepped onto the platform. Before she spoke she walked to the back of the dais and took down the Australian flag. There was a burst of applause. Leo wouldn't have wanted it, she explained to the shocked civil celebrant. This time there were no outlandish stories, no off-colour jokes or declarations. She told the assembled mourners of how she had first met Leo when they were volunteers at the Aboriginal Legal Centre in Fitzroy, of how frightened she had been of the Aboriginal men, of how Leo had never succumbed to white guilt, how one youth had hurled a barrage of abuse at them one afternoon, to which Leo had stood his ground and answered, 'You pay me and you can call me a white cunt—but if I'm a volunteer and you insult me then you're a black cunt.'

Tom Jords spoke next, about Leo's work and activism in those first terrible years of the AIDS epidemic, Leo's sense of humour, how the door of his flat in the Cross was always left open in case any of the working girls or boys needed a safe house to escape to.

Margaret Cannon got up after Tom and read Leo's favourite poem, 'To Posterity' by Bertolt Brecht.

Then it was Saverio's turn to speak. He scanned the crowd. Mel was up the back of the room in a black dress, a chunky silver crucifix around her neck, holding hands with an Islander woman who wore black jeans and a black T-shirt.

His eyes came to rest on Anna. He spoke to her. To her and to Julian. He began by telling them that Leo's real name was Luigi, how Leo had hated that name because it was yelled at him with such derision and spite by the Aussie boys.

'Once he started university, Luigi became Leo. You're his family, you were the ones he learned with and experimented with and found so much joy with. You looked after him, you protected him, you understood him. Thank you for that.'

The room had fallen quiet except for the screams of the birds, the steady hum of the distant ocean.

'I'm not going to speak about Leo but about Luigi, my younger brother. When he first started school Dad made sure I understood that I had to walk with him every day, that I was not to let him out of my sight. "He's your brother," he said to me, "you will always have to look after him. Do you understand?" But from the second day of school Luigi was determined to walk on his own. I guess he was an anarchist from birth.'

There was a ripple of laughter.

'I knew I couldn't change his mind. I knew it even back then. So I said, yes, you can walk ahead of me. That's my favourite memory of him, him walking ahead, a hundred metres in the distance, but every now and then turning back to look at me to make sure I was still there. That was what he was like: always wanting to be independent, free, not reliant on anyone. But I have to believe that from time to time he was still turning back, searching for me.' At this Saverio's voice cracked. 'I have to believe he never forgot me.'

The applause that followed him back to his seat was warm and generous. Anna's claps were the last to die out. Saverio looked over at Julian, who was walking onto the dais. Thank you, the younger man mouthed. It was Julian who spoke at the end, and he spoke simply about love. There were no hymns, there was no religion, no prayers. The service finished with Lou Reed's voice singing 'Perfect Day'.

•

Rachel was waiting for him at the airport and as she folded him into her arms he submitted to the sweet calmness of their life together.

At home, as he unpacked, she sat on their bed, took Leo's painting of their kids and scrutinised it closely. 'I always liked this painting.'

She took it and walked out of their bedroom.

He followed her into the lounge room where she held up the canvas against a stretch of blank wall above the stereo.

'Here,' she said. 'I think it will be perfect here.'

Sticks, Stones

MARIANNE HAD WORKED ALL WEEKEND AT a trade fair in town. She'd risen just after dawn on Saturday morning, and detoured to collect Darren and Aliyah on the way so they could help her set up the stall at the exhibition hall and make sure that their brand-new cyan and white T-shirts with the dark blue company logo had been delivered and were available to give out to any potential clients. As usual Darren had left the women to set up and staff the stand and had spent both days 'networking', slipping out for beers with Arnie from Northern Territory Travel, Marty from Travelworld, and whoever else he could find to ensure he spent as little time as possible actually working. It had been exhausting but Marianne enjoyed the fair, chatting with colleagues, catching up on gossip, making contacts. Her effusiveness, her straight-talking honesty, had as always made her popular. Unlike Darren, she never pretended to be able to offer more than was possible. Aliyah found it hard to step out from behind the table; her attempts to overcome her timidity made her voice sound shrill and unconfident. On the Sunday, Siobhan, the head of sales and their immediate manager, had come to see them. Darren had butted in immediately to tell her about the deals he had nearly struck, the contracts just about to be signed. Siobhan had smiled politely and told the three of them they could take the Monday off. Then she had whispered to Marianne, 'You can take off the Tuesday as well; just keep your phone on, okay?'

Marianne had smiled to herself. Siobhan could tell a bullshitter.

•

Now it was Tuesday afternoon and Marianne experienced a frisson of guilt over how much she had enjoyed her time off. All Monday she had worked in the garden, pruning the apricot tree, weeding, spreading compost on the vegetable patch to prepare the soil for its slow-brewing hibernation and regeneration. She had put on and hung out two loads of washing, and on Tuesday morning had woken up just before six to take a long walk down to Darebin Creek along the path that ran by the back of the high school, and finished off with a coffee at Carmen's. She was back in time to wake Jack for school and to make another coffee for herself and Rick before he headed off to work.

He had looked at her with a bemused grin when she brought in his work shirts off the line and piled them on the redwood dining table. 'You going to iron my shirts?'

'Mm-hm.'

He pulled her close to him and kissed her. 'But it isn't my b-b-b-b-b-birthday.'

She flicked her finger at the snub of his nose, made a face. 'Just this once, boyo.' She stretched, arched her back. 'But I am enjoying being a lady of leisure. I think I might quit my job.' The quick flush of panic that crossed his face made her collapse into laughter.

He began laughing as well and slid up behind her, placing his large long-fingered hands across her shoulder, his left hand slipping underneath her gardening shirt, under her bra strap, his thumb lightly brushing her nipple. 'Maybe I should take the day off as well.'

'Mmm.' Please don't, she thought, I want another day just to myself. They heard Jack slam the bathroom door and Rick jumped back and sat down again to finish his coffee.

'Mum, I can't find my laptop.'

She winked at her husband and called out to the hallway, 'It's in the lounge where you left it last night.'

'Thanks, Mum.'

No, she thought wickedly to herself, thank you.

•

She liked working, appreciated her job and the freedom it gave her. Most days she was on the road, visiting clients, travel agencies and tourist bureaus; once a month she would fly to Adelaide to take agents on a tour of the South Australian wine districts or beaches. She hadn't worked for five years while Jack and her daughter, Kalinda, were preschoolers; by the end she was bored and unhappy. It had been just before Jack started at primary school that she'd mutinously informed Rick she was not ever going to iron his shirts again. More than any other of the myriad household chores, it was the ironing she had focused on to distil her rage. Rick hadn't put up a fight, an anticlimax that had annoyed her no end. It had been the worst period of their marriage—they had just taken out the mortgage on that first house in Watsonia, Kalinda had been diagnosed with dyslexia, and Jack, not adjusting to kindergarten, was still wetting the bed. Her life seemed a constant cycle of washing, cleaning, drying tears, intervening in squabbles, driving, driving, driving. She had come to hate the family car, the smell of it, the metallic trace of Kalinda's vomit that they could never seem to wash out of the back seat, the stereo trapped forever on Classic Hits FM. There had been three months back then when she would wake up every night from a nightmare in which Australian Crawl's 'The Boys Light Up' seemed to be playing endlessly on an infernal loop.

It was Rick who had suggested that she go back to study, and it had been great advice. In the short term, the two evenings a week at college had seemed only to add to her exhaustion, but she had completed a diploma in tourism in three years and by the time Kalinda had started high school she was working full-time for Harvey World Travel. She and Rick could now joke about her aversion to ironing; for the last few years Rick would bounce out of bed on his birthday and announce, taking off Cartman from *South Park*, 'It's my b-b-b-b-b-b-birthday, you have to iron my shirts.'

She didn't want to retire, didn't even want to think about it, but these days she appreciated the rhythms and meditative pace of housework, the pleasure that came from cooking and organising the running of a home. She and her girlfriends would chuckle and complain about the laziness and unreconstructed apathy of their suburban husbands, but she was always a little annoyed when Rick wanted to cook or thought it a good idea to reorganise the lounge or bedroom. No, damn you, she would think, that's my terrain. She went to the gym twice a week, had recently joined a Pilates class. Housework was part of her relaxation. It had ceased to be a job long ago.

She had baked an upside-down pear and caramel cake, washed the dishes, scrubbed the stove top, got rid of the out-of-date bottles gone grey at the back of the pantry, when she glanced at the clock and realised it was time to pick up the boys for soccer. Her hair, unwashed, silver at the roots, was a mess. She quickly stripped off her gardening shirt, put on a blouse, tied a scarf around her head and ran out to the car. She knew the boys would be waiting for her outside the school gates, checking the

time on their phones. As she waited at the lights, she texted her
son a quick message, keeping her eyes out for the police. The
woman in the four-wheel drive in the next lane beeped her horn
at her and Marianne threw her a tight grimace. Come on, lady,
you've got kids, you know what it's like. The lights went green,
she pressed send and took off.

Jack was waiting with his mates Stavros and Billy and they
didn't seem at all concerned about the time. As she made her way
slowly up St Georges Road, she could see them mucking around
with a soccer ball on the footpath. Freda Carlosi's daughter,
Amelia, was with them. As always happened, Marianne felt
a small tremble of sadness go through her on seeing the girl
Amelia had been born with Down syndrome, and even though
she was Jack's age, Freda and Anthony still dressed her in pink
hoodies and track pants that were more appropriate for a girl
half her age. The one she was wearing today had Walt Disney
bunny rabbits printed on it, but her body could scarcely be
contained in the children's clothes: her breasts were enormous,
her bottom fleshy and prominent. As Marianne pulled into the
kerb near them, she could see that the girl was trying to get the
boys' attention. Billy, the tallest of them, was holding the soccer
ball high above her head and Amelia was trying to grab for it.
Her son and Stavros were laughing. Marianne pushed the button
to wind down the passenger window and call out to them, tell
them to stop teasing Amelia and fooling around, when the girl's
fingers hit the ball and it bounced back off her hand and flew
onto the road. She felt a jolt of terror, thinking Amelia would

rush into the traffic, but Bill reached out and pulled her back. The ball had gone under a car and unleashed a torrent of horns.

It was then she heard Billy's voice pierce the noise: 'Freakin' hell, Meels, watch what you're doing!' She saw the girl's face blush red and then she heard her son: 'Yeah, Meels, why are you such a dumb mong?' Stavros broke out into mocking giggles and Billy gave her son a slap across the back. 'Mong,' Jack repeated, even more loudly, and that was when he looked up and saw Marianne. His face broke into a grin and he grabbed his schoolbag off the ground. 'Come on, Mum's here.' The traffic had come to a complete halt and Billy took the opportunity to dash across the road and scoop up the ball.

Jack and Stavros scrambled into the car, Billy following with the ball tucked under his arm. 'Hey, Mrs P,' 'Hello, Marianne,' 'Why are you late, Mum?'

She ignored them. Her eyes were fixed on Amelia waving at them. She waved back uncertainly. She looked over at her son. 'Who's picking up Amelia?'

'I don't know—her mum.'

'We can't leave her here alone.'

Jack rolled his eyes and pointed to the groups of boys and girls at the tram stop, straddling the school fence, drifting down the school drive in pairs, in trios, in groups of four and five.

'She'll be fine, Mrs P,' Stavros said from the back, wrestling the soccer ball off Billy. 'She knows she has to wait for Mrs C.'

'She nearly ran out on the road before.'

'Mum! We're going to be late.'

Marianne put the car into drive and hit the indicator. As the car pulled into the traffic, she could see that the girl was still waving at them. The boys ignored her.

'I heard what you called her.'

'What?' Jack shrugged his shoulders. He was pulling off his jumper and white shirt, fumbling in his bag for his soccer shirt.

'I heard what you called her.'

In the back, Stavros and Billy had fallen silent.

She could smell her son's day-long musty pong. His boyhood sweetness was all gone. It appalled her, the overwhelming vigour of his stink.

'I think it is disgusting, calling her names.'

Jack mumbled something.

'What did you say?'

He was struggling to pull his soccer shirt down over his chest, his middle, wriggling in his seat, all sinewy arms and sprawling legs. 'I said, whatever.'

I could smack you.

'It's alright, Mrs P.' Stavros was leaning forward. 'It's just a word—she doesn't mind. It's like when they call me a wog.'

'That's right.' Billy leaned forward as well. 'Or when they call me a Maco dickwad.'

'You are a Maco dickwad.'

Billy grabbed the ball off Stavros and threw it hard at the back of Jack's head.

'Stop it!' It felt good to scream at them. She wished she could stop the car and order them out into the traffic on St

Georges Road, force them to walk all the way to the game. She felt overwhelmed by the stench of them, the size of them, their vanity and arrogance. Billy was eyeing himself in her rear-view mirror. She glanced over at her son. He had his arms crossed and his neck and face were flushed. She had embarrassed him in front of his friends. Good. He should be ashamed. No one said a word all the way to the oval at Pascoe Vale.

•

All three boys played well that afternoon and their team won 3–1. At one point Jack took the ball all the way up the field, kicked it across to Billy, who then flicked it expertly with his left foot back across to Jack, who kicked it long and smooth into the corner of the goal. The boys wrapped themselves around her son, their screams filled the air. Jack emerged from the scrum with his hands held aloft, his eyes searching the stand for her. She looked down at her feet, pretending to studiously observe a small streak of mud on her heel. She would not catch his eye. She had wanted him to miss that goal, had wanted him to be disappointed, to feel nothing but shame.

She continued her silence on the drive home, dropping off Billy first and then Stavros. Both boys thanked her but neither apologised for teasing Amelia. Her goodbyes were short, gruff. She had not congratulated them on the game.

Jack combated her silence with his own, his eyes fixed on the world rushing past the window. As soon as she had driven up

their drive, Jack was out of the car, slamming the door behind
him.

She caught the word he muttered as he heaved himself out
of his seat.

Bitch. He had called her a bitch. Another word not supposed
to hurt.

You called her a mong. A mong? What kind of animal are you?

•

Rick was home and cooking a stir-fry. She kissed him curtly on
the cheek, annoyed that he had taken the ritual of preparing the
meal away from her. She'd been looking forward to the routine
of chopping the vegetables, grinding the spices and chillies.
Jack was already in the shower.

Rick turned to her and gestured with his chin towards the
bathroom. 'What's wrong with him?'

'I heard him call Amelia Carlosi a terrible name. I'm not
speaking to him till he apologises.'

Rick started to laugh and then, wary of the look in her eyes,
stopped mid-chuckle. He turned back to tossing the beef and
vegetables. 'You two are exactly the same.'

I am nothing like him. Nothing.

'He'll calm down, you'll calm down, then he'll apologise.'
Rick lifted the wok off the flame. 'He's a good kid, he wouldn't
have meant anything by it.'

'I can't believe you're defending him.'

'Can you check the rice cooker?'

Check it your fucking self. He looked over his shoulder at her, sighed, put down the wok and moved over to the cooker. He turned around with a wounded smile. 'It's ready.'

She knew it was childish, pathetic really, but she couldn't help it. She kicked off her shoes into a corner. 'I'm not hungry,' she growled as she walked out of the kitchen.

•

She tried reading a book but couldn't concentrate. Amelia's blurred babyish features, the old woman's eyes in the young girl's face, kept appearing in and out of the words, flooding the spaces between paragraphs and sentences. She turned on the television instead. Hunger scraped at her insides but she couldn't bring herself to leave the bedroom. In a while there was a knock. Jack walked in with a bowl of food in one hand, a fork in the other. He laid them sheepishly on the bedside table and then sat awkwardly at the foot of the bed. An episode of *Seinfeld* was playing, a rerun they had both seen two or three times before. 'I'm sorry,' she heard him mutter. She knew exactly what she should do. She should reach out to him, rub his shoulder. She should. But she couldn't. She picked up her bowl and started eating, her eyes fixed on the screen. He sat there till the ad break, then left the room.

•

Marianne woke just after four, the bedroom in darkness, Rick snoring softly beside her. She couldn't recall a dream, there was dryness in her throat. She carefully slid out of bed. Rick turned over, called out for her, and she whispered to him to go back to sleep. She pulled on a T-shirt and walked out into the kitchen. Let it go, she kept whispering to herself, let it go. But she couldn't. The dirty word kept repeating itself in her head. Mong. Mong. Mong. Wog. Maco. Nigger, slope, bitch and cunt and slut and fag and poofter and dyke. She did not trust their ease with words that hurt so much. She refused to believe that they had been exorcised of their venom and their cruelty. She squinted, tried to make out the hands of the clock. It was four-twenty. She switched on the light and put on the coffee.

•

She got to the gym just as the morning staff were switching on the computers. She spent forty minutes on the treadmill, running on an incline at a tremendous speed. She did fifteen minutes of weights, swam twenty-five laps. Exhausted, she drove home and showered. She woke Rick and called out to Jack to get up. She dressed for work, brewed another coffee and, while Rick was dressing and Jack was showering, she went into her son's room and looked around. The photos of Beyoncé and Gwen Stefani, of Harry Kewell and Ronaldo, tacked on the walls, the poster from *True Blood*, the shelf of soccer and swimming trophies, his books on a pile by his bed, his laptop on the desk, his clothes strewn across the floor. She quickly snatched up his soccer shirt, his socks, his track pants, lifted the lid off the cane basket, tossed the clothes inside. But not before she noticed the handkerchief rolled into a ball at the bottom of the basket. She jumped when Jack entered the room, a towel around his waist. The hairs around his belly button tracking down beneath the towel were wiry, thick and black. There was a sprout of thin curls around his nipples. When had they appeared?

Her son tightened the towel around himself. 'What are you doing?'

'I think it's about time you did your own laundry.'

'What are you talking about?'

'I was not put on this earth to be your slave.'

'No, but you are my mother.'

He thought he'd won, she could see a half-smile flicker across his face. She could smell the cologne he'd splashed on his face, under his arms, a cheap birthday present from Rick's mum and dad. All-chemical imitation of spice. You're so full of it, you think you're God's gift. It delighted her that the odour was so awful, that it revealed his ignorance, showed that he knew shit.

'I'm not washing your clothes anymore.'

'Oh, piss off.'

'And that includes your handkerchiefs.' Her eyes dared his. 'I don't want to touch them.'

That wiped the smile off his face; he dropped his gaze. For a moment she thought he might cry. And then he sneered and she flinched, as though he was about to strike her. 'Get the fuck out of my room!'

She knew her son, she knew his fears, his shames, his strength. She had received a warning. She knew she had hurt him. She had hurt him more than if she had raised a hand to him. She was in a daze as she walked down the corridor. My God, she thought, a coldness settling in her, do I hate him?

•

At work she could forget. She joked with Aliyah and Siobhan, listened to Darren boasting about the woman from Jet Start Travel he had picked up at the pub on Sunday night, smiled at Aliyah making faces at her behind his back. It felt so good to laugh. She went to visit agencies in Elwood, Sandringham and Elsternwick. She had lunch on her own by the beach at Elwood, and took off her shoes and stockings and paddled in the freezing shallow waters of the bay. When Kalinda and Jack were babies, they had taken them down to this beach, stood with them as they fearfully entered the water, squealing at the cold, their eyes growing enormous with astonishment at the roll and pull of the waves around their little feet. Rick had never been a swimmer and it was she who had first taught them to swim. She'd been awed by their trust in her when they had first battled with the power of the sea—she had held them, released them, held them and released them, till they understood they could master the waves, the rolling of the sea currents, till they were able to laugh and relax and enjoy the water.

She loved Elwood Beach. On achingly hot Melbourne summer days, the whole esplanade would be filled with families from across the world: Greeks and Italians with baskets of food; Muslim families, the women in their heavy dresses and their veils, hoisting their skirts above their knees like strange black birds at the water's edge; Tongans and Vietnamese, Turks and alabaster-white families like her own caking on layers and layers of sunscreen to protect themselves from the unforgiving glare of the Australian sun. Her kids had played in the water, in between the wading Muslim women and the beautiful young gay men cruising each other as they tanned on the beach. Holding them, releasing them, wanting them to be free and good in this world. Mong, mong, mong. Wog, Maco, poofter, nigger, faggot.

She met up with Joyce from Tourism Tasmania for an afternoon coffee in Richmond and they gossiped about the weekend trade show. Joyce worked with a man as conceited and deluded as Darren was. He too had boasted about picking up some bright young travel agent at the drinks session at the end of the trade show. I mean, do they honestly think we believe them? Joyce giggled incredulously over her coffee. Don't they ever look in the mirror? They talked about work, then the conversation moved on to their husbands and then their sons. Marianne said nothing to Joyce about the word that had made her so contemptuous of Jack or about how she had humiliated him that morning. She listened as Joyce rolled out her usual complaints about her own son, how lazy Ben was, how absent-minded and forgetful. But there was no harshness in the complaints, no bile. Her love tore the sting from her words.

Marianne returned to the office though there was no reason to. She didn't want to go home. She deliberately left at the hour the traffic would be at its worst, drove twice around the block to finish listening to an interview on ABC radio with the minister for transport justifying the terrible performance of the state's public transport system. Round and round the blocks of her suburb: past young men with their ties loosened, swinging their backpacks as they trudged up the hill from the railway station, groups of Indian students waiting at the bus stops, the drinkers and the smokers crowding the café tables on the footpath of High Street. The sun had set by the time she got home.

Rick had phoned earlier in the day to tell her that he was going to be late, and there was a message from Kalinda saying she was coming over for lunch on Sunday. Marianne slipped off her work blouse and skirt, stretched out on the bed. She thought she might sleep but the silence of the house was too intense, created its own din. She turned onto her side, rolled her hands across the fleshy padding of her belly, looked across to Rick's bedside table, at his jug of water, the clock radio, the book on the history of the Ottoman Empire that he had been reading for months. What if he didn't come home? What if there had been an accident? She gave herself over to the shameful release of imagining the funeral, the never-ever again of having to explain herself, the run of an empty house. She reached for the table next to his side of the bed, touched wood, mouthed Rick's name and lightly sketched a cross on the naked skin above her breasts.

•

She sat up suddenly. She must have dozed off but now she was sharply awake. Jack had left no message on her phone, nor was there any word from him on the answering machine. There was no training tonight, no soccer, no swimming. The silence pressed on her, seemed to be slowly suffocating her. A slow nauseating wave of panic uncurled in her stomach, pushing upwards, tugging and clutching at her heart. She scrambled off the bed, put on a jumper and her pyjama bottoms and walked into Jack's room. Its emptiness startled her. She wanted it to be full of him, his smell, his presence; she wanted to fill the house with him. She lifted the cane basket under her arm and walked, stumbled, to the laundry. She pulled the clothes out one by one and tossed them into the machine. His school shirts, his trousers, his T-shirts, his shorts, his singlets, his socks, his underwear, the crusted handkerchiefs. Come on, Jack, she pleaded, please come home. She was carrying the cane basket back to his room when the exterior light on the back verandah flicked on. She waited, holding her breath, listening for the sound of the sliding door.

Her son walked into the dark kitchen. 'Mum?'

She could breathe. She inhaled. She could breathe him in. He switched on the light and the brightness hurt, making her close her eyes. No, it wasn't the brightness. She opened her eyes. He had come up next to her, his shirt untucked, his schoolbag over his shoulder, looking down at her (how much taller could he grow, how much more handsome?), alarm in his eyes, concern.

He moved towards her. 'Mum,' he said softly, 'are you alright?'

She shut her eyes again, kept them closed. She could hear the washing machine chugging through the cycle, she could hear his shallow anxious breaths, smell the day and the sweat and the boy of him. She couldn't open her eyes. She didn't dare look at him. Looking at him, how it hurt.

Civil War

AFTER DRUGS THERE IS ONLY GOD. I don't want to forget that it was drugs that taught me how to feel. Before drugs, I was immersed in a stultifying mediocrity where the cold, clammy hands of the modern world reached deep into my heart and psyche. There was no joy in school, family or the tense bravado of adolescent friendships. When I was a very young child, it's possible I may have felt moments of great elation. I remember fragments of intense light: staring at the wings of a fly, tracing the path of a slug and watching the sun reflect off the slime. In those moments I may have experienced that phenomenal pleasure of intoxication which begins as a pinprick deep in the gut and then grows to flood the physical body. But these fragments are stray pieces from a jigsaw and I cannot imagine what whole they belong to. Was I a happy child? I have no idea. My first memory of being happy is as a teenager, smoking a joint with a cousin after school.

I am thinking about God, what it would look like, taste like, smell like. Outside the window of the truck the ochre ocean of the Nullarbor spreads out before me. The massive vehicle I'm travelling in is dwarfed by the grandeur of the prehistoric earth. Its deep guttural snorts, its thundering wheels are no competition for the explosive silence of the desert.

God is absent from this landscape. Or rather, God too is eclipsed by the rocks and the dirt, the scrub and sand. I began this journey across the desert to search for some intimation of spirit. Unable to perceive it in my usual urban environment, I am hoping to catch a glimpse of it out here in the naked wilderness. I cannot pretend to know what it may look like or what it may feel like but I am determined to experience it if it exists. If I fail to uncover divinity out here I will slink back to the city, tired and cynical, and I will pursue again the euphoria of chemical intoxication. It will be a pursuit of death, the day-to-day, minute-by-minute abandonment of self to dissembling and forgetfulness. Every step I have taken in my worship of the chemical I have been aware of the stripping away of myself. First the body, then the mind and finally the abandonment of soul. (I cannot offer an exact or universal definition of what I mean by the word 'soul' except to say that it is the part of me which resists being numbed, be it by drugs or money or inertia.) It is my soul, not my intellect or my pride, which has led me into the desert, searching for a divinity that does not eschew life.

The truck driver, overweight and ravaged by sun, offers me a Marlboro. I suck on it gratefully.

'Where are you heading, mate?' he asks me.

'Over east,' I reply. Aware that the question demands more of me, I make up a destination. I say Sydney, though I am not yet sure of where this journey will end. Probably when the one hundred dollars in my pocket is spent.

'Is this your first time across the Nullarbor?'

I nod.

'I must have done this journey a few hundred times.'

I glance over at him. His skin, shockingly pale at the edges of his singlet, is coarse and dark where it has been exposed to the sun. In particular his face, which is still handsome but lined with the history of too much alcohol and too many cigarettes, is the colour of the desert earth. We pass the skeletons of abandoned vehicles on the side of the road. In time the scrub grows over the decaying bodies and forms shrubs in the shapes of Volkswagens and EJ Holdens. Nothing can withstand the hold of the desert. The truck driver, over a working life of breathing in this landscape, is also becoming part of it.

'Don't you ever get bored by it?'

He laughs loudly and points out to the plain. 'You can't get bored by this. I get real fucking bored by this road, by the asphalt and the bloody white lines. But you can't get bored by this,' and again he points across the scrub. 'This land that looks like an atom bomb hit it is the most beautiful thing I've ever seen.'

He lights a cigarette and offers me another one. I again accept gratefully.

'Why Sydney?' he asks. 'I hate the place.'

'To get away from Perth,' I tell him.

•

Perth, all bland office buildings and vast suburban stretches, is a modern city at the edge of the world. It is an automated, clean city. The railway stations don't have toilets in them, as though it wasn't a city for human use, for the daily animal cycle of eating, drinking, shitting, pissing and sleeping. People there are proud of their trains. But the landscape makes a mockery of their attempts to control and master the environment. Even in the middle of the business district, in the dead centre of the city's heart, the ancient sand seeps through every crack. With every strong gust of wind the sand rises and swirls and dusts the concrete and plastic with a faint orange tinge.

The sand is not the only ancient element which taunts and threatens the city. This white city lives in fear of the shadows cast by its black inhabitants.

They drink too much.

They are lazy.

They hate work.

They steal cars.

They are dirty.

They are animals.

Like the sand, the shadows remind the city that it too will decay.

•

It was a thin young man with beautiful dark eyes who taught me that the sand is one of the weapons the landscape uses to fight back against the arrogance of the city. The unfathomable sky is another. Dwarfed by the sky and breathing in sand, Perth feels like a make-believe city. I kept meeting people who told me how in a few years it would be one of Australia's great cities. A few even suggested that one day it might be one of the *world's* great cities. But when I got to Perth I had no time for claims of a grand future. I was not impressed by the swiftness of the electric trains and the efficiency of the state-of-the-art communications systems. Instead I loved hearing him talk about the soil eating away at this baby metropolis. By the time I'd arrived in Perth I had stopped believing in cities.

We met when he asked me if I would buy him a drink because the barman would not serve him. I started an argument with the barman and got both of us thrown out. We then wandered into another pub and I bought him cigarettes and drinks till my money ran out. He was genuinely surprised that I only had twenty dollars on me. We then went back to his house and fucked. I fell asleep on his mattress while he stayed up listening to music on a cheap ghetto-blaster, getting stoned on a bong.

In the morning he made me a disgusting coffee and smoked my last cigarette. When I snapped at him he offered me a drag. I watched him go to the wardrobe, search behind a pile of T-shirts and lift out a plastic mineral-water bottle. He sat by me on the mattress and covered the opening of the bottle with his mouth. After taking a few short sharp breaths he offered the bottle to me. I smelt strong chemical fumes and backed away.

'I'm all out of dope,' he said, shrugging his shoulders. 'You can either sniff this or it's nothing.'

Glue sniffing is harsh on the lungs. I coughed into the bottle and he started a melodic chain of laughter. I lay back on the pillow and tried to chart the rush from the solvent. I experienced nothing except the faint throb of a hangover. But when I tried to lift my head up again, to take in another snort from the bottle, he had to help me. Again, the laughter. I sniffed some more and felt the beginning of a rhythmic tattoo beating at the back of my head.

His room was bare except for the old wardrobe and the single mattress. A pile of dirty clothes lay in a heap against a wall, and a torn tie-dyed sheet was nailed across the window. Two pictures were Blu-tacked to the wall, a poster of an American rapper and a photo of a very old Indigenous woman.

'Who's she?' I asked.

'My nan. She's up north.' He got up and pulled a T-shirt over his slender frame. 'I'll be back soon. You want to wait for me?'

I was touched that he trusted me with the care of his tiny kingdom. I nodded and sank back into the mattress. He left me with a kiss, and placed the plastic bottle with its clear liquid contents by my side.

•

The truck driver begins to tell me about his life. I'm not really listening, more intent on being lulled into a trance by the landscape we are gliding through. I'm making a mental note of the number of carcasses we pass. Twelve roos. Eight wombats. A score of large birds. The trucks must be going exceedingly fast, for the bodies are torn apart, smashed by the velocity of the impact.

'There's gonna have to be a war soon in this country.'

I look up at him and he's glancing over at me.

'People are getting ready,' he continues, 'arming themselves. And who can blame them? The fucking government is in cahoots with the niggers, giving them all this land, paying them money so they can get drunk and piss it all away.' He snorts angrily and accelerates. I offer neither resistance to nor approval of what he is saying. 'Do you know those bastards get money to send their kids to school? And what do the parents do with all that money? Drink it or spend it on drugs. The pricks up in Canberra keep giving them our money, buying them houses and cars.' He is animated now, anger and passion softening the hard surfaces of his skin, making him seem younger. 'It's our money that pays for all those gifts to the bloody blackfella while he sits on his lazy arse and sells his kids and wife for extra cash. They're cunning bastards. No natural intelligence at all, just animal cunning.' He spits out this last insult. 'They know how to use the system. But the bastards are making use of my taxes to live the good life.'

His voice drops. 'I hate them. Every last fucking one of them. I work my arse off to feed and clothe my family, drive these bloody trucks across the continent three, four times a month, and then have to pay most of it back to the government so it can waste it on these ugly bastards who won't work, can't make anything, have never been any good for anything.' The hate in his voice is hot. It blows hard into my face. 'I reckon we need to kill each and every one of them. The women and children too. I'm mad about kids, myself, I can't wait to be a grandfather. But when I see one of those black babies and know what it's going to grow up to be, I want to take it and smash it against a wall or on a rock. I want to see it die in front of me.'

We pass a sign announcing a roadhouse a few dozen kilometres up the road.

'I need to take a leak,' I tell him. Then I close my eyes and try to shut out the world.

•

The roadhouse has been worn dull by the weather. Even the huge orange and yellow advertising sign is faded and dirty. Two trucks are parked on the other side of the road and I get ready to jump out. The driver tells me to join him in the truckies' section of the restaurant when I finish up in the toilet.

'Grab yourself a coffee,' he tells me, 'and sit next to me. If they think you're with me you won't have to pay for coffee.'

The toilet smells of piss and mice. I stand up for a long time before I can get any urine to flow, and when it finally comes it is a slow and puny stream. I rest my head against the cool ceramic of the cistern. Outside a wind is murmuring. I look down at my soft dick and start pulling it. I think of fucking the truck driver in the mouth and come quickly, dripping three days' worth of semen onto the toilet lid. I wipe the lid, flush the toilet, and wash up at the sink.

Inside the restaurant, a bored young girl in a black T-shirt is smoking a cigarette at one of the laminex tables. She gets up when I come in but I shake my head and immediately she sits back down. Tina Turner is playing on the radio. A partition separates the dining room into two sections. The first section is empty. I walk past it and into the section marked TRUCK DRIVERS ONLY. Four men are sitting around a table. One of them is my driver but he fails to acknowledge my wave. I blush as I shuffle towards the coffee urn, conscious of my slender weak limbs, of the heaviness of my T-shirt, dark jeans and runners. The broad-shouldered men around the table are all in singlets and shorts, and they all wear their masculinity easily. So easily that their brutish physicality seems effortless, almost elegant. I sit down awkwardly next to them, pulling a chair from another table and placing it a little off to one side of the main group. No one bothers with introductions.

The coffee is scalding and tastes awful. I put it down and wait for it to cool. One of the men is talking about the blackfellas claiming back ancestral land. He too has skin marked by sun and wind, but the tight curls of his blond hair and the metallic grey of his eyes temper the erosion of his body. A delicate weave of blond hair creeps up his arms and his singlet fits tightly around a firm roll of flab and a well-muscled chest. He leans forward as he tells his story and I take in his aroma over the burnt fumes of the coffee.

'You know who's paying for them?'

'The government,' answers my truck driver.

The blond man looks exasperated. 'Fuck, mate, of course, but who else?'

The other men wait for the answer.

'The Jews, of course, and all the other fat businessmen they have in their back pockets. They're all in it.'

'They're in what?' My question booms around the circle and they all turn towards me. The blond man tilts his head at my truck driver, who gives him a slow nod.

'Arming the bloody boongs,' he replies.

It takes a moment for the words to sink in. 'Arm them for what?'

'The war.'

I fight back the urge to laugh in his face.

He shifts his chair closer to me. 'Some of us have already started storing away guns, started building a militia. The fucking politicians are in the pocket of the black man. We can't depend on them.' He leans back and smiles at one of his friends. 'At least there ain't too many of the pricks left, eh, Davo? With enough warning we should be able to kill the fuckers off in a few days.' He turns quickly back to me. 'As long as we're all in it together, right, mate?'

I release some sort of pathetic squeak, pretending to myself that it can pass for dissent.

He cocks a finger to my head. 'Yep, that's right. Bang bang. I can't wait.'

•

At first I thought he was asleep. Then I noticed the syringe still sticking out of his arm, and the vomit coating the front of his T-shirt. I sat down next to him and I am embarrassed to admit that the first thought in my head was whether I should run away, leave someone else to find the corpse. That thought didn't last for long though, just long enough that I'll never forget it. I sat next to him and gently pulled out the syringe and took off his T-shirt, wiping away the vomit from around his mouth and chin.

I cried, but I'm still not sure if it was for him or for myself. I had not yet got to know this man who was still so very much a boy. I had been up his arse, I had sucked on his cock, but I knew very little about him. I knew that there was someone I should call: the police? the ambulance? When my crying had been exhausted, I got up and made my way to the kitchen where I boiled some water over a small electric stove. Then I went back into his room and went through the pockets of his jeans. I found nothing and began to panic. No, it wasn't even panic, just a shortness of breath, a quickening in the beating of my heart, but I knew that if I did not find what I was searching for soon then the anxiety would escalate to full-blown hysteria. I searched through all his pockets, in his shoes, hoping to spy the dull sheen of aluminium foil. When I couldn't find a thing, after scouring every inch of carpet, going through every item of clothing in the wardrobe, I sank exhausted onto the mattress. My panic, laced with desperation, turned into anger at the dead man beside me. But I refused to look into his face, as if even with his eyes shut forever, my shame would still be reflected back at me in the clear black surface of his skin. After another bout of crying, I slowly dug my hand under his thighs and found a metallic object with my finger and edged it out from under him. I opened the foil and sniffed at the powder.

I used his fit to shoot up. If there had been more heroin I may have taken the whole lot and willed myself into a narcotic death. I knew so little about him that I did not know if by injecting drops of his blood into my body I would be infecting myself with disease. At that moment I did not care. When the euphoric wave of the rush swept over me I was able to lie back on the bed and grasp at sanity. I smoked a cigarette and went to call the ambulance.

•

They asked me his name. I could give them that. They asked me his next of kin. That I could not answer. The smack was good, very good, and I wondered if he had touched heaven when he died.

They asked me if I knew his friends, a relative, someone who could vouch for his past. I shook my head. The ambulance men gave me twin looks of disgust as they dismissed me and put him on a stretcher. Outside, the neighbours had gathered to bear witness to his death.

'What happened?' a young woman holding a baby asked me.

'He OD'd.'

She clicked her tongue in distaste and wandered back to her house.

I thought I heard one of the ambulance men say that 'picking up after these black bastards is a waste of time'. I might have been mistaken. But the thought was definitely in the air.

•

I fall in and out of sleep watching the endless straight road, half dreaming of Led Zeppelin. When I awake the road is still stretched out before me but now darkness has fallen on the plain. Melodic country and western is playing on the stereo. I stretch, yawn and reach for my pack of fags.

The driver chuckles and turns to me. 'Good sleep, mate?'

I nod and light my cigarette. The air blowing in my window is now cold and uncomfortable and I reach into my backpack to pull out a jumper. The driver, wired on speed and lack of sleep, is impervious to the cold in his singlet and shorts.

The shapes in the desert are now dark shadows suggesting bush phantoms, but I am aware that these are only fantasies drawn by my imagination and that what lies before me is the same flat earth that I have already spent an age watching. The only object which I can be sure of is the road. Lit by the high beams of the headlights, the straight narrow chasm across the continent appears to be leading us towards infinity.

A mounting hunger is gnawing at my stomach. I turn around in my seat and look in the back of the cabin for a bag of chips I bought at the last stop. When I turn back I see a small dark shape move out of the shadow landscape and into the path of the truck. The driver shouts out a warning, I hold my breath and there is a loud bang which seems to explode right inside my head. In that moment the desert evaporates and only the shock of the collision is real. Then the moment passes and the wind howls back through my open window; there is only the cocoon of the black desert earth and sky, and Bonnie Raitt.

The driver turns to me and gives a sheepish laugh. 'Sorry, mate, I think I might've just hit some pissed coon.'

•

I wasn't the only white person at his funeral, but I was the only one who looked like he didn't belong there. I spent the whole day in a stoned haze, a wall of opiates protecting me from the harsh outside world. I may even have pretended that my exclusion was of my own choosing. I chain-smoked cigarettes on the porch and watched a procession of men carry in slabs of beer from the pub down the road. The women sat in groups drinking beer or cask wine, telling each other stories or holding each other's hands. No one was rude to me but nor did anyone welcome me. I assumed I was an uncomfortable presence, a reminder of the way their son, nephew, brother, cousin or friend had lived and died.

I was struck by the very Australianness of their mourning. Here there was no Mediterranean lamentation or hushed silences. No women in black forming a shrill fresco of despair. Instead everyone was getting pissed.

An old woman sat in the backyard, surrounded by a circle of other women. She sat there not moving and it seemed she was looking past the timber fence, past the suburb and into another world altogether. I managed to find some courage and stepped off the porch. As I walked towards her the group surrounding her looked suspiciously at me.

I ignored everyone else and walked straight up to the old woman. 'I'm sorry.' She didn't seem to hear me. But I was determined to proceed with my confession. 'I wish I could tell you something about him.'

She did not avoid my eyes but I felt that she was looking through me, ignoring me with all her senses.

'He told me about your place up north. I think he missed it very much.' Was I making this up? He had never spoken those words to me, we had never been so intimate that he revealed emotional desire, but I do remember one conversation in which sex and drugs did not figure but instead he told me about swimming with crocodiles while an old woman chanted a song that kept the beasts tame.

'I'm sorry,' I repeated lamely.

This time she turned to me and started a low quiet laugh. Tears filled her eyes. She said something to me but I did not understand her. A young woman sitting beside her started to laugh with her and soon the circle of women were all laughing and crying together. I stood there, humiliated.

The young woman tugged at my shirt sleeve and whispered to me, 'It's okay. She just called him a silly young poof. Maybe he wanted to come back home but he was too busy running around after you white guys in the city.' She shook her head at my obvious dismay. 'Hey, boy, don't worry. We're not upset at you. His spirit be happier now.' She looked into my eyes and gave a soft whistle. 'You look after yourself, boy.' She offered me a beer.

I refused the beer and instead pointed to the old woman. 'Tell her I wanted to say I'm sorry.'

The young woman whispered my apologies to the grandmother, who turned her head to me one last time and nodded. With that I was dismissed. The circle fell back into conversation and drinking.

I turned away, walked back through the house and out onto an ugly suburban street. My anger finally conquered the chemicals in my blood and I spat a large glob of venom onto the dry pavement.

And what about you, you bastards? I was thinking. What about you lot? You were family. You should have done something. And now you insult him. You were too busy drinking and getting out of it in your own way. You fucking good-for-nothing lazy black bastards.

I'm ashamed even as I write these words. But it would be more shameful to pretend I did not think them.

•

The truck keeps thundering through the night and I am stunned and frozen. As the driver's words sink in I mutter a pathetic, 'Are you serious?'

He laughs at my unease. 'If I've put one of those black arse-holes out of their misery, I'm happy.'

'Stop the fucking truck.' I grab for my knapsack and clutch it to my chest. 'I said stop the fucking truck.'

He says nothing for a moment, he does not slow down. Then he points a finger out into the dark. 'Look out there. It is real easy, dead easy, to lose someone in this place. You could lose a body here and no one would ever find it.'

I am pierced by his menace and I am shivering with hate and fear. I cannot stand the stench of him, the poison of his amphetamine sweat.

The truck slows down with a loud scream. I open my door and prepare to lower myself down. As I am about to jump, he slams a fist into the back of my head. I sprawl onto the hard road and I let go of my pack. He revs the truck and I am scared he will run me over. Though my body and face are hurting I roll off the road and he roars away, the lights of the truck carving up the thick black night.

The first thing I do is fumble for my pack in the pitch dark. After a few minutes of fruitless searching I sit exhausted on the ground, massaging my aching jaw. I look up to the sky. The astonishing celestial dance pacifies me and I begin to grow accustomed to the dark. I watch the stars, let myself breathe, then attempt another search. I find the pack close to where I fell. My relief is quashed when I remember the reason I am here alone in the middle of an empty world. Shivering from the cold and the thought that somewhere close is a dead human body, I make my way back down the road. The asphalt shimmers in the night light and I have little difficulty keeping along it. But I have no concept of how much distance we had travelled between the accident and my undignified fall from the truck. As I walk along I keep looking up to the sky, asking the stars for warmth and light.

There are sounds out here. Alien sounds. Of course there is the wind but underneath its whistle there seems to be a soft pounding booming coming from the very depths of the earth I'm walking on. Time too has no concrete shape in this terrain and I have no idea how long I have been walking. The black night is now forming faces and bodies which change shape with every breath I take, as if they are breathing along with me.

Somewhere in the distance I hear a rustle and I am scared. The cold night air digs through the wool of my jumper, runs

up and down my legs and reaches far into the core of me. The
shapes are now forming lizards and snakes writhing in front
of me. The road itself seems to pulsate, as if keeping a beat to
the disconcerting pounding of the earth. I'm beginning to feel
foolish and almost regret leaving the truck. But then I remember
the driver's malevolent laugh and I keep walking.

I first smell the body. The scent is very much animal.
Nervously I kneel to touch it. It does not move. I run my hand
along a thick hide which still feels warm. Excited and relieved
I trace the curves of its body and feel thick liquid. The blood
has not dried yet. 'It was a roo,' I scream into the night, 'it was
only a fucking roo.'

I find my cigarettes squashed in my shirt pocket and put
a battered one in my mouth. I smell the blood on my hand.
Appalled, I spit out the cigarette and wipe my hand in the scrub.
I light myself another cigarette and lie back in the dirt.

The sky is raining down sharp slivers of light and I'm
disappearing into the fire. Around me the earth is still shifting:
animals and flora come in and out of view. It is almost as if an
acid trip is coming on, but though my body is sinking into my
mind, there is no bitter pharmaceutical aftertaste. I'm vanishing.
Reptiles and insects are weaving around my legs and the night
no longer seems cold. Up in the sky the familiar constellations
have gone, replaced by ancient primeval clusters. A collection
of stars forms the outline of a great lizard and in its centre one
large star pulsates to the rhythm of my heart.

My fear has gone. In the distance a mountain is forming, a large purple dream at the edge of a pitch-black horizon. The mountain becomes the giant face of a black girl and as I look at her, earth starts to crumble down her face and she begins to age. I cannot tell how long this takes. I think that perhaps I'm dying. But if this is death it does not hurt and it does not touch my body.

The old woman of the mountain surrounds me and I can make out the hollows of her eyes. Her mouth opens and she sucks in the world. The ancient stars do a final dance, a mad symphony of colour, then they too disappear into her mouth. I shut my eyes and when I look up again the stars of the Milky Way are back in their place. I look around me, I look back up at the sky, I grab a fistful of dirt but all that I can sense are the physical shapes, sights and smells of the desert. The vision has gone.

I remain in the scrub, exhausted. The cold begins to eat into me again and I curl into a tight ball. I'm aware that I have just experienced a kind of magic, that I have finally been touched by the caress of gods, but I'm also sure that the magic sung tonight, all the colours and light, the fire and music, were not meant for me. My presence here is not needed. I sink into sleep, grateful for that accident of fate.

I will wake the next morning bathed in sand. I will spend most of the day thirsting for water and running a dry tongue across burnt lips. A truck will pick me up late in the afternoon and the driver will tell me stories of women and drugs and how the boongs control the economy. I will neither agree with him nor argue with him, but he will find security in the colour of my skin and proceed to offload hatred as if talking to a close friend. At Port Augusta I will get off and wander the streets seeking food. It will take me another two days to get to Sydney and when I arrive there I will avoid my old friends and acquaintances. I will not touch chemicals and instead I will slip quietly into a peaceful life in the inner western suburbs. I will gather a new circle of friends and I will learn how to play cards, and how to bet on the horses. I will feel safe and I will not question this safety. But occasionally, when a hot wind blows in from the west, I will remember that they are gathering guns in the outback.

The T-shirt with a Fist on it

for Malcolm Hay

AMANDA RETURNED FROM THE AIR FRANCE counter shaking her head. She took her book out of her backpack and sat on the plastic seat next to Daniela. 'Sorry, honey, it's going to be another thirty minutes before they even open the counter.'

Daniela slumped further in her seat. All over the lounge, distressed and anxious travellers were volleying between the one television monitor listing departures and the other showing an episode of *CSI: New York* dubbed into Arabic.

Daniela's lip curled up sharply in frustration. 'Damn, I'm bored,' she announced loudly.

Amanda placed an arm around her lover's shoulders but Daniela shrugged it off. 'Not here,' she warned.

Amanda mouthed an obscenity and opened her book, a detective novel she had picked up in an English-language bookshop in Cairo. The story was lurid, the writing soporific and the mystery self-evident, but she and Daniela had exhausted their supply of books and it was the only one she hadn't read. It was an awful book but a rapid read, and in all likelihood with the plane delayed she would finish it before they boarded. She read two paragraphs and then slapped it shut. It was terrible. She saw that Daniela was rereading *The Edible Woman*.

Amanda peered over her spectacles at a young broad-faced Egyptian man in thick grey overalls leaning on his mop. He was staring intently at both of them. She frowned, but that only made his face break out in an inane grin. He stared even more intently. She was sure that his right hand was jiggling in the pocket of his overalls. For God's sake. She was so weary of that, but this time she didn't groan out loud, not wanting to alert Daniela to the man's attentions. Daniela would be both offended and confused, her feminist ire conflicting with her cultural sensitivities. Amanda's Arabic was limited to *Salaam Alaikum*, *Merhaba*, *Shkrun*, *Bekam* and *La*. When they reached Amman she was determined to find someone who would translate for her the phrase 'I am old enough to be your mother'. She was probably much older than his mother.

The tender-aged mothers and the boyish fathers: she had noticed them from their first day in Istanbul. It had been the same throughout southern Turkey and Egypt. She was sure it would be no different in Jordan. She had expected it of the women; all the usual prejudiced crap, of course, that the Arabs kept their women barefoot and pregnant, as if Arabic culture was some ludicrous mirror of backwoods Georgia or outback Western Australia. Nevertheless, all that bigotry had to be there in her head too, because she had not been thrown by the young women who looked like girls holding their babies or chasing after their children. The youth of the fathers had been more shocking. She had been taken aback to see baby-faced Turkish youths carrying their sons through the markets; and a working man in a small town south of Izmir arriving home for lunch, his son and two daughters rushing around him, his oil-streaked uniform almost slipping off his slight shoulders. He had seemed so young. Back home, boys his age were still locked in their rooms playing video games and delaying the responsibilities of adulthood for as long as possible.

Wherever she and Daniela had travelled, she could not help thinking about Eric. She wished she had fallen pregnant younger. Eric's adolescence was exhausting. She loved him, but he could be such a snappy, moody little shit. It seemed fantastical to imagine him coping with a job and three young children, but surely he was only a few years younger than the boy she'd seen on the outskirts of Izmir? She kept telling herself that being away from Eric for six weeks was not a bad thing; in fact, it was positive: good for him to be spending more time with his father and stepmother. But wherever they went she was constantly reminded of her son.

In the end she didn't manage to finish the book. The plane lifted, they flew across a stretch of golden desert and then seemed to follow the coastline of the dazzling sea. Every few minutes it seemed Daniela was exclaiming, *I think that's Beirut, no, maybe that's Tyre, oh I think that's Tel Aviv, is that Tel Aviv? Oh my God, is that Jerusalem? No, I think that's Haifa.* Then all of a sudden, first in Arabic, then in French and finally in English, a steward was announcing their descent into Amman.

The proximity of the world in the northern hemisphere was startling, astonishing. They had just passed over three countries, a desert, two seas and the juncture of three continents in less time than it took her to drive across Melbourne to visit her mother. Amanda gripped tight to her armrests, preparing herself for the stomach-churning moment when the plane's wheels unfolded and it prepared to touch the earth. She refused to cross herself, thought touching wood superstitious. Her ritual was to count to seven, over and over.

They had landed. They were safe.

They had booked three nights in Amman, and that was one night too long. After the ferocious scale of Istanbul and then Cairo, the compactness of the Jordanian capital was pleasing. But after a visit to the Roman ruins, a half-day getting lost in the labyrinth of the ugly, congested downtown area, and another half-day wandering the national museum, there was nothing much left for them to do. It was not impossible to buy alcohol but the cafés and restaurants they found themselves in did not serve any, and the nightlife—at least that which was visible to tourists—was not the kind to attract two middle-aged women.

It did not help that on the second day Daniela developed a stomach bug. Amanda thought she should stay in the room and rest, but Daniela would not hear of it. She was determined to see the ancient amphitheatre of Philadelphia.

'Don't worry about me, I'll be fine,' she said, but she wasn't bloody fine. She followed Amanda around with a pained expression, putting on a stoical smile whenever her lover glanced back at her. It nearly drove Amanda mad. That smile *oozed* martyrdom.

The stone steps of the amphitheatre were steep, and the desert sun was already broiling by mid-morning. Daniela looked sullen when Amanda announced that she wanted to climb to the top.

'It looks slippery.'

'It looks perfectly manageable.'

'Can't we head back to the hotel? I don't feel well.'

'Then you should have stayed in the room.' And with that, Amanda started to climb, not once looking back. When she reached the summit, sweat was running down her neck and back. There were only a few other tourists wandering the ruins below. She spotted Daniela sitting on a large slab of stone shaded by the eastern wall. Her frustration and annoyance vanished at once. A stomach bug was a miserable thing on a holiday; it was bad enough when it happened at home. She took one last look at the miniscule world below, the jumble of concrete and power lines, the narrow streets and laneways of the city.

She carefully walked back to earth and sat down beside Daniela. 'Let's go back to the hotel. I want to escape this bloody sun. I'll write postcards and you can rest.'

'Are you sure?' Daniela's tone was timid. Amanda nodded vigorously. Daniela's answering smile was grateful and relieved.

•

'Your driver is waiting for you, madam.'

The young clerk at the desk spoke English with a faint American accent. He was spindly thin, with a neatly trimmed black goatee, which he would stroke gently when faced with a request or a question. On their first afternoon there, the women had returned to the hotel to change for dinner and had found him praying on a small mat next to the desk. They had waited for him to finish before asking for the key and he had bowed to them and thanked them profusely. Amanda wondered what he thought of them, these two women sharing a room, no wedding rings on their fingers, no sign of husbands. But if he thought it at all unsavoury, his manner did not show it. He had been charming and polite from the beginning.

'*Shukrun*, Ahmed,' she said as she handed him back the key. 'It was a wonderful stay.'

Their driver, Hassan, was a large stout man in an olive-coloured ironed shirt and white linen trousers. He picked up both their bags as though they weighed nothing at all, and grinned cheerfully as he opened the rear door of the car for them.

'Would you mind if I sat in the front seat?' Amanda asked.

He frowned, just for an instant, and then immediately his warm smile returned. 'Of course not.'

He had been recommended to them by their friends Archie and Colm, who had visited Petra two years earlier. Amanda had rung the mobile number they had given her from Cairo, not sure if the number would still work or whether he would still be working as a driver, but it had been picked up on the second ring. A male voice had answered, 'Salaam' and then 'Hello'. Flustered, she had attempted a polite greeting in Arabic but then quickly asked, 'You speak English?' She thought she heard the hint of a laugh in the man's quick response, 'But of course.'

His English was indeed excellent. The car sped down a dusty highway and then slowed as it neared a small caravan by the side of the road. 'Would you like a coffee?'

Daniela was still concerned about her stomach, and refused, but Amanda willingly agreed. She went to unclasp her purse but Hassan motioned with a quick lift of his head as his tongue hit the roof of his mouth—that gesture and sound that throughout the Middle East seemed to indicate, *No, I'll take care of it, don't worry.*

Within a very short time they had reached the outskirts of Amman and were ascending the last hilltop. The narrow streets were cluttered with squat concrete cabins, lopsided electrical and telephone poles, precarious apartment blocks and the occasional villa. Then, the car accelerating, they dropped and were speeding along a straight motorway; on either side there was only the endless sea of burnished desert sand.

Hassan asked if they wished to listen to music and when Amanda nodded he put in a cassette of old disco. Daniela leaned forward in her seat and asked if he had any Arabic music. Pleased, he inserted another cassette. A male voice sang a deep, plaintive lament, its strangeness exhilarating and uncanny to Amanda's ear, but the music beneath was chintzy and slick, little different to the monotonous beat of the disco it had replaced. But Hassan was nodding his head to it as he drove; in the back seat Daniela too was gently swaying, her eyes hidden behind the thick lenses of her prescription sunglasses, gazing out to the unrelenting desert that surrounded them. At one point Hassan sang along to a chorus and Amanda wished she could turn off the stereo and just listen to the man sing. His was a rich baritone, and though not always faithful to the tune, it seemed to her an apt accompaniment to the sparse, brutal landscape. He was a handsome man, overweight, no doubt because of the sedentary life of driving—and also, Amanda supposed, from his wife's rich cooking—but he was naturally thick-bellied, with a broad chest, and the heft suited him. His face was as slate, strong lines, a jutting jaw and elongated cheekbones. She could well understand why Archie and Colm had been so taken with him. Silly old poofs, she chuckled to herself, they would have fallen in love with him.

Thinking of her old friends, a wave of homesickness overtook her. This desert earth seemed cleansed of scent. The first thing she would do when they returned to their home in Sydney would be to push open the small attic window of her study and take in the perfume of the jacaranda tree.

As they drove they passed groups of men crouched wearily in long lines at the side of the road. They were all startlingly thin. As the car approached, the first man in the line would jump to his feet, waving his arms in the air as if he were dancing. As the car zoomed past he would return to sitting back despondently on his haunches.

'They are Egyptians,' Hassan explained. 'Looking for work.'

Again, the incredible propinquity of the Old World: the road ahead could lead them into Saudi Arabia or Egypt; to turn back would take them through Syria and Lebanon. If they turned right there would be Israel, or left they would be in Iraq. There is a war on, she reminded herself; to the east of this desert, a civilisation has been destroyed by war.

Earlier, Hassan had talked about his family, his two sons and two daughters, his pride in them all. He spoke of his love for his mother and father, of his brother's studies for the civil service, of his sister married in Damascus. 'You must miss her,' Amanda had said, and Hassan replied with a laugh, 'Damascus is two hours from Amman in the car.'

No wonder the family was a bedrock in this part of the world, she thought. If Australia was defined by the tyranny of distance, here was determined by its subjugation to proximity.

At a crossroad leading to the Dead Sea in one direction and the River Jordan in the other, their passports were examined by a dark-skinned youth who was smoking a cigarette in his sentry box. He spent an age glancing at the three passports, looking at one face, then another, at one point asking Daniela to remove her glasses. Finally, as if reluctant to do so, his eyes still flicking from face to face, he returned their papers.

As soon as Hassan had driven away, he let out a stream of Arabic that hinted at the sour fury of an expletive or a curse.

'Are you okay, Hassan?'

'He is a Bedouin. He doesn't know how to read.'

Amanda wondered if that could be true. He had seemed such a child, no more than Eric's age. She tried to imagine her son in a military uniform. She couldn't bear such a thought.

When they arrived at the Dead Sea, Daniela annoyed her by asking her in the women's changing room whether it was appropriate for them to be swimming. She was concerned that Hassan would be offended by the sight of them in bathing suits. Amanda snorted, kept on disrobing and did not dignify the question with a response. Hassan had asked them whether they wanted to swim, he had taken them to the small resort beach, had organised chairs for them, and had suggested a restaurant in which to have lunch. This was the man's living, taking tourists and travellers from one end of his country to the other. He was not some fundamentalist warlord who recoiled at the thought of a woman's bare flesh. He was an urbane, intelligent man who spoke at least two languages. He was certainly not wealthy, not of that Old World class at all, but he was working hard to support his family. Amanda and Daniela were probably the same age as his mother. It was absurd to think that their ageing bodies would have any effect on the man at all.

Once in the water, Daniela's reservations disappeared. The two of them floated in a state of surrender on that strange soup of sea, the brutal glare of the sun off the barren hilltops and motionless water affirming that they had indeed returned to an antediluvian world. A French family were swimming near them, the mother repeatedly warning the children to be careful of their eyes. There were not many in the water, but they all seemed to be European. The only Arabs were the assorted drivers and waiters watching from the shore. Amanda spotted Hassan. She fought back a childish urge to wave at him. Instead, she lay on the warm, viscous water and looked up at the sky. Even that looked seared by the intensity of the sun, the blue washed out to a near white.

She had never been particularly religious, but being there she could not help but think of the stories from the Bible. It was no wonder this land gave birth to prophets. The earth here was forbidding, the very air ascetic. She thought of the verdant foliage of home, of the emerald harbour, the dense kingdom of forest that spread south from the edges of their city all the way down to Wollongong.

She swam over to Daniela and they brushed shoulders. 'I think God was lying when He said that this shithole was the Promised Land.'

Daniela, who had experienced a fierce longing to have faith as a devout Catholic schoolgirl, could not stop laughing.

On the beach they showered off the salt, then lay back on the lounge chairs. Amanda asked if Hassan wanted a seat, but he declined, indicating he was just as happy to sit behind them on the sand. She had just closed her eyes when two whiplash booms thundered through the valley. Hassan sprang to his feet, staring at the opposite shore. The Europeans glanced nervously at one another, as did Amanda and Daniela. The Arabs stood still, guarded, waiting, but there was the faintest of echoes and then the return to arid silence. Hassan sat back down.

'What was that?' Amanda asked.

'Gunfire from Palestine,' he answered.

She looked across the placid tepid water. You could swim over there, she thought. You could swim there in less time than it would take you to cross Sydney Harbour.

They invited Hassan to join them for lunch and when it came time for paying the bill, he tactfully excused himself from the table. Amanda left a generous tip, assuming the driver would receive a part of it for recommending the restaurant. On his return, Hassan glanced at the money on the small plate, and smiled at both of them. Amanda was pleased her instincts had been right.

It was late afternoon when they reached the hotel in Wadi Musa. Amanda had booked it over the internet and was delighted by her choice. It was an old stone villa, with an enormous terraced verandah that looked down to the hills of Petra. Their room, it was true, was tiny; also, the edges of the carpets in the lobby were frayed, the garden could have been better maintained, and the tiles on the verandah were cracked and stained. But it was inexpensive, the dining room was grand, and she felt as if she and Daniela were characters in an Agatha Christie novel.

They asked Hassan to join them for a drink and after a moment's hesitation he agreed.

The women quickly freshened up. Amanda changed her shirt and Daniela wore the bright yellow silk shawl she had bartered for in the bazaar in Cairo.

'How do I look?' she asked, turning to show Amanda.

'You look beautiful,' she said and kissed her on the lips. And she did. The colour perfectly suited her bronzed Mediterranean skin.

Hassan was standing on the balcony when they came down-stairs, looking down across the valleys. At one table an elderly couple were sitting quietly with their beers and at the other end of the patio sat another couple, very much younger, the girl with big streaks of silver in her black hair, the boy in bright red shorts. They were drinking cocktails and laughing loudly.

Hassan walked over when he saw them, and stayed standing while they took their seats. Amanda looked around, spotted a waiter standing at attention at the bar, and gestured for him to come over to their table. He arrived, bowed and smiled, with just a flicker of anxiety evident as his gaze fell upon Hassan.

'*Salaam*,' said Amanda. 'We'd like to order some drinks.'

'Yes, of course.' He looked again at Hassan.

'Two white wines and . . .' She looked over at Hassan, who

spoke in Arabic. The waiter nodded and returned with the glasses of wine and a bottle of German beer.

In the car, at the restaurant and on the beach, conversation between them all had flowed quite easily. But now it seemed they had little to say to one another. Hassan's English was perfectly adequate but his vocabulary was limited. They had exhausted the topics of family and of work, and it somehow did not seem possible to speak freely about any other topics.

Amanda realised that Hassan had not once alluded to her and Daniela's relationship, that he had avoided any remark that would lead to a declaration or an explanation. Though it would not have been fair to blame Hassan for that. She and Daniela had avoided the subject too, had not spoken of their home or their life together, of their having raised her son, of having lived, breathed and loved one another for over twenty years. She liked the man; indeed she felt that even though she had only known him half a day, she respected and admired him. His courtesy reminded her of her grandfather, and of Daniela's Italian father, men whose civility was underscored by a gentle kindness. But inviting him for a drink now felt like a charlatan act, as though they were striving to be some stereotype of the egalitarian Australian abroad. So here they were, awkward, uncomfortable, staring into their drinks.

'I think they're from home.' Daniela was looking over her shoulder to the young couple in the corner. Amanda strained to hear them, but couldn't catch any of their conversation. Hassan also looked over at the same time as the young man happened to glance their way. He turned so he was looking straight at them, and gave them a wide smile. He said something to the woman, who also turned to look at them.

'May we join you?' It wasn't really a question, as they were on their feet already. He was most certainly Australian. They had been in shade at their table and Amanda had not been able to discern much about their appearance. But now, as they approached, she found herself a little taken aback. They were both in their twenties and she thought them outlandishly dressed for the Middle East. The youth's scarlet shorts were almost skin tight; his legs were hairless, shaven. The woman was wearing a man's tuxedo jacket and underneath that a tight Bonds singlet that fully displayed her prominent breasts. Her nipples were clearly visible beneath the fabric. But what disturbed Amanda more than anything was the young man's T-shirt. It would have once been black but had faded to a wintry grey. On the front was a crude outline in red of a fist atop a circle with a cross beneath it, the symbol for women's liberation. Amanda herself had worn such a T-shirt in her twenties, when she was first discovering feminism at university, and first fell in love with a woman.

As the boy sat down across from her and they made their introductions, Amanda found she could hardly speak. Noting the direction of her gaze, he laughed loudly and slapped his chest. What a horsey sound, she thought spitefully, what a silly show pony.

'This was my mother's,' he explained, laughing, 'when she

was slumming it at uni.' He then turned around and motioned ostentatiously to the waiter for another round of drinks.

Amanda looked over at Hassan but his eyes were firmly fixed on the girl's bosom. He might as well have his tongue hanging out, she thought. It is a wonder he's not salivating all over the table.

The boy's name was Frankie and his friend was Keira. They were friends from university where they had studied law, and were travelling together for six months before going back to Melbourne to begin their Articles. On a whim they had caught a plane from Nicosia to Amman, and had come to Petra because Frankie had always wanted to see the ancient city.

'From when I first saw *Raiders of the Lost Ark*,' he explained. 'I've wanted to see it since I was a little boy.' He sighed contentedly. 'And it was worth it,' he continued, then giggled. 'But alas, I didn't meet my Harrison Ford.'

There was an uneasy silence, as both Amanda and Daniela quickly glanced across to Hassan. But he gave no indication that he had heard or understood anything of what Frankie had said. Too busy staring at the girl's tits, fumed Amanda.

'We're going to Petra tomorrow,' Daniela said. 'I've always wanted to see it too.'

'Another Harrison Ford fan?'

'Oh, shut up, Frankie.' Keira tapped Hassan's packet of Marlboros. 'May I?' He nodded. She lit up.

Daniela was explaining how she had become fascinated with

Petra when she studied archaeology in first year. 'That was a long time ago,' she added.

Keira smiled. 'How long have you two been together?'

Amanda was mortified. She didn't know why she felt the flush of humiliation. She was proud of her love for Daniela; her whole life had been lived in the amity of lesbians. She felt wretched for asking the driver to join them. If he hadn't been there, she and Daniela would have enjoyed the company of the two young people, been grateful for the opportunity to chat and gossip, to talk about home, to openly be a couple after weeks of walking around the Middle East as though they were Victorian spinsters. She envied Frankie his unashamed campness, Keira her fearless sensuality. Nevertheless, nevertheless, could they not shut up?

'Twenty-two years,' answered Daniela, winking at her lover.

'Wow!' Frankie clapped his hands. 'Lesbians are so committed. We fags are hopeless at it.'

Keira snorted. 'Speak for yourself. Dad's been with Michael for fifteen years. Maybe *you're* the one hopeless at commitment.'

'It's been twenty-two terrific years,' said Daniela. 'But we've never had the opportunity to come to this part of the world before and I'm so glad we did.' She smiled at Hassan. 'Jordanians are very generous.'

Thank you, sweetheart, thank you, thought Amanda. For changing the conversation, for saying exactly the right thing.

'We should get another drink?'

Amanda shook her head. 'We're off to the dining room for dinner.'

'Oh, but why?' said Frankie. 'We've just met—how about one champagne to celebrate twenty-two years?'

She didn't want anything more to drink, she didn't want to have to look at his stupid T-shirt that he had no right to wear, she didn't want to spend another moment in their idiotic company. 'No, we really must be off.'

'How about you, Hassan? You'll stay for a drink, won't you?'

Hassan nodded, not at Frankie but at Keira.

Amanda was suddenly furious, the force of it hitting her like a wave. She turned to Hassan and said sharply, 'I hope you understand that any further drinks you have you must pay for yourself.'

The silence was dreadful. Frankie and Keira were looking down at their drinks; Daniela, who had been getting up to follow Amanda, froze in mid-motion. And Hassan. Hassan looked as if he had been struck. As he probably had, thought Amanda, the red flame rising from her chest, burning her throat, her neck, her cheeks. There was such dismay in the man's deep-set eyes, but it only lasted an instant. He composed himself, a genial smile returned to his lips and he lifted his head, tapping the roof of his mouth with his tongue.

'Of course, I would not have done otherwise.'

Daniela took the man's hand. Surprised, he looked down at where she was touching him, as if he could not quite believe it was true.

The burden of Amanda's mortification was unbearable, as if she could not breathe from the immensity of it. Insensibly, almost tripping over herself, she fled the verandah. She could hear Daniela's heels hurriedly clicking along the tiles, following her; she heard the scrape of Hassan's chair as he must have sat back down. The last thing she heard was Frankie saying, 'It's alright, Hassan, don't worry, we've got plenty of money.'

It wasn't until she had crossed the lobby, past the long front desk, and was about to enter the dining room that Daniela finally caught up with her.

'How dare you?' she exploded.

Amanda couldn't answer. Daniela was waiting impatiently for some kind of response and she did not have one to give her. She didn't know where she could begin, how to explain the shame she had experienced at the table, the jealousy she felt towards Keira. But worst of all was her shaming of that wonderful, gentle man who had won her heart that day; by his gravity and subsequent equilibrium, by his unforced instinctual civility. These were the traits she so wished she could find in Eric; it was that kind of man she wanted her son to be.

That wasn't all, though. How could she explain that Hassan's gentleness had exhausted her? As had Daniela's constant anxiety to respect cultural niceties, to not offend anyone, to always do the right thing. She did not only envy Keira her youth, but also her and Frankie's exuberant arrogance, their bolshiness, the fuck-you audacity she herself had once had as a militant student feminist. Amanda couldn't bear her lover's stony opprobrium a minute longer. She tried to find the words.

Daniela surprised her by listening without interruption except for gentle urgings to continue when Amanda stumbled over words as she tried to shape sense and order out of the panic of thoughts in her head.

When she had finally exhausted herself through talking, and started to cry, Daniela, oblivious to the waiters, to the other guests, had taken her hand and held it, squeezing it tight.

Amanda took a sip of her wine, wiped her eyes and blew her nose. 'I'm fine,' she whispered. 'I'm fine.'

'My love,' said Daniela, 'you're absolutely right. We are fools to think we can just walk into a different country and a different culture with some facts and figures taken from the opinion pieces in the Sunday papers and think we can fit in and remain unobserved.' She let go of Amanda's hand and signalled the waiter for another two glasses of wine. 'At the very least, to even begin to be able to do that, we would need to know the language. *Shukrun* and *Salaam Alaikum* will only get you so far.'

She cupped her hands around her mouth and blew a secret kiss to Amanda. It made them both laugh. It had started years ago, when they were just getting together, their secret, something they would do at weddings and christenings, at family barbecues and family birthdays.

'That's better,' said Daniela. 'Now go and fix your make-up, it's all smeared.'

In the toilets the attendant was a scarfed young woman. She watched as Amanda carefully reapplied her pink lipstick, as she carefully wiped the inky smudges from under her eyes. The girl's curiosity was unabashedly forthright. The spark in her honey-coloured eyes reminded Amanda of Hassan's implacable intensity.

She slipped her lipstick back in her bag and smiled at the girl. She wanted to say, Yes, my clothes look like a man should wear them but I also like lipstick. Yes, the reason I do not have a wedding ring is because I love women and they love me. Yes, I am fifty-five, the age of grandmothers, but my son is still only sixteen. And the girl might reply, I know all of that or have guessed most of that and still all I want to know is where you got that lipstick. But because she knew no Arabic, Amanda said nothing and instead just handed the young woman a large tip.

She asked for Hassan at the front desk, having to check the surname on the card given to her by Archie and Colm. She was directed to a room on the top floor.

As soon as she stepped out of the lift, she almost keeled over from the force of the heat. There was no air-conditioning on the sixth floor, not even overhead fans. The air was heavy, and she had to stay herself a moment. She took a deep breath; already a sheen of perspiration was glistening on her arms, her face and neck. Apart from the syrupy heat, the smell of cigarettes and chemical cleaning agents was overpowering. The corridor looked as though it had not been painted for generations; the walls were peeling, with enormous patches of damp and mildew.

The thin acrylic carpet was threadbare. A maid's trolley, laden with cleaning equipment and detergents, blocked her way and she had to hug the wall to pass it. She could hear the tinkle of music from somewhere; also shouts and male laughter. She found Hassan's room and knocked.

There was the sound of scraping on floorboards, a questioning shout in Arabic, and the door opened a fraction. Hassan appeared, dressed in a singlet, his belt buckle loosened. On seeing her, his face registered disbelief and for a moment she thought he was going to close the door on her. He raised his arm, as if blocking her view, and she caught a whiff of his robust odour. He was drenched in sweat. She could see little behind him and did not want to look, but could tell that the room was tiny, and it had to be insufferably hot. So these were the shitboxes where the drivers slept, where the menials who catered to the wealthy tourists like herself in the air-conditioned lower floors came for rest. This thought strengthened her resolve.

'Dear Hassan, I have come to apologise. What I said before was unacceptable and shameful. I do hope you can forgive me.'

There was a giggle from inside his room, girlish and quickly muffled. Hassan was looking straight at her and his eyes were moist, so dark that the pupils seemed to disappear within the blackness. She was shocked at the weariness they expressed, the fatigue and sorrow.

He's ashamed, she realised. He has some woman in this room and he is ashamed. She would not judge him, she refused to judge him.

He lowered his arm and offered her his hand. She took it, he clutched hers tight—it was as if a life was passed on to her in that grip—and then he released her. 'There is nothing to forgive. Thank you.'

He was a bear of a man, he was a husband and father, but to her he looked so young, she could still see the boy in him.

'We'll see you in the morning.'

He returned her smile and closed the door.

Only then, only then did she allow herself a tremor of disbelief. For when he had dropped his arm to shake her hand, she had seen behind him. A pair of bright red shorts lay crumpled on the floor.

She turned back to the corridor and there was a short, thin-necked young man, with two long scars on his left cheek, smoking a cigarette by the cleaning trolley. She had to slide past him and as she did she felt his body shift and press hard against hers.

While she waited for the lift, she berated herself for not having shoved the dirty little pervert back against the wall. She was twice his size and over twice his age. He hadn't scared her at all.

She glanced back and he was staring at her, his hand was sliding up and down the furrows of his jeans pocket.

She burst out laughing. 'You stupid, stupid boy,' she called down the corridor, 'I am probably older than your mother.'

His quizzical expression, the lift of his head, the click from his tongue hitting the roof of his mouth, all said that he hadn't a clue what she had said. She was still laughing when the lift doors opened.

In their room Daniela was reading her Margaret Atwood, naked on the bed, the top sheet crumpled loosely around her feet as the overhead fan whirred noisily. Amanda stood in the doorway, taking in Daniela's pudgy body: the full roundness of her breasts, the almost lavender smudge of her areola, her stubby nipples, the rolls of fat around her belly, the wide inviting girth of her hips that always reminded Amanda of the sensuous contours of the guitar.

Daniela lowered her reading glasses. 'Did it go well?'

'Yes.' Amanda sat on the bed, and gently kissed her lover's nipples, her belly, buried her face in the salt and pepper thistles of Daniela's pubic hair. She inhaled her lover's odour: the sourness of her sweat, the bitter hint of urine, and the delicious pungency of her cunt. Amanda breathed her in, and the world of men disappeared.

'Come to bed,' whispered Daniela, throwing aside her book. 'Just come to bed.'

The next morning Hassan drove them to Petra. That evening, writing a postcard to Eric, she tried to distil her wonderment at the vastness of the site; the terror of a city of such scale and endeavour built on the most inhuman and unforgiving of ground; the melancholy of the ancient city succumbing to the relentlessness of time. She had watched a Bedouin shepherd walk his flock over the decaying marble floor of Aphrodite's temple; she had brought rainwater to her lips from a Roman aqueduct, still functioning in the desert millennia after the empire that had built it had gone. She tried, but words could not take the measure of such splendour.

In the end, across the back of the postcard, she wrote: *My Darling Son, it is indescribable.*

Porn 1

THE HARSH FLUORESCENT LIGHTS WERE A shock. She had been expecting the store to be dark and dingy, everything in disguising shadow. However, the young man nonchalantly flicking through the newspaper at the counter was an unremarkable, common-place youth, with a mop of ginger hair and a rash of acne beneath his bottom lip. He was not that different to the bored young men who served her at the supermarket. Except that he was smoking a cigarette in brazen defiance of the no-smoking sign at the entrance; that was the first sign that she was indeed entering an illicit world.

She coughed and the young man looked up. His lazy pose snapped to deference. 'Can I help you?'

She was suddenly flooded with shame. She shook her head, turned and quickly walked further into the store.

She looked everywhere and saw nothing, she had to will colour and light and shadow into form. In one of the aisles, a middle-aged gentleman in a suit was flicking through magazines. He looked up at her, stiffened, and quickly grabbed his briefcase off the floor. He walked to the back wall, opened a blue door— sunlight, true light—and rushed out into the alley.

She breathed in deeply, a moment of relief. She had almost laughed, so boyish had he been in his embarrassment.

She scanned the shelves. Everywhere there seemed to be images of women proudly pulling at their nipples or cupping their breasts and smiling lasciviously at the camera. Most of them were young, of course, girls really, but she was surprised to see quite a few older women on the covers of the videos and DVDs.

There seemed to be no faces of men. Instead there was a dizzying display of penises: short, long, thick, white, black, brown, erect, outlandishly enormous, even some puny and limp. At the age of fifty-nine, for the first time in her life, she finally understood that every man she knew and every man she had known, in fact every man in the world, had a unique and identifiable penis. And every one of them was hideous. She was overtaken by rage. Every one of them was ugly. She turned into the next aisle.

The homosexual videos and DVDs filled one narrow panel. She tensed and walked towards the shelf. These penises had naked bodies attached to them. Those bodies had faces. Without thinking, she blindly stretched out her hand and grabbed a video from the shelf. She turned it around, silently read the names on it, and then placed it back. She took the next one, then the next, then the one next to that. The actors' names were all silly, all-American: Randy and Calvin, Lance and Kirk. If not all-American they were exotically European: Sven, Hans, Lazlo or Misha. As she methodically scanned the videos and DVD slicks, she refused to engage with the images. Of course she was aware of the naked bodies twisted around each other, the stark close-ups of genitalia, the carnal directness of the images, but she did not think about them, did not allow herself any emotion. She felt neither curiosity nor disgust. She was seeking a name.

Men would approach the shelf and then, spotting her, swiftly turn around and walk away. A portly bearded man reeking of tobacco and aftershave looked at her with undisguised spite, but he too did not dare come close. Let them wait. Let them bloody well wait before indulging themselves in filth.

When she found what she'd been looking for, she froze. The image on the cover was of a man in uniform, a grey sheriff's attire. A preposterous erection strained the actor's tight pants. His name was there, in red type: Ricky Pallo. She held the video cover in her hand, noting the baton in the actor's hand, the deep black void of the sunglasses that hid his eyes. She willed herself to turn over the cover, to look. But she couldn't; her hands were suddenly clammy, her breath restricted. She thought impulsively of praying, but it seemed blasphemous to ask for God in this place.

She took a breath. Foolish woman, she sharply reprimanded herself. She turned over the video cover.

She caught her breath. He looked so very handsome. She was unaware of it but her tongue fiercely ground against her teeth, her lips were suddenly parched. She carried the cover back towards the entrance.

The young man at the counter was clearly bemused by her choice but he said nothing. He searched under the counter and found the cassette. 'Twenty dollars.'

'What?' She was staring at a poster for a magazine called *Kink*. A woman's ecstatic face was drenched in a thick paste of semen.

'That will be twenty dollars.' The man's tone was patient.

'Of course.' She fumbled with the catch of her purse, took out a fifty-dollar note and gave it to the youth. She knew her face was flaming red; she did not look at him again. He handed her the change and put the video in a brown paper bag. She allowed herself a smile at this small conceit. Like a greengrocer, she thought to herself; only greengrocers and, evidently, pornographers still use brown paper bags. She accepted the package and stuffed it deep into her bag, covering it with her scarf.

'Goodbye.'

She did not answer him. Making her exit she nearly collided with a man. He too was young, with slightly chubby cheeks on which the unshaven down could not quite muster to form a full beard. He stepped back, threw himself against the wall, and turned his face away from her. He cringed, his cheeks and neck flushing to bright pink.

She walked quickly into the light, into the street, making rapid strides away from the store, looking at no one, experiencing a humiliation that was visceral. She was terrified that one of the shadows rushing past her in the city street would not belong to a stranger. She only stopped when she reached the corner of Russell and Lonsdale.

That boy she had so nearly collided with—he was still a boy to her—who had been mortified by her presence, he had a sweet, charming face. She had wanted to hug him, stroke his hair, his cheek. She had so wanted to comfort him.

•

'A packet of Supa Mild cigarettes, thank you.'

'What?' The girl at the counter was surly. Customers waited impatiently behind her.

'Supa Mild.'

The girl stared back blankly. 'Never heard of them.'

'They finishing to make them long time ago. I smoke them too once. They very good cigarette.'

She turned. The man behind her was beaming; he was her own age and his trim beard was speckled with silver.

'Oh, I'm sorry.' She was apologising to everyone. She scanned the tray of cigarettes and recognised a brand from her past. 'Peter Stuyvesant, please.'

•

She had not had a cigarette in over fifteen years when she had asked for one in Los Angeles, in the tiny grim office at the back of the police station. She and her husband had flown across the Pacific, mostly in silence, to collect their son's body and take it home.

There had been two policemen. The older, white one had seemed a little bored, as if detailing the particulars of an overdose to distressed kin was a familiar, tedious routine for him. As it probably was. But the young black officer had been courteous and gentle. His broad face had worn a sad smile throughout. She had found herself talking to him, asking him questions, though it was often the other one who answered her, reading directly from his notes. They had found a combination of heroin and cocaine in their son's body, he explained, as well as traces of alcohol, marijuana, Viagra and Zoloft. Had their son been suffering from depression? There had been an embarrassed silence. She was ashamed to admit that it had been years since they had seen Nick, that they had not spoken since that phone call in the middle of the night, when he had been slurring, making outrageous accusations, making no sense at all. Her husband had grabbed the phone from her and slammed it down so hard that the casing had cracked.

Clearing his throat, the white officer had then informed them that their son had been HIV positive.

Her husband had made a whimper, like a frightened animal, and then, rising, his voice cracking, he had excused himself. She had put out a hand to him but he had refused to take it. She was alone with the strangers.

'I don't understand. AIDS?'

The white officer had nodded.

'Oh.' She felt nothing. He was dead, what did it matter?

The older man swallowed. 'Mrs Pannini, did you know your son was homosexual?'

'Yes.' She knew, she had guessed. Of course, she had always known. Always.

'Did you know the work he was doing in LA?'

She stared confusedly at the man. 'Acting? That's what he wrote to us.'

'Mrs Pannini, I'm sorry to inform you of this, but your son worked as an actor in pornographic movies.'

There was silence. The black officer had lowered his eyes.

'Did he use his real name?'

'No.'

She then addressed the black officer. 'Can I please ask for a cigarette?'

He rose immediately to obey her request but the white officer frowned and looked directly above her shoulder at the no-smoking sign next to a portrait of the grinning President Bush.

She turned again to the younger man. 'Please, I must have a cigarette,' she pleaded.

'Of course, ma'am.' She was astonished at his old-fashioned courtesy.

The first inhalation of smoke hurt, she had a fit of coughing, and then she felt a dizzying euphoria. 'Thank you.'

'I'm a smoker too, ma'am.'

For the first time she glanced down at the tag on his shirt. James B. Franklin. 'Thank you again, Mr Franklin.'

'You're welcome, ma'am.'

'Can you please not tell my husband about my son? The pornography? Please, let me tell him—I need to tell him in my own time.'

She saw the two men glance at one another. They seemed unsure of how to proceed. They were embarrassed. Of course they were. It was sordid and awful and disgusting. The foolish, foolish boy; so easily led, never thinking of consequences.

'We thought it best to inform you directly.' Officer Franklin cleared his throat. 'Sometimes people can be cruel.'

She thought immediately of her sister-in-law. Oh, how Sonja would gloat over it all, her sympathy poisonous and insincere. 'Thank you, I do understand you had to tell me.'

When her husband returned, his eyes were red and there was a trickle of snot on his top lip. She moved to wipe it, and he broke out into wounded, terrified sobbing. They had collapsed into grief, watched quietly by the two Americans. Her arms encircled him, she held him tight. He must never know. It would destroy him. She made up her mind: if he ever found out she would deny it. Of course not. *Of course not.* How can you say such things? Nick would never do such things.

•

On entering the house, she was conscious of a strange vibration all around her: the walls, the floor, the very air seemed to be pulsating. She walked through every room, her hand still clutching her bag, as it had done throughout the train journey. She was alone. She opened her bag and laid the video on the coffee table.

She looked around and closed the lounge curtains, blocking out the daylight. She deadlocked the front door and took the phone off the hook. The house still seemed to be breathing.

She slotted the video into the machine and fingered the remote control: there was the hum of the television coming to life, the sunburst of snow, and then colour flooded the screen. The volume blasted music and noise, a woman was exercising on a bike. She grabbed the second remote and pressed a button. The screen went black and there was silence. She waited.

The music began and she was struck by the harshness of its sound. She pressed the remote, and the five green bars became four, then three, and then finally one. She had reduced the volume to a whisper. She fixed her eyes on the screen and took her glasses out of their case. Names flashed across the screen, and then a series of close-ups. Her son's face appeared, his hair shorn to the scalp in a military cut. He was smiling, and winked at the camera. The pseudonym he had chosen for himself, Pallo, had been the nickname of Con Pollites, his best friend in primary school. They had lived in Brunswick then, at 33 Edwards Street, and the Polliteses had lived at number sixteen. The children were always running in and out of each other's houses.

She almost laughed at the contrived nature of the first few minutes of the film. A tall, blond young man entered an office where another man was sitting behind a desk, largely empty except for a few pens and a notebook. There were two long close-ups of the actors, one licking his lips, the other raising an eyebrow. The man at the desk was playing the boss of the younger man, who was apologising for being late for work.

Is this necessary? She was furious. Just fornicate—that's what it's about, isn't it? That's why men pay money for this filth. Just fuck!

It was not her first experience of viewing pornography. Early in their marriage her husband had brought home a few reels of Super 8 film and he had made her watch them with him, taking out the family projector and showing the images on one of the walls of their lounge room. She had been unnerved by them, most repulsed by the hairiness of the women's privates. That night in bed she had been silent and unmoving as he mounted her. He had never shown her such films again.

She told herself to look at the screen. The man playing the boss had removed his trousers and his shirt was unbuttoned. Both actors had smooth, waxed skin. It reminded her of the burnish on a not-yet-ripened Fuji apple. She did not fast forward though her fingers were curled tightly around the remote control. She was glad that this first scene featured two strangers, other women's sons. As the men kissed, she experienced a sensation akin to nausea. Disgust. But it rapidly dissipated as she watched the gyrations of their mouths. The two men were handsome, strong, and the kiss was passionate. She reached for her cigarettes, her eyes firmly on the screen. The boys were now undressed.

Oh, sweet Lord, oh, Mother of God. This was a different world. She felt a sweeping melancholy as she watched the two men kiss and fondle each other. She had been with only two men in her whole life, and the first had been a quick humiliating moment in her sister's bedroom during a party. She and the man had remained clothed the whole time and he had pressed her against the bedroom door and rubbed himself on her for a few minutes. They had not kissed once. When he had finished she discovered that he had stained her skirt, and she had spent the next hour in the bathroom, washing and squeezing dry the garment, crying the whole time. And after that, it had all been with her husband.

Who are you? she quizzed the screen. They were American, obviously, they looked fit, healthy, they looked as if they had enough to eat. The images had relaxed into an inert succession of poses and she was distracted, bored even. Did *their* parents know? No, of course not. She could not conceive of a parent knowing. She was alone in this.

She turned away in distaste. The blond man was on his knees, mechanically devouring the other man's penis. She noticed a fine spider's web beginning from the light globe in the lounge room and reaching the cornice just above a portrait of her mother and father. Her parents' faces looked down at her, stern and distant. Her father, standing, was wearing a suit and a collarless shirt. Her mother, sitting so her head was level with her husband's chest, was wearing the pale yellow summer dress that he had given her after she had accepted his proposal.

Aware suddenly of the muted grunts and moans coming from the television, she turned away from her parents' forbidding gaze and forced herself to watch the screen again.

They were having intercourse now, sodomy. She scrutinised the blond's face every time there was a close-up. Surely he could not be enjoying this. He was grimacing but his words seemed to be encouraging the other man. She had to stand up. She went into the kitchen and wet her lips. Didn't the silly *finocchio* know how much he was debasing himself? They were not actors. Whores. That's what they were. Whores.

When she returned to her armchair, the same monotonous exertions were taking place. Her disgust had disappeared. She had expected that she would find the images foul, not necessarily because they were pornographic, but because they depicted sex between men. Yes, the actors had seemed effeminate and ridiculous when they were kissing or performing oral sex on one another. But now that the older man was sodomising the younger one, frowning in concentration as he pounded away at the prostrate body spread over the desk, it seemed all too familiar. It was shockingly normal.

She closed her eyes. She would not look, she would keep her eyes shut. She heard the men on the screen barking out their orgasms. When she finally opened her eyes again the boss was zipping up his pants and the blond youth was sheepishly putting on his shirt. Now don't ever be late again, the boss counselled. She laughed out loud.

Her body tensed as the next scene began. A large stocky man, older than the previous actors, was entering a toilet. He unzipped in the cubicle and lowered his pants. His penis was thick, so unlike her husband's lean organ. The actor took off his shirt, revealing a flabby belly covered in fine brown hairs. She thought him ugly, obscene; he reminded her of all the sweating rude men who called her *love* at work, the men who scoffed down their meat pies.

He was the man who was going to abuse her son. She knew it even before Nick appeared. There was a hole in the wall of the cubicle. Her jaw clenched when Nick came in, stood at the urinal.

Her gaze was still locked onto the screen but the images had fallen away. She had removed herself into a memory, nothing concrete, not a vision or an image; the tender sensation of Nick falling asleep at her breast. She fell back into the room. Outside, birds were trilling and she heard schoolchildren laughing on their way home.

'Fuck me.'

It wasn't Nick's voice. It was an American voice. For one small moment, happiness descended—this was not her son.

But her relief quickly vanished. It was Nick, his wide grin, his lazy left eye that made his face still seem goofily adolescent. She saw the Scorpio tattoo on his neck, the tattoo that had caused her husband to hit out at him that first time he had run away.

It was not Nick's body. She knew him as a skinny young man, still vividly remembered his embarrassment as the first sprinklings of black hair appeared on his belly and his chest, how he would try to hide his body at the beach by crossing his arms. 'Don't be embarrassed, Nicky,' she would laugh at him, scratching at his belly. 'You're becoming a man. Be proud.' He would snap at her, push her away from him.

This was not Nick's body. He had muscles now, his torso and chest were smooth. She rose, began to pace, not looking, looking. He was on his back, the ugly man was sodomising him. She hated him, she detested him.

'Why?' It was a scream. 'You didn't need money. We gave you everything. Why? Why? *Why?*' The choked word was her defence, she threw it at the screen, no longer caring who heard: the neighbours, the laughing children, the whole world. She wanted Nick to hear it, wanted him to understand her fury.

She roamed the room, cursing him and wounding herself, smashing her palms against her temples, sinking her fingernails into the flesh of her arms, making herself bleed. She strode around and around the room, damning him to the devil. On the mantelpiece was a photo of the family. Nicky, her little Nicky.

She stopped and turned back to the screen. She watched,

appalled, as Nick, with joy in his eyes, licked at the semen dripping from the other man's penis.

She took the remote and shut off that world. There was a last fleeting glimpse of her son, the camera in his face, his eyes to heaven, as his mouth and jaw were bathed in semen. The video whirred to a halt inside the VCR.

An advertisement was on the television. She watched a young woman hold up a box of detergent, the pristine whiteness a shock after the muted yellows and oranges of the video. It too seemed obscene, contaminated by all that she had just witnessed. Her breath was retching. She threw the ashtray against the wall with such force that she stumbled and collapsed. She lay curled up on the floor, with no tears but with her entire body shaking and convulsing.

When she finally rose, the room was dark. She turned off the TV and threw open the curtains, allowing in the winter's fading sun. She ejected the video from the player, and dropped it and its cover into the kitchen sink. She opened the window, switched on the fan above the stove, and took out a bottle of methylated spirits from the cupboard underneath the sink. She doused the video, struck a match, threw it and moved away. The flame leapt, grabbed the edges of the curtains. She rushed to put out the flames, ripping apart the fabric, throwing the still-burning material into the sink. She stood in awe as the flames flared and leapt almost to the ceiling, washing the kitchen in their fiery light. Slowly, the fire stopped dancing and she approached the sink. The video was now two shattered solid white wheels afloat

in a thick black ooze. The smoke smelt toxic. She coughed and
fanned the smoke towards the window. Covering her mouth,
she leaned over the sink and blasted the foulness with water.
There was a sizzling, more black smoke, then finally nothing.
She scooped the coagulated mess into her gloved hands and
threw it in the bin, spitting on it before she slammed the lid.

She scrubbed, scoured the kitchen with disinfectant. The
sink she attacked mercilessly, her face, her arms, her back
dripping with perspiration; she bathed the sink in vinegar till
it shone silver, till all signs of blackness had disappeared.

When she had finished, when the house was once again neat
and clean, when the shards of the ashtray had been collected
and deposited in the bin, when all was as before except for the
reproving nakedness of the kitchen window, she took a bottle
of brandy and sat cross-legged in the spare room, his old room.

She took out the family photo albums, and drank and
remembered. There was Nick at his confirmation, grinning
proudly at the camera. There was Nick as she knew him, the
real Nick, in a singlet by the sea, his arm around his cousin's
shoulder, laughing so hard his eyes were squeezed shut. There
was Nick at two and Nick at five. There was Nick in his school
uniform, Nick as a surly thirteen-year-old in a village square in
Italy. She filled and refilled her glass, poring over the photographs, remembering, replenishing her memories, filling her
eyes and her mind with *her* Nick.

She finished the bottle, going through the photo albums again
and again. When her husband found her, she was whimpering

her son's name, over and over, a blanket of photos spread around her. He took her in his arms, placed her gently in bed, whispered to her that she should sleep.

But sleep would never again be peace. She lay there still, listening to the muted words of his praying.

Porn 2

WHERE DOES JESUS LIVE? I KNOW. He lives deep down in the sewer with me.

I saw Jesus just the other night. I was with Mickey. He was shit-scared, couldn't stop looking over his shoulders, jerking his body this way and that, jumping around, grinding his teeth from all the goey he had shot up. He was petrified cos he owed Dick Cheese Saunders, that big fat fuck, two thousand bucks. Mickey didn't have two thousand bucks. He could barely scrape together a lousy twenty.

I saw Jesus in Mickey's eyes. For a brief moment they had stopped twitching and had swerved back to look at me. Our Saviour stared straight out.

Then a fleshy, hairy paw landed on Mickey's shoulder and I heard a gruff, bass voice say, 'Where ya been, cunt?'

Dick Cheese Saunders had found us.

I waited outside the kebab shop, my hands deep in the pockets of my tracky daks, trying to keep warm. I tried to scam money off some drunk working stiffs going past but the turds wouldn't even look at me.

I was freaking out that Dick Cheese Saunders would kick the shit out of Mickey. Saunders was capable of anything when he lost it, and two thousand bucks was a lot to lose. Please, Jesus, I kept thinking to myself, please look after him. Please. That made me feel a bit better. Jesus wouldn't let anything bad happen to Mickey. Jesus was in Mickey, I'd seen him.

And Jesus was there alright. Straight after, Mickey galloped up to me, all gangling arms, skinny long legs and the biggest shit-eating grin spread on his face. He wrapped an arm around me and pulled me to the ground, pretending to dry hump me. I punched him off. I had a stiffy.

Saunders had offered a deal: if Mickey agreed to do some porno scenes in a video he was shooting, Saunders would forget about the debt. He'd even promised to chuck in a baggy of heroin.

Mickey said yes straight away. 'I'm gonna get fucking high,' he told me. 'So fucking high that it won't be me on the video. Then I'm out of here. I'm gonna catch a bus back to Adelaide, find my mum and go cold turkey. I miss my mum, I even miss that hole of a city.' His eyes were wide and shiny. 'That way,' he continued, 'I won't have no more debts, no reason for anyone to look for me. I can fucking disappear and never have to think of frigging Sydney ever again.'

•

Mickey was an angel and all of us were in love with him. All of us. There are whores in the brothels and on the streets tonight crying as they're getting fucked because Mickey is on that bus back to Adelaide. There are men driving down to the Wall, looking for their sandy-haired seraph and returning home disappointed. After Mickey, no one else would do. I bet those faggots are crying as well. I'm not crying. I'm not sooking like a baby. I'm sitting on the beach, the waves crashing in the blackness, the waves that go all the way back and forth, back and forth, from here to America. I'm not feeling the cold. The heroin is liquid honey inside of me.

•

Mickey took me with him to the shoot. It was in some warehouse apartment in Annandale, around the corner from Booth Street. There was no furniture in there and the windows had all been blacked out. The whole joint was crammed with lights and cameras, microphones, cables and coloured plastic that went over the lights.

There was me and Mickey, Dick Cheese Saunders, and two young blokes, one holding a camera and the other the sound equipment. There was an older man, who said he was the director. He had a camera as well. He spoke in a thick accent that I couldn't place, that I never heard before.

Mickey asked if I could come in on the shoot. He wanted me to make some money too. The director looked across to Dick Cheese Saunders, who shook his head. 'The kid's fucking cross-eyed!'

I looked down at the floor, humiliated, and then I went spastic, wanting to knife the cunt, but then I remembered what Alex, who was my sponsor at the Congregation, had taught me. He taught me that when I get pissed off, I should just pray, instead of losing it. So I started to pray and the director bloke came over and lifted my chin.

He smiled and asked me in that strange accent of his if I could open my mouth. 'More, open more wide,' he ordered me and I stretched it open so much it began to hurt. He checked my teeth, checked my profile, left and right, got me to take off my T-shirt, show him my dick, to bend over and stretch open my arse. He was like a doctor. 'Is okay,' he said finally, 'we can use.'

Mickey winked at me.

But Dick Cheese Saunders still said no. Then his tone softened. He said something about the next time. He offered me something to get me high, an E crushed into a powder, and asked me to stay out of the way and be quiet. So I sat in a corner and got high and kept quiet.

A scrawny red-haired kid came rushing in. He had zits all over his chin and he was obviously speeding off his nut. Dick

Cheese Saunders introduced him to Mickey but no one bothered about me.

It took ages and ages to set up, I smoked five cigarettes before it even started, and Mickey came over to sit with me. Saunders wouldn't hand over the baggy till the shoot was finished, cos he was scared Mickey wouldn't be able to get it up if he was high, so Mickey snorted some of the E instead.

Then they were ready. A white sheet had been pinned against a wall and some crates were piled in front of it. Mickey and the red-haired kid were sitting on the crates kissing, which I knew Mickey didn't want to do, but he seemed to be getting into it, which caused a tingling sensation in my stomach which I knew was jealousy. They had to keep stopping and starting, something to do with the cameras.

When Mickey stripped to his underwear, the director couldn't help himself. 'Fuck,' he called out in admiration, pronouncing it *furrk*. 'Fuck!'

Mickey is so fucking beautiful. Mickey makes the whole world go Fuck!

Mickey says his mum is from the bush and his dad was from a place overseas called Caracas, which I'd never heard of but which always makes me laugh when he says it. Carac-*ass*. His dad was in South Australia one year picking fruit and fucked Mickey's mum under a full moon. She got pregnant. She wanted to get pregnant to him, even though she was only sixteen, even though he was a stranger, a backpacker travelling through, because he was dark and handsome and she thought that with his genes and her Irish blood they would create a beautiful baby. And she was right. Mickey has a photo of his brother and his sister, and they're alright, good-looking enough, but both their dads are strictly Aussie and the kids are nothing like Mickey. They don't make your stomach crunch up like he does.

At the Congregation—it's not a church, they don't call it a church—they give you free coffee and sandwiches and you can crash there for the night. It used to be a movie theatre, back in the old, old days, and I like falling asleep in the ticket box, curled up in there. The place is always full of ferals and punks and whores and druggies, and then there are the old men and women who stink of their own shit, and everyone is snoring and cursing, but sometimes they are praying and sometimes we all pray together. That's the best, when we are all praying and then I can get to sleep because I know I'll be safe, that Jesus is in the old picture house with me.

Sometimes Alex is there. He always seeks me out. And always takes me out and buys me a feed. He asks how I'm doing, where I'm sleeping, how I'm getting my money, and even when I tell him I'm doing fine, that Mickey's looking out for me, tears will always well up in his eyes and that makes me feel crap, like I done something to him, and I have to look away. Alex is twenty-six but he doesn't look that old and he has a job and rents a house and is a normal civilian. Mickey, who never goes to the Congregation, who says he can't stand their holy God-bothering bullshit, reckons Alex is like any other mug, that he just wants to fuck me. I tell Mickey he's wrong, but he won't believe me.

Alex isn't like that, he's not evil. I'm the evil one. I wish Alex *would* take me home, that he *would* fuck me. I wish I could live with him forever.

I drift back into the warehouse. Even without the scag, Mickey was taking ages getting hard and the director was starting to get pissed off. The red-haired kid was on his knees sucking Mickey off and from time to time he'd drop Mickey's cock out of his mouth and shrug at the men filming.

'Nothing's happening,' he complained, sounding bored, like he wished it was all over.

The director was getting wilder and wilder, screaming out instructions, some in English, some not, and the room was boiling with all the lights like it was a sauna. The director called Mickey a useless junkie whore and I could tell Mickey was about to lose it.

So from the corner of the room, the lights so bright that they seemed as big as the sun—it was a really trippy E—I yelled out, 'Close your eyes, Mickey!'

Dick Cheese Saunders turned around at me and then he started yelling, telling me to fucking shut my mouth or I'd be thrown out.

I said, really scared, 'But he's got to close his eyes and think of girls, otherwise he can't get it up.'

At that, Dick Cheese Saunders just started running towards me, like some wild animal in a television documentary, and it looked slow motion except for his voice, which was screaming, *Didn't I tell you to shut it, didn't I tell you to say nothing, you ugly cross-eyed cunt*, and when he reached me his boot flew up and kicked me right in the gut. My head hit the wall, and I hated myself for it but I started crying. I saw Mickey tense up but he and the others did nothing. There was nothing anyone could do. There was no one who could beat Dick Cheese Saunders in a fight. He bent down, grabbed my hair. 'Not a word, right, not one fucking word.' Then he turned and walked back. I wiped his spit and my tears off my face.

Later, in our flat, watching *The X-Files*, Mickey told me what I said wrong. 'Poofters don't want to hear that straight guys have to think of girls to get off. They want to believe that straight guys can get off on faggot sex.'

'But I was right. Once you closed your eyes, you were fine.'

'I know,' he said. 'You were right, but you shouldn't have said it in front of Saunders. I'm not angry, I'm just trying to explain why the fag got mad at you.' He stood over me. 'I'm leaving tomorrow, I won't be around to look after you. Don't forget any of what I taught you.'

'I won't.'

He slapped me playfully on the back of the head and smiled.

I will not get into a car without first chalking the rego on a street pole.

I will ring Mum at Christmas and on her birthday.

I will not allow mugs to fuck me up the arse without a condom and I'll keep my eyes shut real tight when they come on my face.

I won't jack up heroin on my own.

I will go back to school one day.

And one day, I will move away from here. Like Angie going up to Cairns or Mickey going to Adelaide. He got me to promise that one day I would move away, to somewhere smaller, further away from the world. Sydney, he always says to me, is a city of dead souls.

Mickey knows I am in love with him and he says he doesn't mind. In fact, he jokes that he's honoured. He's the second guy I've been in love with. The first was my father's friend Roman, who was a big loud Polish guy who lived in the same street we grew up in. Roman had been married and had two kids but he had murdered his wife when their youngest kid was still a baby. His wife had been fucking someone else. He had been locked away for thirteen years. He lived across the street from us and only Dad and my mum would talk to him. He was fifty-five when we got together. Dad would chuck me out of the house every second day, for giving lip, or refusing to speak Greek to my *giagia*, or just because he had drunk too much, and I'd go across to Roman's house. At first we just watched TV together and then we started watching it in his bedroom. Then one day he kissed me and jerked me off. I wanted him to do other things to me but he said no, that it wasn't right. Then when I was thirteen I got pubes and he told me that it was not a problem now, if I wanted to, it was alright for him to fuck me. We did, for two years, until I busted my *giagia*'s jaw and kicked my dad almost to death and had to run. From home, from Melbourne. I knew I had to run as far away as I could. So I ran to Sydney.

It was Roman who taught me about Jesus. Above his bed he had a huge picture of Jesus holding a bleeding heart. In the picture Jesus was crying. If the room was dark, the bleeding heart glowed orange, and Jesus's eyes would shimmer. I'd fall asleep looking at His eyes. Roman taught me the Lord's Prayer and told me how if I prayed and looked down at the ground, Jesus would listen to me.

Roman told me how back in his village one day the Germans had come to take all the boys and men, and he had looked down at the ground and prayed, and the Germans completely overlooked him. He said he heard the Virgin speak to him, tell him, 'Shh, it will all be fine. You will go live and travel far away and you will find a beautiful wife but she will betray you and you will suffer but I will never leave you.' Roman would sometimes cry when he told me this; he would tell me how lovely his wife had been. But there were no pictures of her in the house and the pictures of his children were all hidden from me. He wouldn't tell me their names because what he and I did was wrong and shameful and he didn't want someone like me to know who they were because he said people who had fallen under the sway of Satan were granted evil powers while they were on earth. He said that I could make someone die by just wishing it. But I had to have a vision of them in my mind before I could curse them. That was why I was going to burn in hell for eternity.

That's wrong, Alex says. Jesus forgives all sins. That's the promise. Jesus is not going to cast me into the fires of hell, even though I am a sinner and a junkie and a pervert, because he loves me, and when I am reborn in heaven I will not feel the urge to sin anymore. I will be as one with the angels.

Like Mickey. He's an angel already and that's why Jesus is inside him.

Mickey had to fuck the redhead. The room was so damn hot that his body was all wet with his sweat. They kept having to stop the shoot and wipe him down, his face and arse and shoulders. It was really slow and made me think being an actor would be boring. With all the stopping and starting, Mickey was taking ages to come and the redhead started whinging that he was getting sore. Dick Cheese Saunders made a sudden move and the kid shut up immediately.

I was watching the ceiling turn blue and grey, then green and pink. I was so warm in the light that I fell asleep.

Mickey woke me, and asked me if I wanted a bite to eat. He had his clothes back on. Dick Cheese Saunders gave us ten bucks and we went outside and my body expanded. I could breathe clean air again.

I walked behind Mickey, who was shivering a little from the chill.

'Is it finished?'

'Nah. I've got some more to do in the afternoon.'

'What was it like?'

'Okay. But it's not like having sex with a mug. It's different because the kid I'm fucking is being paid as well. Do you remember Show and Tell at school?'

I nodded.

'It's like that. I was really nervous. Until I closed my eyes. And then I didn't think of sex. I thought of how much I like the beaches in Adelaide and I thought of being on that bus and how happy Mum will be to see me. Then it was fine. Then I just did it.'

'I wish you weren't going.'

He was silent. He hadn't given me a phone number of anyone in Adelaide. I knew Mickey liked me. But I was part of what he wanted to leave behind. All the dead souls of Sydney. I wasn't going to take it personally. He was leaving behind four million people and I happened to be one of them.

●

Last summer I saw the body of a young girl in Potts Point. She was sitting against a wall on Macleay Street with her head down. Everyone was walking past her. I stopped and looked more closely at her. The syringe was still clutched in one hand and her skin had turned the colour of ash. I checked that no one was around and then I touched her skin. I jumped back: it was freezing and felt like leather. Eventually one of the drag queens noticed her and called over a cop, who lifted her arm, dropped it, and called through for an ambulance.

'Did you know her?'

I said I had no idea who she was.

'A scrag,' said the drag queen and started walking away. The ambulance came and so did the nuns. They started praying and I joined in with them.

That night I told Mickey and he must have had a hard day

because he went ballistic at me, started hitting me and kicking me, called me a fucking lousy Jesus freak. 'She's gone to hell, you know, being a whore and a junkie and all that shit. That's what you believe, isn't it?'

He kept punching me, kept hitting me; I was screaming and every part of me hurt like I was burning and then I passed out.

In the morning I was in the bed between him and Angie, and he held me tight and kept saying sorry. 'I didn't mean to, I didn't mean to.'

Angie made me toast and taught me a little maths, which she was really good at, and afterwards I crept back into bed with Mickey

I told him that I didn't believe in hell, there was only heaven. 'That's because Jesus loves us and he wouldn't let there be a place worse than earth.'

Mickey touched the corner of my eye. 'Sorry, mate,' he said, and his voice was way sad. 'It's going to bruise. I've given you a black eye.'

'I don't care.'

'Go to sleep.'

But I remembered that I'd touched a dead body. I went and washed my hands, just let the hot water run and run till the skin went red.

•

When we got back to the warehouse, Saunders and Mickey had an argument. Mickey doesn't get fucked. It don't matter how much the mugs offer. He just doesn't do it. He'll suck cock, and he'll let the mugs lick him out down there and if they pay extra he may lick them there too but no way will he get fucked. Saunders wanted to see him get it. I realised that this was what it was all about. But Mickey said no, he wasn't going to do it and he wasn't going to budge. Saunders reminded him that Mickey owed him.

'That's why I'm doing this shit, you pervo cunt. I owe you nothing.'

'We made a deal.'

'And I'm sticking to it.'

'No, you're not.' Dick Cheese Saunders was standing over him, jabbing his finger into Mickey's chest.

Mickey went to shove him away and Saunders clocked him a backhander. *Thwack!* It rang through the warehouse. Everyone went dead quiet.

'Listen here, you maggot. You promised me that you'd do this. My exact words to you were would you make a porno for me in which you have to get fucked. Up. The. Arse. Do you remember me saying that?'

Mickey sullenly nodded.

'And what did you say in reply?'

Mickey was silent.

Thwack! Dick Cheese Saunders backhanded him again. I wished I *could* make people die with my thoughts. I'd make Saunders die a million times, in burning oil, vultures tearing at his innards, a spike up his arse to his throat. I could watch him die a million times.

'What did you reply, maggot?'

'I said I'd do it.'

Dick Cheese Saunders turned to the director, all smiles. 'Let's start.'

While we'd been out they had built three cubicles, fitted out to look like they were public toilets, with sleazoid graffiti all over the walls and glory holes punched in the masonite.

A man with a thick grey moustache who had not been there before lunch was joking with the sound guy. He was wearing a checked shirt and his jeans were unzipped. He was smoking, and from time to time he would pull out his dick and tug at it. The thing was a monster, the hugest I'd ever seen. Long, thick as a beer can, with a hideous droopy foreskin.

The lights were switched back on and the moustache man went into the middle cubicle and started pissing. The camera guy was on his knees filming it all. The director ordered Mickey into the first cubicle and he too started pissing. Then it was the red-haired kid's turn but he couldn't get a stream going so they had to stop.

When they started again the older guy's cock was rock hard and he was getting sucked off by both Mickey and the redhead. Then the director ordered Mickey to stand up and the kid had to go down on both of them. He was finding it hard and starting to gag. Then they stopped the filming again to wipe everyone down.

This time Mickey had to fuck the kid. There was no condom but I knew it was okay because Mickey didn't have the disease. The kid's face was all screwed up, he wasn't used to getting fucked yet, and his cock had shrivelled up completely. I could see the veins straining, popping out on his neck.

Then Mickey pulled out and the older guy started fucking the kid. As soon as he was in, the kid was screaming, 'Stop! Stop! It fucking hurts, it fucking really hurts.' He was crying, actually sobbing, and it made him look even younger.

But they didn't stop filming for a long time, by which time the kid's sobs had stopped and he was just groaning, making gurgling, incoherent sounds, with his eyes shut and his teeth clenched.

I didn't want to look, I just kept staring up at beams on the ceiling, but then Dick Cheese Saunders came over to me and yanked me to my feet. He had his cock out too and grabbed my hand and made me touch it. I started jerking him off but still tried to look anywhere else but at what was happening in the middle of the room. Saunders' breathing was both loud and slow.

I looked over when I heard the director call out, 'On the boy's face, come on his face.' Mickey blew but the director and his camera were interrupting my view and I couldn't see it. The older guy was still fucking the red-haired kid.

Dick Cheese Saunders slapped my hand away from his cock. 'Not yet.' I didn't know if he was talking to me or to himself.

The red-haired kid stumbled away, crouched over, holding his stomach. He was wiping the cum off his face, making a face at the foulness of the taste. The sound guy gave him a bottle of water. He sat in the corner across from me and I could see he was crying again. But I didn't care about him.

It was Mickey's turn. He was on all fours under the intense, blazing lights. I didn't want to look. I snatched a glance. There was a steely, determined look on his face and his jaw was jutting out. He looked over at me and I turned away and looked down at the floorboards.

'Have you got a condom on?'

I turned back to look. Mickey was standing up. 'I won't do it if this cunt won't put on a rubber.'

Dick Cheese Saunders stepped forward. 'No condoms.'

'Then I'm not doing it.'

Saunders seemed bigger than I had ever known him. I thought he might wallop Mickey, but instead he just nodded his head. 'Alright, kid, that's fair.'

The guy who was going to fuck Mickey shrugged and held out his hand. Everyone searched in their pockets for a rubber and the sound guy eventually found one. The guy with the moustache started putting it on but it only covered half of his freaky monster dick.

Mickey was back on all fours and I didn't want to look. I crouched and looked up at the ceiling. I noticed that on one of the beams a bird had built a nest. But there was nothing in it now. I could hear grunts, the older guy talking dirty like they do in pornos, the on-again, off-again, on-again of the cameras starting and stopping. But Mickey was making no sound.

Saunders had me on my feet again, jerking him off. It seemed to go on forever, the heat and the light, the grunting, the spinning and buzzing and humming of the cameras, the fucking, my hand going up and down, up and down Dick Cheese Saunders' pongy little dick. The bastard wouldn't come. I wanted it to be over. A sparrow. I decided it had been a sparrow's nest.

Dick Cheese Saunders suddenly grabbed my jaw and jerked my head around so I had to look at the room. 'Do you like seeing your mate getting it up the arse?'

Mickey was no longer on his hands and knees but on his back. The guy was holding his legs up, fucking him fast, pulling out then thrusting back in, which was what hurt the most when mugs fucked me. But Mickey was still not making a sound, just looking up at the two cameras. From time to time he'd wince, but that was all.

The older guy suddenly stopped. He stood up, winking down at Mickey, and pulled the condom off his dick. 'I'm ready.'

'Sure, very good, sure.' The director motioned for Mickey to get on his knees. The cameras were right up on his face. Saunders' hand was on the back of my neck now, his grip tight. I had to keep watching. The guy with the moustache was jerking himself off, and even with the cameraman and the director filming around them I had a clear view of Mickey's face. He was waiting, his mouth closed, his eyes screwed shut, exactly how he had taught me, so that the semen won't get in your eyes and through your eyes into your blood so you don't get the disease. The guy grabbed hold of Mickey's hair and was pulling Mickey's face closer to his cock all the time, shouting stuff like *I'm going to come all over your face, fag*, and Dick Cheese Saunders was breathing faster now, and under his breath he was going *do it, do it, do it*, and I couldn't bear to look so I pulled away from his grasp and he was so focused on what was happening that he let me, though I was still jerking his cock. I looked out through a crack of the boarded-up window, and I saw a flash of blue and white, sky and cloud, and then the guy finally blew and he started howling, exactly like one of the dinosaurs in *Jurassic Park*. Dick Cheese Saunders shuddered beside me and his cum spilt all over my hand and when I shook it off, it fell on the floorboards in front of us.

I looked over at Mickey, I looked over to see he was alright. His eyes were still shut tight; screwed so tight that deep creases had appeared on his brow. Sprog was splashed across his cheeks and the bridge of his nose, and it was dripping down his chin. The guy with the moustache was wiping his cock with some tissues. He passed the box to Mickey, who wiped his eyelids; only then did he finally open his eyes. He was looking straight at me and his eyes were shimmering. The sadness—no, the misery—of the world was looking at me. But then his mouth twitched towards a small smile and I saw Our Lord's mercy.

I stood up, stepping over the cables and past the men. As I walked over, I ripped off the bottom of my T-shirt, and when I reached Mickey, I wiped clean his face and his neck. I kissed his mouth. As I did that I could see Jesus again in his eyes.

But as soon as I'd finished wiping away the spoof, Jesus had gone and it was just a sandy-haired black-eyed laughing boy staring back at me. 'Don't you dare kiss me again, ya crazy poofta.'

We were laughing like little kids at Luna Park, going down down down, fast fast fast on the Big Dipper. And just as we stopped laughing the red-haired kid stood up and was pointing at his arse. 'I'm fucking bleeding,' he screamed, and that just started us up again. We were crying from the laughing.

For my fifteenth birthday, Mickey got me a ticket for the Big Day Out. We took acid, it was my first time, and when it started, first with the tingling and then with the rush of colour and sound and smell and movement, I knew that this was how heaven will be. Angie and Mickey walked through the crowd, hand in hand, and I bumped into friends and even glimpsed one of my mugs in the crowd. Mickey slipped me an E as the sun was going down, and I watched Courtney Love bare her tits to the crowd. Afterwards I wandered to the techno tent and bumped into Angie and Mickey. The DJs were wicked and I was peaking and the crowd was going off and the music was in my body and in my soul and I was jumping around like a madman and so was Angie and so was Mickey and so was the whole world. Everyone was shining and screaming and dancing and I climbed onto Mickey's shoulders and I was looking straight into the light and into the night, and the music was the sound of the angels and the bass beat was the sound of heaven and I raised my hands towards the stage and one of the DJs pointed at me I swear electricity shot from his fingers towards me and I was happier than I had ever been. I was happier than I would ever be.

That same night, on the train going back to town, Mickey was sitting in the middle of the seat, holding Angie, and I was next to him, resting my head on his shoulder. Then Mickey grabbed me, all of a sudden, and gave me a long kiss, his tongue in my mouth and his hands on my chest. His eyes were looking into mine. He stopped and Angie was laughing and the young kids on the seat opposite, straight kids, civilians, were looking away embarrassed. Then Mickey sat back with one arm around me and the other around Angie. He was smiling a huge motherfucking shit-eating grin.

I had fallen asleep by the time the train got to Central. Later, Angie told me that Mickey had carried me all the way home.

Porn 3

GHASSAN HAD NEVER TOUCHED A EUROPEAN before, not even to shake hands with. He had never smelt one up close. He was finally to do so. It was fated to be this pale young man beckoning him to come closer. As he approached, the man's features became more distinct, emerging slowly from the hellish darkness. The only light came from the video screen behind them and a solitary red globe above them in the corridor. The blood-hued flickering illumination distorted everything, so that the man's fair hair appeared orange and there were deep shadows across the bottom half of his face. Still, Ghassan could espy the white scar on the left side of his top lip, that there was stubble on his chin. The man reached out and tugged at the front of Ghassan's shirt, bringing him closer so that their lips were almost touching. Ghassan had to resist sniffing at him: he wanted to search the man's body with his nose, as if they were dogs, not men; he wanted to determine the source of the man's distasteful odour. He pulled away from the European, who then offered him an anxious shy smile. He reached for Ghassan's crotch and had his hand swiped away. Ghassan breathed in.

The man smelt of offal, of guts and stomach and lungs. He did not smell of skin. He smelt of the foul secrets inside the body.

Aware that something had changed, the man tilted his head to one side, his eyes now alert and suspicious. The two men stared at each other, as if daring each other to make the first move, to speak, to reignite or disavow their earlier intimacy. This is a dance, thought Ghassan to himself with some disappointment, not so different from the one we dance with whores. The man suddenly coughed, an abrupt sharp sound, but it acted as a concession. The man had coughed, and then he had raised his arm to scratch his head, the gesture reminding Ghassan of something a little boy would do, an act that seemed to encompass shyness and diffidence and assertiveness all at once. It was a sweet, simple movement. As the man had raised his arm, Ghassan had glimpsed swirls of fine wet hair under the sleeve of the man's shirt; as well, his nose had detected the tang of citrus. The man's deodorant banished thoughts of decomposition, visions of flesh and meat. As did the sight of the dark hair against the man's pallid skin. Ghassan's cock pumped with blood; he placed his hand on the man's shoulder and drew him close. This was desire.

He had first noticed this European in the orientation week at the university; he always sat two rows in front of Ghassan, and he was clearly equally bored by the lecturer. They all were. The professor for Chemical Engineering Applied Methods was one of those men who seemed never to have been touched by youth, one of those insipid sexless European men who spoke in a hushed monotone that squeezed any passion or interest from the words. Granted, there was little musicality or emotion to be gleaned from the dry calculus and rules of applied engineering, but the man's dullness caused spontaneous yawning, restlessness and fidgeting among the students within the first five minutes of the lecture. Ghassan dutifully scribbled down the notations and equations the lecturer wrote on the whiteboard, but the words the man spoke were nonsensical. Ghassan trusted his own intelligence, he knew that his command of the English language was adequate—no, better than adequate, he had a true aptitude for languages—but the man behind the lectern might as well have been speaking an obscure dialect of some ancient lost civilisation. It was as if the tedium of his delivery drained the words of their meaning. Ghassan found he did not understand a word of what was being said.

The only thing that saved him from being bored senseless over the interminable creep of the hour was the freedom he had to examine his fellow students. The margins of Ghassan's notebook were filled with quick sketches of the faces and bodies of the young women and men who sat around him in the lecture theatre. For the most part, the sketches were of the young blonde girls with their shamelessly exposed breasts. Tits filled the margins of his notes. His friends would lean over to look at his sketches and then giggled conspiratorially. They'd take turns guessing which girl he had sketched. They'd surreptitiously point to a young woman and ask in Urdu, Is it that slut there? Ghassan would smile and never confirm or deny their queries.

For him, sketching those interchangeable European women was a smokescreen for his real purpose. If any of his friends had taken the time to really study his drawings, if they had properly paid attention to his work over the year, they would have noticed that two portraits kept reappearing. They would have also noticed that these portraits were never mere caricatures, unlike Ghassan's sketches of the European women, which were always crude and often insulting, their expressions either those of imbeciles or showing a trace of animal cunning. But it was different with the two recurring portraits of the men. The first portrait was that of the elegant, lean and dignified Omar. Ghassan's love for his best friend was pure, a love beyond the degrading treacheries of lust and desire. Omar was untouchable, incorruptible. In every sketch Ghassan drew of him, he was unsmiling and straight-backed. He floated in the white margins of Ghassan's notebook, separate from the vulgar sketches around him. The other recurring portrait was that of the young European man with the broad sloping shoulders who always took that seat two rows in front of Ghassan and his friends. Whenever Ghassan sketched this portrait, he would drop his free hand to his crotch. He did not dare do more than feel the bulk of his cock through the cheap fabric of his trousers. His love for Omar was pure. The European he wanted to fuck.

And now it was happening. The man was on his stomach, his jeans around his ankles, naked and vulnerable. Ghassan was shocked by the amount of hair that covered the man's plump arse. It was unexpected. Ghassan realised at that moment that in his masturbatory imaginings of Europeans he had really always dreamt of youth, of boys between childhood and manhood. These were the degenerate fantasies that fed his lust. He had assumed that a European man would be hairless, smooth, that to touch white skin would always mean touching feminine skin. As with the sexless lecturer who had bored him all year, he had never thought of virility being something that European men could possess.

He could hear the man's slow heavy breathing. His face, now hidden from Ghassan's view, pressed against the filthy black vinyl of the couch, was most likely tensed, grimacing, anticipating Ghassan's first thrust. The man had tried to kiss him but Ghassan had quickly turned him over. It wasn't that he didn't want to kiss him—in fact, there was no act between men that Ghassan preferred to kissing. Sometimes after their final evening prayers, Omar would hold Ghassan, they would stroke each other's hair, and they would kiss, as Omar specified, as brothers, as friends, as comrades. Skin never touched skin. Omar's purity was such that his passions were never inflamed.

Only afterwards, alone on his own mattress, did Ghassan give himself over to the corruption of his imaginings. And now the sight of the man's naked body was making him swoon with an intoxication that was humiliating. He had expected a boy and he had to confront a man. A man like himself but viewed in a false and diabolical mirror. The dark thistles of hair on the man's chest, the masculine abundance of the belly, the thickness and solidity of the man's cock, so much like his own except for the serpentine hood covering the head. Yes, he had swooned. He had wanted to fall to his knees and take the man into his mouth. Instead, unable to bear the unfamiliar beauty of the sight, he had savagely turned him around so he was facing away from him. The man had resisted for a moment, and Ghassan had thought that they would struggle, that they both could only legitimise their passion through violence. He had pushed harder on the back of the man's head. The man resisted, then allowed his body to go limp. It was the moment of submission. Ghassan had loosened his grip and the man had tumbled forward, unresisting, onto the stained black vinyl couch. Ghassan unzipped.

They had not spoken a word to each other all year. Ghassan could not now recall when he had first become aware of the handsome European. He had no recollection of a defining moment, the way there was when he thought back to his first meeting with Omar. That memory was as distinct as the material world created by God that was always before his eyes. He and Saleem were waiting for the 5.15 train to Epping. Saleem had greeted a lonely figure waiting on the crowded platform with a small black bag between his feet. Omar's greeting had been warm, his eyes piercing. Ghassan had fallen into those eyes and had swum in them ever since. He knew those eyes better, more profoundly, than he knew himself. They were shaped like almonds; they were the colour of the darkest, most luscious honey.

He had no idea of the colour of the European stranger's eyes. Yet at some point this man had indeed begun to seep into his consciousness; he'd realised this when he was flicking back through his notebook and registered the recurring portrait. In lectures, Ghassan found himself searching for the man's freckled pale neck, enjoying how the glare of the bright fluorescent lights in the lecture hall made the fine blond hairs glisten on the man's arms. Dew on snow. He did fancy that there were moments when the man turned and searched for him. But in those moments, Ghassan would avert his gaze and focus instead on the glacial movements of the lecturer.

The European youth only existed within the lecture theatre. Ghassan never saw him around campus, never in the cafeteria or the libraries, never in other lectures or tutorials. He was only ever there on Tuesday mornings at ten o'clock, always sitting two rows ahead of Ghassan and his friends. His fair hair was always kept neat and cut short. His clothes were simple and unadorned, masculine, eschewing vanity. Ghassan desperately wanted to believe in the European's moral rectitude. He could not imagine him drinking or being intoxicated, could not imagine him surrendering to vileness or perversion. Ghassan wanted with all his will to believe that the emotions stirred inside him by this stranger could also be divine in their essence, as pure and unsullied as his love for Omar. It was the European man's unfamiliarity, the exotic pornographic danger of his skin, that was threatening. Omar represented all that was worth celebrating in a man—strength, dignity, keen intelligence and resolute faith. Was it possible that this stranger too could embody all these virtues? Was it possible that the young man was a mirror, one that reflected back to Ghassan an image of himself in white skin? Could the European truly be such a man, stripped of degeneracy, decadence, sloth, lust and greed? Maybe one day it could be possible. This was how much he had come to love the stranger.

'Fuck me.'

The coarse, ugly English words. He had become detached from the savage animal act in which they were engaged. His cock was still erect, he was mechanically thrusting into the man, but his mind had been elsewhere, inside the warm, timeless cocoon of the lecture theatre. The obscene, brutal words brought him back to earth. *Fuck me.* He increased the speed of his thrusts as he became conscious of the electronic music that was piped through the cubicle, the groans, expletives and screams coming from the frantic couplings in the cubicles on either side of theirs, or from the porn playing on the monitors in the corridor outside. He could no longer block out sound, or sight; he resigned himself to looking at the blood-like stains of the semen marks on the bare walls. He was wrenched back to the body he was sodomising by its smell, a chemical, unnatural stench, but also earthy and nauseating. That smell of offal again.

'Fuck me.' The insistent words now almost shouted. The demon words did their work, they aroused him further. Ghassan looked down at his cock, wet from lubricant and spit, flecks of shit visible on the shaft. He stared in fascination at the pink hole that was stretching, opening up to receive him. It was the raw red of blood and the pitch black of night. Ghassan was not wearing a condom and the stranger had not asked for one. He wished for death, he trusted in death, his words were a call to death. *Fuck me*. Ghassan pushed the whole of himself into the European, as if through his cock he was splitting in two the very universe itself. Ghassan moaned in the darkness and from deep inside his ecstasy and his loathing, he spilt himself. He shuddered, jerked like an epileptic as he dissipated into the whiteness. The body underneath him also began a relentless jerking. The stranger groaned, he called out into the void. Shamelessly, he was calling out to God, not knowing that God abhorred him. A trail of white splattered across the vinyl arm of the couch.

Omar had pointed out the building to him not long after they had first met. He had described, coldly, what went on inside it. Ghassan had listened, shocked, as Omar told him that children were taken there and violated, how iniquitous orgies as vile and blasphemous as those of the time of Sodom and Gomorrah were committed there inside the deceptively innocuous simple brown brick facade of the building, how men were ensnared and made insane by demons who corrupted the holy books with their bodily excretions. A small rectangular plaque the colours of the rainbow was the only indication of the depravities performed inside. Is it not scandalous, Omar asked, that the very symbol of God's promise to man has been taken by these devils and become a promise of death and sin?

The building sat tucked in between an alley and a large warehouse stocking parts for automobiles and motorbikes. Across the road was a bank. On the corner diagonally opposite was a twenty-four-hour convenience store. Their friend worked there and they were waiting for him to finish his shift. As they were talking, an emaciated girl turned into the alley next to the store and crouched behind a large square industrial bin. Ghassan had been trying to take in Omar's words, could not believe what he was hearing, was ashamed by how those words made him feel. The girl walked back out from behind the bin and he was staring right at her. She looked startled but then flung a syringe at his feet and jeered, 'Fuck off, curry muncher.' She stumbled as she lurched past them and then her gait slowed. Her white skin was the pallor of ghosts.

'She is the walking dead,' Omar said quietly. 'They let their young die on the streets here, alone. And inside, they have their orgies.'

Omar must always be proud of him. Omar would never know his shame.

The stranger wiped his wet cock with a tissue, and then, shyly, again like a little boy, he offered a clean tissue to Ghassan. Wordlessly, Ghassan took it, wiped himself clean and then pulled up his trousers. The European did the same, both of them with their backs to each other, ludicrously embarrassed by their nudity, as if the last few minutes of primal intimacy had not occurred.

Ghassan was about to undo the latch on the door when the stranger spoke.

'Do you smoke?' He was offering a cigarette. Ghassan reached over and took one. The man lit the cigarette for him and their hands touched. Ghassan pulled away.

'I think you are in my lecture. At uni. I do engineering as well.' There was a hopeful glint in the man's eyes. He was waiting expectantly for Ghassan's answer.

And for a moment Ghassan wished to answer thus: I know you and I know who and what you can be. I have loved you for months now, and I have wanted to communicate to you all the wonder and joy and pain that is in this world. I have dreamt that together we would discover God and in our submission and faith we would also discover that there is a union of souls in love that the body and its base functions can never compare to. Oh, how I have wished for this and how I regret that this is not possible. Come now, take my hand, and I will lead you out of here. This place is death and destruction, and if it did not occur today, it would happen tomorrow or the day after, for this place is an abomination. Will you come with me?

Instead, Ghassan shook his head. He made his accent deliberately thick, his speech broken. 'No, no me. I no go university, I no student.'

He thought the man would object, contradict his deceit. But instead the man nodded, and a rueful half-smile appeared on his face. 'My mistake.' The smile vanished. 'Got a girlfriend, have ya?' Then, more spitefully, 'Or maybe a wife?'

Ghassan said nothing. He dropped the cigarette and stubbed it out on the dirty wet floor.

The man sat back on the couch and unzipped his jeans. 'You can fuck me again.'

Ghassan unlatched the door and pulled it open. The whiff of chemicals and offal, men visible in the shadows.

'Leave the door open,' the man called out, in a tone both defensive and accusing. 'I'm not finished.'

The corridor was full of shadows, naked ghouls—luminescent, poisonous white skin—whose hands groped at him. Ghassan pushed them all away, refusing to look at the bodies surrounding him. The noise of fornication was all around him, but he ignored it and maintained his purposeful walk. He walked past the showers and sauna and into the small alcove with the lockers. He pulled the key from his pocket.

Ghassan began the countdown in his head. He looked out past the locker room to where a bored attendant was sitting at the counter flicking through a magazine. Behind him was the exit, the door that led to the street and to the light. Ghassan hesitated, he panicked, his resolve gone.

Every second of every minute of every hour of every day, awake or asleep, we must pray in order to resist sin. In the diabolical din of this hellhole he heard Omar's words break through, a ray of illumination that cleaved the darkness. The words, their light, wrapped themselves around him. He would not flee; he secured the bulky belt that contained God's fury tighter around his middle. He patted, and he set forth.

As soon as he had entered this inferno, paid the surly attendant twenty dollars and spotted the youth in the alcove, Ghassan knew that he was doomed to sin, he did not have the resolve to resist temptation. Their magazines, their videos, their films, their dirty words scrawled on toilet walls, their nakedness, their parading of their bodies, their hatred of chastity, their decadence, their sadism, their brutality, their filth: it had infected him, it was in his blood. And like a cancer, it fed on itself, bred on itself, so that the fever intensified. He had once wondered what it would be like to touch another man's skin. Now that was not enough. He had seen too much; nothing was sacred, nothing was safe, not even a child. He had become one of them but soon he and all of them would be gone. By doing God's work he could atone. There would be no more magazines, no more films and filthy words, no nakedness, no brutality, no sadism, no filth. He was bringing the fire.

He walked out of the alcove and back up the stairs that led to the cubicles, to the violent red and orange light. A frail old man was desperately stroking at his crotch and clutched at Ghassan as he shoved past him. He stopped in front of the scene of his sin and saw that the European was once again bent over the vinyl couch, and another man was entering him.

Ghassan was the fire. He turned away and looked down the corridor. A dark-skinned man with the fleshy jowls of a bourgeois Punjabi was looking away from him, ashamed. Your false gods cannot save you. There is only one God, *my* God. At the end of the corridor, a television monitor looked down at them all. On the screen a scrawny pale-skinned youth had his eyes screwed shut as a man furiously ejaculated all over the boy's cheeks, his chin, his naked shoulder, his hair, his lips and mouth. This was what they did to their children.

He was counting down. Only a few seconds now and he would be free.

On the screen, the boy's eyes opened and looked straight at Ghassan. The boy was smiling and the semen on his face sparkled as tears.

Then there was only the unforgiving, intransmutable silence.

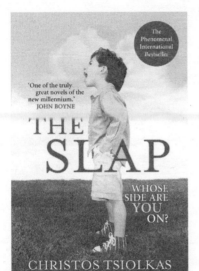

Barracuda

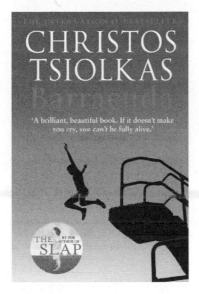

'A brilliant, beautiful book. If it doesn't make you cry, you can't be fully alive' *Sunday Times*

'I finished *Barracuda* on a high: moved, elated, immersed … This is the work of a superb writer' *Guardian*

'Masterful, addictive, clear-eyed storytelling' Viv Groskop, *Red*

Daniel Kelly, a talented young swimmer, has one chance to escape his working-class upbringing. His astonishing ability in the pool should drive him to fame and fortune, as well as his revenge on the rich boys at the private school to which he has won a sports scholarship. Everything Danny has ever done, every sacrifice his family has ever made, has been in pursuit of his dream. But when he melts down at his first big international championship and comes only fifth, he begins to destroy everything he has fought for and turn on everyone around him.